Murder on the Rocks

This Large Print Book carries the Seal of Approval of N.A.V.H.

A GRAY WHALE INN MYSTERY

MURDER ON THE ROCKS

KAREN MACINERNEY

WHEELER PUBLISHING

An imprint of Thomson Gale, a part of The Thomson Corporation

Detroit • New York • San Francisco • New Haven, Conn. • Waterville, Maine • London

This is a work of fiction. Names, characters, places, and incidents are either the product of the author's imagination or are used fictitiously, and any resemblance to actual persons, living or dead, business establishments, events, or locales is entirely coincidental.

Wheeler Publishing Large Print Cozy Mystery.
The text of this Large Print edition is unabridged.
Other aspects of the book may vary from the original edition.
Set in 16 pt. Plantin.

LIBRARY OF CONGRESS CATALOGING-IN-PUBLICATION DATA

MacInerney, Karen, 1970–
Murder on the rocks : a Gray Whale Inn mystery / by Karen MacInerney.
p. cm. — (Wheeler Publishing large print cozy mystery)
ISBN 1-59722-389-1 (pbk. : lg. print : alk. paper) 1. Hotelkeepers — Maine — Fiction. 2. Bed and breakfast accommodations — Maine — Fiction. 3. Murder — Fiction. 4. Large type books. 5. Cranberry Isles (Me. : Islands) — Fiction. I. Title.
PS3613.A27254M87 2006b
813'.6—dc22
2006030343

U.S. Softcover:
ISBN 13: 978-1-59722-389-8
ISBN 10: 1-59722-389-1

Published in 2006 by arrangement with Midnight Ink, an imprint of Llewellyn Publications, Woodbury, MN 55125 USA.

Printed in the United States of America on permanent paper
10 9 8 7 6 5 4 3 2 1

ACKNOWLEDGMENTS

So many people go into a book project; it's hard to know where to start! So I'll start at the beginning, with Carol and Dave Swartz, for always being there and always encouraging me to shoot for the moon; and Dorothy and Ed MacInerney, without whose love and support so many things — including this book — would not be possible. I also want to thank the late great Barbara Burnett Smith for her enthusiasm, her keen critical eye, her effervescence, and her encouragement . . . I miss you every day. Thanks also to Bethann and Beau Eccles, for their insightful comments — and their friendship. And, of course, everyone at Austin Mystery Writers for their great critiques, insights, and above all their support: Mary Jo Powell, who was there from the beginning; Andrew Butler, Dave Ciambrone, Laney Hennelly, Kimberly Sandman, Rie Sheridan, and Sylvia Dickey Smith.

Thanks also to Sandi Heimsath, for her early words of encouragement; Maryann and Clovis Heimsath, for introducing me to Maine and the Cranberry Isles; Dana Lehman, for helping me open the door; and Marsha Moyer, for her support and friendship. I cannot say enough wonderful things about the world's best agent, Jessica Faust at BookEnds; thanks also to everyone at Midnight Ink team, particularly editors Barbara Moore, whose enthusiasm is contagious, and Connie Hill; I also want to thank Brett Fechheimer and Alison Aten, my wonderful publicity team, for all their help. And last — but definitely not least — my wonderful husband, Eric, for his critical eye, his plot ideas, his unflagging encouragement and support, and his ability to put up with an occasionally neurotic and slightly obsessive spouse. I want to say thank you also to Abby and Ian, the lights of my life, for their love, understanding, and ability to entertain themselves while their mom pounds away at the keyboard.

Author's Note: Although there are several endangered tern species, the black-chinned terns are not among them; they exist only in the pages of this book. Those familiar with the Cranberry Isles will also fail to recognize many of the nautical features surrounding Cranberry Island; that is because they are figments of the author's imagination.

Dedicated to my grandmother,
Marian Quinton;
and to the memory of my grandfather,
Harold Quinton.

One

The alarm rang at 6 AM, jolting me out from under my down comforter and into a pair of slippers. As much as I enjoyed innkeeping, I would never get used to climbing out of bed while everyone else was still sleeping. Ten minutes later I was in the kitchen, inhaling the aroma of dark-roasted coffee as I tapped it into the coffeemaker and gazing out the window at the gray-blue morning. Fog, it looked like — the swirling mist had swallowed even the Cranberry Rock lighthouse, just a quarter of a mile away.

I grabbed the sugar and flour canisters from the pantry and dug a bag of blueberries out of the freezer for Wicked Blueberry Coffee Cake. The recipe was one of my favorites: not only did my guests rave over the butter-and-brown-sugar-drenched cake, but its simplicity was a drowsy cook's dream.

The coffeepot had barely finished gurgling when I sprinkled the pan of dimpled batter with brown-sugar topping and eased it into the oven. My eyes focused on the clock above the sink: 6:30. Just enough time for a relaxed thirty minutes on the kitchen porch.

Equipped with a mug of steaming French-roast coffee, I grabbed my blue windbreaker from its hook next to the door and headed out into the gray Maine morning. As hard as it was to drag myself out of a soft, warm bed while it was still dark outside, I loved mornings on Cranberry Island.

I settled myself into a white-painted wooden rocker and took a sip of strong, sweet coffee. The sound of the waves crashing against the rocks was muted, but mesmerizing. I inhaled the tangy air as I rocked, watching the fog twirl around the rocks and feeling the kiss of a breeze on my cheeks. A tern wheeled overhead as the thrum of a lobster boat rumbled across the water, pulsing and fading as it moved from trap to trap.

"Natalie!" A voice from behind me shattered my reverie. I jumped at the sound of my name, spilling coffee on my legs. "I was looking for you." Bernard Katz's bulbous nose protruded from the kitchen door. I stood up and swiped at my coffee-stained jeans. I had made it very clear that the kitchen was off-limits to guests — not only was there a sign on the door, but it was listed in the house rules guests received when they checked in.

"Can I help you with something?" I couldn't keep the anger from seeping into my voice.

"We're going to need breakfast at seven. And my son and his wife will be joining us. She doesn't eat any fat, so you'll have to have something light for her."

"But breakfast doesn't start until 8:30."

"Yes, well, I'm sure you'll throw something together." He glanced at his watch, a Rolex the size of a life preserver. "Oops! You'd better get cracking. They'll be here in twenty minutes."

I opened my mouth to protest, but he disappeared back into my kitchen with a bang. My first impulse was to storm through the door and tell Katz he could fish for his breakfast, but my business survival instinct kicked in. Breakfast at seven? Fine. That would be an extra $50 on his bill for the extra guests — and for the inconvenience. Scrambled egg whites should do the trick for Mrs. Katz Jr. First, however, a change of clothes was in order. I swallowed what was left of my coffee and took a deep, lingering breath of the salty air before heading inside to find a fresh pair of jeans.

My stomach clenched again as I climbed the stairs to my bedroom. Bernard Katz, owner of resorts for the rich and famous, had earmarked the beautiful, and currently vacant, fifty-acre parcel of land right next to the Gray Whale Inn for his next big resort — despite the fact that the Shoreline Conservation Association had recently reached an agreement with the Cranberry Island Board of Selectmen to buy the property and protect the endangered terns that nested there. The birds had lost most of their nesting grounds to people over the past hundred years, and the small strip of beach protected by towering cliffs was home to one of the largest tern populations still in existence.

Katz, however, was keen to make sleepy little Cranberry Island the next bijou in his crown of elite resorts, and was throwing bundles of money at the board to encourage them to sell it to him instead. If Katz managed to buy the land, I was afraid the sprawling resort would mean the end not only for the terns, but for the Gray Whale Inn.

As I reached the door to my bedroom, I wondered yet again why Katz and his assistant were staying at my inn. Bernard Katz's son Stanley and his daughter-in-law

Estelle owned a huge "summer cottage" called Cliffside that was just on the other side of the preserve. I had been tempted to decline Katz's reservation, but the state of my financial affairs made it impossible to refuse any request for a week in two of my most expensive rooms.

I reminded myself that while Katz and his assistant Ogden Wilson were odious, my other guests — the Bittles, a retired couple up from Alabama for an artists' retreat — were lovely, and deserved a wonderful vacation. And at least Katz had paid up front. As of last Friday, my checking account had dropped to under $300, and the next mortgage payment was due in two weeks. Although Katz's arrival on the island might mean the eventual end of the Gray Whale Inn, right now I needed the cash.

Goosebumps crept up my legs under the wet denim as I searched for something to wear. Despite the fact that it was June, and one of the warmer months of the year, my body hadn't adjusted to Maine's lower temperatures. I had spent the last fifteen years under Austin's searing sun, working for the Texas Department of Parks and Wildlife and dreaming of someday moving to the coast to start a bed-and-breakfast.

I had discovered the Gray Whale Inn while

staying with a friend in a house she rented every summer on Mount Desert Island. I had come to Maine to heal a broken heart, and had no idea I'd fall in love all over again — this time with a 150-year-old former sea captain's house on a small island accessible only by boat.

The inn was magical; light airy rooms with views of the sea, acres of beach roses, and sweet peas climbing across the balconies. I jotted down the real estate agent's number and called on a whim, never guessing that my long-term fantasy might be within my grasp. When the agent informed me that the inn was for sale at a bargain price, I raced to put together enough money for a down payment.

I had had the good fortune to buy a large old house when Austin was a sleepy town in a slump. After a room-by-room renovation, it sold for three times the original price, and between the proceeds of the house and my entire retirement savings, there was just enough money to take out a mortgage on the inn. A mortgage, I reflected as I strained to button my last pair of clean jeans, whose monthly payments were equivalent to the annual Gross National Product of Sweden.

I tossed my coffee-stained jeans into the overflowing laundry basket and paused for a last-minute inspection in the cloudy mirror above the dresser. Gray eyes looked back at me from a face only slightly plump from two months of butter- and sugar-laden breakfasts and cookies. I took a few swipes at my bobbed brown hair with a brush and checked for white hairs — no new ones today, although with the Katzes around my hair might be solid white by the end of the summer. If I hadn't already torn all of my hair out, that is.

When I pushed through the swinging door to the dining room at 7:00, Bernard Katz sat alone, gazing out the broad sweep of windows toward the section of coastline he had earmarked for his golf course. He looked like a banker in a blue pinstriped three-piece suit whose buttons strained to cover his round stomach. Katz turned at the sound of my footsteps, exposing a line of crooked teeth as he smiled. He was a self-made man, someone had told me. Apparently there'd been no money in the family budget for orthodontic work. Still, if I had enough money to buy islands, I'd have found a couple of thousand dollars to spare for straight teeth.

"Coffee. Perfect." He plucked the heavy blue mug from the place setting in front of him and held it out. "I'll take cream and sugar." I filled his cup, congratulating myself for not spilling it on his pants, then plunked the cream pitcher and sugar bowl on the table.

"You know, you stand to earn quite a bit of business from our little project." Katz took a sip of coffee. "Not bad," he said, sounding surprised. "Anyway, there's always a bit of overflow in the busy season. We might be able to arrange something so that your guests could use our facilities. For a fee, of course."

Of course. He leaned back and put his expensively loafered feet on one of my chairs. Apparently he was willing to cough up some change for footwear. "I know starting a business is tough, and it looks like your occupancy is on the low side." He nodded at the room full of empty tables.

"Well, it is an hour and a half before breakfast." He didn't have to know that only two other rooms were booked — and one of those was for Barbara Eggleby, the Shoreline Conservation Association representative who was coming to the island for the sole purpose of preventing his development from happening.

"Still," he went on, "this is the high season." His eyes swept over the empty tables. "Or should be. Most of the inns in this area are booked to capacity." My first impulse was to respond that most of the inns in the area had been open for more than two months, and that he was welcome to go to the mainland and stay at one of them, but I held my tongue.

He removed his feet from my chair and leaned toward me. "Our resort will make Cranberry Island *the* hot spot for the rich and famous in Maine. Kennebunkport won't know what hit it. Your place will be perfect for the people who want glitz but can't afford the price tag of the resort."

Glitz? The whole point of Cranberry Island was its ruggedness and natural beauty. So my inn would be a catchall for poor people who couldn't quite swing the gigantic tab at Katz's mega resort. Lovely.

I smiled. "Actually, I think the island works better as a place to get away from all the 'glitz'. And I don't think a golf course would do much to enhance the island's appeal." I paused for a moment. "Or the nesting success of the black-chinned terns."

"Oh, yes, the birds." He tsked and shook his head. The sun gleamed on his bald pate, highlighting the liver spots that had begun to appear like oversized freckles. "I almost forgot, you're heading up that greenie committee. I would have thought you were smarter than that, being a businesswoman." He waved a hand. "Well, I'm sure we could work something out, you know, move the nests somewhere else or something."

"Good morning, Bernie." The sharp report of stiletto heels rescued me from having to respond. *Bernie?*

"Estelle!" Katz virtually leaped from his chair. "Please, sit down." Katz's daughter-in-law approached the table in a blaze of fuchsia and decorated Katz's cheeks with two air kisses before favoring him with a brilliant smile of straight, pearl-white teeth. Clearly orthodontic work had been a priority for her. Her frosted blonde hair was coiffed in a Marilyn Monroe pouf, and the neckline of her hot pink suit plunged low enough to expose a touch of black lace bra. An interesting choice for a foggy island morning on the coast of Maine. Maybe this was what Katz meant by glitz.

She turned her ice-blue eyes to me and arranged her frosted pink lips in a hard line. "Coffee. Black." She returned her gaze to Katz, composing her face into a simpering smile as he pulled out a chair for her.

"Estelle, I'm so glad you could come. Where's Stanley?" Stanley Katz was Bernard Katz's son, and Estelle's husband. I'd seen him around the island; he had inherited his father's girth and balding pate, but not his business sense or charisma. Stanley and Estelle had seemed like a mismatched couple to me until I found out the Katzes were rolling in the green stuff. As much as I didn't like the Katzes, I felt sorry for Stanley. Between his overbearing father and his glamorous wife, he faded into the background.

"Stanley?" Estelle looked like she was searching her brain to place the name. "Oh, he's out parking the car. I didn't want to have to walk over all of those horrid rocks." She fixed me with a stare. "You really should build a proper walkway. I could have broken a heel."

Katz chuckled. "When the Cranberry Island Premier Resort is built, you won't have to worry about any rocks, my dear." Or birds, or plants, or anything else that was "inconvenient." Their voices floated over my shoulder as I headed back to the kitchen. "You look stunning as usual, Estelle."

"Keep saying things like that and I'll be wishing I'd married *you!*" I rolled my eyes as the kitchen door swung shut behind me.

The aroma of coffee cake enveloped me as I ran down my mental checklist. Fruit salad, whole wheat toast, and skinny scrambled eggs for Estelle; scrambled whole eggs and blueberry coffee cake would work for Katz, who from the bulge over his pin-striped pants didn't seem too interested in Weight Watchers-style breakfasts. I tugged at the snug waistband of my jeans and grimaced. At least Katz and I had one thing in common. I grabbed a crystal bowl from the cabinet and two melons from the countertop.

As the French chef's knife sliced through the orange flesh of a cantaloupe, my eyes drifted to the window. I hoped the blanket of fog would lift soon. The Cranberry Island Board of Selectmen was meeting tonight to decide what to do with the land next door, and Barbara Eggleby, the Shoreline Conservation Association representative, was due in today. I was afraid the bad weather might delay her flight. *Save Our Terns,* the three-person island group I had formed to save the terns' nesting ground from development, was counting on Barbara for the financial backing to combat Katz's bid for development. As I slid melon chunks into the bowl and retrieved a box of berries from the refrigerator, my eyes returned to the window. The fog did look like it was letting up a bit. I could make out a lobster boat chugging across the leaden water.

The berries tumbled into a silver colander like dark blue and red gems, and as the water from the faucet gushed over them, the small boat paused to haul a trap. A moment later, the engine growled as the boat turned and steamed toward the mainland, threading its way through the myriad of brightly colored buoys that studded the cold saltwater.

Since moving to the island, I had learned that each lobsterman had a signature buoy color that enabled him to recognize his own traps, as well as the traps of others. I had been surprised to discover that what I thought of as open ocean was actually carved up into unofficial but zealously guarded fishing territories.

My eyes followed the receding boat as I gave the berries a final swirl and turned off the faucet. Lately, some of the lobstermen from the mainland had been encroaching on island territory, and the local lobster co-op was in an uproar. I strained my eyes to see if any of the offending red and green buoys were present. The veil of fog thinned for a moment, and sure enough, bobbing next to a jaunty pink and white one was a trio of what looked like nautical Christmas ornaments.

The boat had vanished from sight by the

time the fruit salad was finished. I eyed my creation — the blueberries and raspberries interspersed with the bright green of kiwi made a perfect complement to the cantaloupe — and opened the fridge to retrieve a dozen eggs and some fat-free milk. When I turned around, I slammed into Ogden Wilson, Katz's skinny assistant. My fingers tightened on the milk before it could slip from my grasp, but the impact jolted the eggs out of my hand. I stifled a curse as the carton hit the floor. Was I going to have to install a lock on the kitchen door?

Ogden didn't apologize. Nor did he stoop to help me collect the egg carton, which was upended in a gelatinous mess on my hardwood floor. "Mr. Katz would like to know when breakfast will be ready." His eyes bulged behind the thick lenses of his glasses. With his oily pale skin and lanky body, he reminded me of some kind of cave-dwelling amphibian. I wished he'd crawl back into his hole.

I bent down to inventory the carton; only three of the dozen had survived. "Well, now that we're out of eggs, it will be a few minutes later." It occurred to me that I hadn't considered him when doing the breakfast tally. Although Ogden generally stuck to his boss like glue, it was easy to forget he existed. “Are you going to be joining them?”

“Of course. But do try to hurry. Mr. Katz has an extremely busy schedule.”

“Well, I’m afraid breakfast will be slightly delayed.” I tipped my chin toward the mess on the floor. “But I’ll see what I can do.”

The oven timer buzzed as Ogden slipped through the swinging door to the dining room. I rescued the cake from the oven and squatted to clean up the mess on the floor. What kind of urgent business could Bernard Katz have on an island of less than a square mile? Most of the movers and shakers here were fishermen’s wives after a few too many beers. I hoped Barbara Eggleby would be able to convince the board that the Shoreline Conservation Association was the right choice for the land next door. The Katz development would be a cancer on the island. Lord knew the Katzes were.

I raced up the stairs and knocked on my niece’s door. Gwen had come to work with me for the summer, cleaning the rooms, covering the phones, and helping with the cooking from time to time in exchange for room and board. The help was a godsend — not only was it free, but it allowed me time to work on promoting the inn — but Gwen was not a perfect assistant.

Part of the reason Gwen was spending the summer at the inn was that her mother didn't know what else to do with her: she'd flunked half of her classes her first year at UCLA and my sister couldn't spend more than ten minutes in the same room with her daughter without one or the other of them declaring war. Her work at the inn, while not F-level, was between a B and a C, when I needed everything to be A+. Still, help was help, and beggars couldn't be choosers. I wished that some of the enthusiasm she showed for the art classes she was taking on the island would spill over to her housekeeping skills.

"Who is it?" answered a groggy voice from the other side of the door. I cracked the door open. Gwen's hair was a messy brown halo in the dim light from the curtained window.

"I'm sorry to wake you, but I need you to run down to Charlene's and get a dozen eggs."

"What time is it?"

"It's just after seven. Please hurry . . . I've got guests waiting."

She groaned. "Seven in the *morning?*"

"I know. But it's an emergency." She grumbled something and began to move toward the side of the bed, so I closed the door and jogged back down the stairs. I'd start with fruit salad and a plate of coffee cake, and bring out the eggs later. Maybe a pan of sausage, too . . . I could keep it warm until the Bittles came down at 8:30.

I was retrieving a package of pork sausages from the freezer when someone tapped on the door to the back porch. I whirled around to tell the Katzes I'd meet them in the dining room shortly, and saw the sun-streaked brown hair of my neighbor, John Quinton.

"Come in!" I hollered, smiling for the first time that morning. John's green eyes twinkled in a face already brown from afternoons out on the water in his sailboat, and his faded green T-shirt and shorts were streaked with sawdust. John was both a friend and a tenant; he rented the inn's converted carriage house from me, as well as a small shed he had converted to a workshop. He was a sculptor who created beautiful things from the driftwood that washed up on the beaches, but supplemented what he called his "art habit" with a variety of part-time jobs. In the spring and summer, he made toy sailboats for the gift shop on the pier. He also held a year-round job as the island's only deputy.

"You're up early. Working on a new

project?" I asked.

"Island Artists ordered a few more boats. I figured I'd churn them out this morning and then start on some fun stuff." His eyes glinted with mischief. "One of Claudette's goats was eyeing your sweet peas, by the way. I shooed her off, but I'm afraid she'll be back."

I groaned. Claudette White was one of the three members of *Save Our Terns,* and was known on the island as "eccentric." Although her husband, Eleazer, was a boatbuilder and popular with the locals, most of the islanders gave Claudette a wide berth. Her goats were almost as unpopular as she was, since they were notorious for escaping and consuming other people's gardens.

When Claudette wasn't caring for her goats or knitting their wool into sweaters and hats, she was holding forth at length about the evils of the modern world to anyone who would listen. I wasn't delighted that she had chosen to join *Save Our Terns,* but since the only other takers had been my best friend, Charlene, and me, we didn't feel we could turn her down.

John watched me pry sausage links out of a box and into a cast-iron pan. "I'm not the only one up early. I thought breakfast wasn't till 8:30."

"Yeah, well, we're working on Katz time today." A thump came from overhead, and then the sound of the shower. I sighed: so much for urgency. Gwen must be performing her morning ablutions. I appealed to John for help. "Do you have any eggs I can borrow? I was going to send Gwen down to the store, but I'm short on time."

"I just picked up a dozen yesterday. Is that enough?"

"You're a lifesaver." He disappeared through the back door, and the thought flitted through my mind that he might stay for a cup of coffee when he got back. I spooned fruit salad into a crystal bowl and reminded myself that John had a girlfriend in Portland.

Five minutes later I sailed into the dining room bearing the fruit salad and a platter mounded with hot coffee cake. Stanley Katz had arrived, and sat hunched in an ill-fitting brown suit next to his wife. Estelle glared at me. "Coffee cake? I can't eat that. I thought this breakfast was supposed to be low-fat!" Then she pointed a lacquered nail at the ginger-colored cat who had curled up in a sunbeam on the windowsill. "And why is there a *cat* in your dining room? Surely that's against health department regulations?"

I scooped up Biscuit and deposited her in the living room. She narrowed her gold-green eyes at me and stalked over to the sofa as I hurried back into the dining room. "I'll have skinny scrambled eggs and wheat toast out shortly," I said. "We had a slight mishap in the kitchen." I shot Ogden a look. He blinked behind his thick lenses. I attempted a bright smile. "Can I get anybody more coffee?"

Estelle sighed. "I suppose so." She turned to her father-in-law, who had already transferred two pieces of cake to his plate. "With this kind of service," she muttered under her breath, "I don't know how she expects to stay in business."

When I got back into the kitchen, a carton of eggs lay on the butcher-block counter. Darn. I'd missed John. The sausages had started to sizzle and Estelle's egg whites were almost done when the phone rang.

"Nat."

"Charlene? You're up early." Charlene was the local grocer, a fellow member of *Save Our Terns,* and my source for island gossip. She was also my best friend.

"I've got bad news."

I groaned. "You're kidding. The Katzes sprang a surprise 7 AM breakfast on me and then his assistant broke all of my eggs. It can't get any worse."

"It can. I just talked to the coastal airport: no planes in or out, probably for the whole day. A big nor'easter is about to hit the coast."

My heart thumped in my chest. "The airport is closed? So Barbara isn't going to make it in time for the council meeting?"

"It's just you and me, babe. And Claudette."

My stomach sank. Without a representative from the Shoreline Conservation Association to combat Katz's offer for the property next to the inn, we could only sit and watch as Katz wooed the board of selectmen with visions of the fat bank accounts the island would enjoy when the Cranberry Island Premier Resort came into being.

I leaned my head against the wall. "We're sunk."

Two

Save Our Terns might not be able to seduce the board with the promise of well-lined wallets, but I'd decided to resort to the best weapon in my arsenal: chocolate. That was my theory, anyway. Charlene had promised to try to schmooze with the selectmen one last time before the meeting. For my part, I'd been trying to reach Barbara all day, and ended up leaving six messages on her voice mail. The weather had only worsened; the fog had been supplanted by fat drops of rain that flung themselves at the kitchen windows, and the wind howled past the inn's eaves. The airport was definitely closed.

Since Barbara was not going to be here to advance our case, the job fell to me. My plan was to coerce the board of selectmen — and the rest of the island — with mounds of decadent desserts. Although I loved the island, it had been difficult getting to know the islanders, most of whom viewed both me (an outsider) and anything related to conservation with a wary eye. I hoped the international language of chocolate would help.

The timer dinged, and as I slid a pan of golden oatmeal chocolate chip cookies out of my twenty-year-old electric oven, I found myself wishing for a larger model. Maybe in another year, after revenue got steady, I'd invest in more appliances. My stomach lurched. If there *was* a second year.

I finished spooning chocolate-studded mounds of batter onto a pan and consoled myself with one of the cookies cooling on a rack. Ten dozen cookies down, ten dozen brownies to go. I rinsed the bowl out in the sink and began to root through the pantry for baking chocolate, crossing my fingers that the box was full. Five pans of brownies required a lot of chocolate, and I didn't relish the thought of a walk to the store in driving rain. Besides, time was running out; it was already three, and I was hoping to have time for a batch of shortbread before the meeting started at seven. I put my hand on the box and gave it a good shake; to my relief, it was almost full.

"Aunt Nat?" Gwen stood in the doorway and ran a hand through her long mass of curly brown hair. As usual, she was artistically dressed in a long, flowing black skirt and a close-fitting purple tank top that accented her slender waist. It wouldn't be my choice for changing sheets and cleaning bathrooms, but she seemed comfortable.

"How's it going back there?"

"I have to show you something." She spoke with a note of urgency, and visions of overflowing toilets, broken water pipes and electrical fires passed before my eyes.

"What's wrong? Is it an emergency?" My hand strayed to the phone. "Do I need to call John?" John often helped out with inn emergencies; plumbers were hard to come by on short notice.

"No, no, it's not that. Just come look." I followed her through the parlor down the long hallway to Ogden's room. When Gwen opened the door, my eyes swept the room. The blue-and-white-checked quilt lay smooth on the bed, and the wood floor shone as if freshly waxed. Either Ogden was a neat freak, or Gwen's housekeeping skills were improving. I hoped it was the latter.

"Everything looks great. Except the weather." My eyes drifted to the window, where starched white curtains were pulled back to expose an ocean of molten lead, interrupted by violent crashes of white as the surf hit the rocks. My throat tightened at the reminder that we were on our own at the board meeting tonight.

"And except for this." Gwen walked over to the rolltop desk in the corner. "I rolled it back to make sure I hadn't missed anything, and I found this." She pointed at a blueprint that lay half-unrolled next to a stack of bank statements on the cherry-wood desk's gleaming surface. My eyes lingered on the top statement; the holder of the account was listed as Holding Construction Company, and the most recent deposit was for more than $400,000. The Katzes must be doing pretty well.

"I'm not talking about the bank statements, Aunt Nat. This is the blueprint for the resort." She unfurled the pale blue paper and I stared down at the familiar coastline of Cranberry Island, disturbed by the sprawl of buildings depicted on the currently pristine property next door.

"Parking lots?" I snorted. "Is he planning on putting in a car ferry, too?"

"That's the least of it, Aunt Nat. Where's the Gray Whale on this map?" I looked at the section of coastline where the building that housed the inn had stood for more than a hundred and fifty years. In its place was an expanse of lined parking spaces. My stomach filled with ice water.

"That creep," I hissed. "Just this morning he was trying to convince me that the resort would be 'good for business', and all along he's been planning to run me out of business so he can raze the Gray Whale."

A footstep sounded in the hall. I froze. Gwen snatched my hand from the blueprint, shoved it back into the desk half-rolled and started tugging at the rolltop.

"Roll it down, roll it down!" Gwen wrenched the handle at the top of the desk, but it wouldn't budge; the humidity from the storm must have made the wood swell. I dropped the blueprint and yanked with her. The footsteps came closer, then paused. Suddenly the top slammed down with a bang, landing on my left thumb. I winced with pain and scurried toward the bathroom, where I was inspecting the sink when the door opened.

Ogden Wilson stepped into the room. His bulging eyes registered Gwen, then flicked to me. "What are you doing here?"

I smoothed my hair back with my uninjured hand and smiled. "Just checking to make sure the room was okay. My niece started a few weeks ago, and I was just looking to see if she'd missed anything."

Ogden's eyes roamed the room, lingering at the desk. A corner of the blueprint was sticking out. Had it been that way when we came in? "What was that noise I heard?"

"Noise?" My brain raced to produce a plausible explanation. "Oh, I slipped on one of the rugs and whacked the doorframe with my thumb." I raised my injured hand. The base of the nail had already begun to darken. "I've been meaning to buy some slip-proof pads," I continued, forcing a smile. "I'd better pick them up soon. I don't need the business shut down over a liability case."

I moved toward the door, and Gwen fell in behind me. "Anyway, it looks like you've done a fine job, Gwen. Mr. Wilson, please just let us know if there's anything you need." I eased the door closed as Gwen slipped through. "Sorry to disturb you."

I hurried back to the kitchen with Gwen on my heels. "Thank you for showing me that, Gwen. I can't *believe* this guy. If he wants to drive me out of business and then buy my inn, why is he even staying here?"

Gwen shrugged. "Maybe he doesn't like his son." She glanced at her watch, then looked up at me. "Hey, I really want to get in a few sketches of the storm; do you mind if I leave the last room to you?"

So much for a reformed helper. "On another day I'd say okay, but I've got 100 people to feed tonight and I still haven't done any prep work for breakfast tomorrow." Gwen sighed and trudged back down the hall. "Thanks for giving me the heads-up on the plans, Gwen," I called after her. She didn't respond.

When the kitchen door closed behind me, I picked up the phone and dialed Charlene. I shouldered the handset and recounted what we'd found in Ogden Wilson's room, unwrapping chocolate squares with my injured hand.

"That dirty rotten fink!" Charlene fumed. "I can't *believe* him! Nat, you should kick him out."

"I can't. I need the money. Besides, what am I going to tell him: that I was snooping through his assistant's stuff and didn't like what I saw?" I unwrapped four sticks of butter and dropped them into a saucepan to melt, then reached for the flour and sugar canisters.

"I guess it's better to keep your enemies where you can see them. So Gwen filled you in on what was going on? That was unusually helpful of her."

"Yeah, I guess it was. Now if only she would apply the same zeal to her housekeeping duties."

Charlene snorted. "Don't count on it.

Jeez, maybe we'll have to start another group: Save the Gray Whale."

"Very funny."

"You know, if Katz is planning to drive you out of business, I wonder why he's not staying with his son instead of paying you to provide bed and board?"

I measured the flour into an extra-large mixing bowl and then rummaged through a drawer for my second set of measuring spoons. "I've been wondering that too. Bad blood?"

"I'll see what I can find out." Charlene was the spider in the middle of the island's web of gossip. As the storekeeper and postmistress, everyone came by to see her, and she was so good at extracting information I was surprised that the CIA hadn't contacted her with a job offer.

"By the way," Charlene said, "I haven't been able to get in touch with Ingrid."

I extracted the spoons from the jumble in the drawer and began measuring out baking soda. "She hasn't been by to pick up her mail?"

"Nope. In fact, she hasn't been by the store in two days." Ingrid was the only undecided selectman, and her vote could make or break us. As of a week ago, she had been leaning toward voting for the association, but she was by no means a shoo-in. "I'm worried, Nat."

"Isn't Ingrid one of your afternoon regulars?" Several of the island women stopped by and had tea and sweets in the front of the store a few days a week, and I had seen Ingrid on a stool at the counter many times. She'd complimented me on my oatmeal-chocolate-chip cookies before; that's why I was baking ten dozen of them for tonight.

"Yup. She never misses two days in a row."

I stirred the dry ingredients together with a fork, and added them to the butter and chocolate. "Well, keep calling her. Maybe she came down with the flu or something."

"By the way, you've got a few letters down here, looks like they might be brochure requests, and Katz has got some sort of package."

"If the weather lets up, I'll send Gwen down to get them."

"Rats. Can't you come instead?"

"I'll tell you what. If I get ten dozen brownies done in the next 45 minutes, I'll be right down."

Charlene sighed. "See you at the church tonight then. And save some for me."

When I stepped into St. James Episcopal Church at 6:45, it was already half-full and buzzing with conversation. Cranberry Island was too small for a town hall, so the antique wooden church did double duty as a meeting hall. Usually, a half dozen islanders at a meeting was considered a good turnout; tonight it looked like the whole island, and even a few from neighboring islands, had showed up.

I headed toward the tables in the narthex with two loaded cookie trays. The room already smelled of coffee; Charlene had brewed enough to fill the two silver pots she'd set up on the folding tables. Charlene joined me in removing the wet plastic wrap from a mound of fudge brownies. We had barely uncovered the rich brown squares when the locals set upon them like a pack of starving wolves. They might not be sure what to think of me, but they certainly knew what to do with a plate of my brownies.

"The Katz contingent is already here," Charlene murmured into my ear. She had dressed for the occasion in a sparkly sweatshirt and jeans that hugged her well-padded form. Despite the rain, her highlighted and artfully tousled light brown hair looked as if she had just stepped out of the beauty parlor. She went to the mainland once a month to get her hair done and was addicted to Mary Kay cosmetics. I liked to tease her about it, telling her that she belonged in Texas, not a small island in Maine. This was usually met with a withering look and a comment regarding what she called my "bowl cut."

I looked down at myself — in my hurry, I had forgotten to change — and brushed a bit of flour from the front of my ragged blue T-shirt. Charlene grimaced at my ensemble and then pointed toward the front of the church. "Ogden is setting up posters and what looks like a big computer presentation."

I sighed. "Let's hope chocolate will triumph over technology." My eyes surveyed the room. Murray Selfridge stood in the corner talking with Bernard Katz and Estelle. Murray had moved away from the island and made his fortune on Wall Street, then retired and returned in grand style, buying up property and promising to establish a historical museum if he were elected to the board. He won the election, established the museum, and then, to the chagrin of most of the people who had voted for him, began courting developers.

I scanned the room, looking for Ingrid. Tom Lockhart, the head of the lobster co-op and the only selectman firmly in our court, was standing next to my neighbor, John, drinking coffee and wolfing down a brownie. John caught my eye and waved a brownie in greeting. I felt the blood rise to my face as I smiled back, then turned to Charlene.

"Where's Ingrid?" I asked.

"I don't know. She's usually an hour early to town events, and the first one at the feeding trough, but I haven't seen a trace of her this evening."

"Any luck getting in touch with her this afternoon?"

"She wasn't home . . . or she wasn't answering the phone. She hasn't gone off-island; I'd have seen her on the pier, and I can't imagine she was out for a stroll all afternoon in this weather." She nodded toward the rain pelting the church's windows.

"I guess we just have to keep our fingers crossed, then." I glanced over at the tables, where the mountains of cookies were dwindling. "Maybe I should have made more."

"Don't worry about it, Nat."

A cold wind blew into the room, and a tall woman with a bright yellow rain slicker swept in, closing the church door behind her. She peeled off her jacket and strode past the plates of cookies without a sideways glance. When a few people greeted her, she nodded, her thin lips stretched into a tight smile, as she made a beeline for the front of the church.

"Well, there's Ingrid," said Charlene. "I wonder what's up with her."

"I don't know, but it looks like we're about to get started." People were making little stacks of the remaining cookies and brownies and moving into the sanctuary. I snagged a brownie and followed Charlene down the main aisle.

Claudette was already sitting at the front of the church, looking grim and stolid in a flowered broomstick skirt and a large black tunic that clung to her ample figure. She looked like an avenging earth goddess, with her long gray hair pulled back into a severe bun and steel-gray eyes above rolling mounds of flesh. As always, her knitting needles clacked in her lap; whatever she was working on tonight was so thick and fleecy that it looked as if she were recreating a sheep out of wool.

"Hi, Claudette. What are you working on?" I asked.

Claudette looked at me as if I were dense, and raised the lump of wool, which now appeared to have at least one sleeve dangling from it. "A sweater."

"Did you get some of Nat's cookies?" Charlene asked. "They're to die for."

"I'm on a new diet; can't have sugar. Besides, I don't want sticky wool." Despite her bulk, Claudette was on a perpetual diet; the beet and spinach diet, the high-protein diet (which, Charlene informed me, might have failed due to heavy consumption of bacon and whipping cream), the cabbage and grapefruit diet . . . she'd tried them all.

"Mind if we join you?" Charlene asked. Claudette lumbered over a few inches to make room for us. Charlene, who was also generously proportioned, deposited herself in the empty spot next to Claudette, and I wedged myself into the remaining six inches at the end of the pew.

Once most of the islanders had abandoned what was left of the cookies and filed into the sanctuary, Tom moved to the pulpit, clearing his throat and calling the meeting to order. After a discussion of trash disposal and pier maintenance, he addressed the real business at hand, and stepped down to give Bernard Katz the pulpit. Ogden dimmed the lights in the sanctuary and Katz began his sales pitch, flashing colorful illustrated pictures of the future resort on the small white screen he'd erected over the cross at the front of the church.

"This resort not only means two million dollars in the town's coffers — enough to build a new school, or a library — but more jobs for islanders, as well as an increase in property values." He smiled broadly and looked around the room. "By making Cranberry Island the home of the next Premier Resort, you're investing in the island's future." My stomach lurched. I knew that the Shoreline Conservation Association's offer didn't even come close.

He turned toward the screen, ready to describe the proposed plan to the assembly. I noticed that the parking lot expansion I'd seen on the blueprints — the one that would presumably be built after he had bulldozed my inn — wasn't featured in the plan he was describing to the islanders. He had begun explaining how the golf course would be available to locals at a reduced fee when Claudette's sharp voice interrupted him.

"What about the terns?"

"The terns?" Katz looked confused for a moment. "Oh, you mean the birds." He chuckled. "I didn't know they played golf."

A few people tittered, but Claudette's voice was strident, and her gray eyes flashed fire. "I'm not talking about your stupid golf course. What are you going to do about the terns' nests?"

Katz smiled at her benevolently, exposing a line of crooked teeth. "Why, we'll relocate them to a more appropriate location, of course. Premier Resorts International is highly sensitive to environmental issues . . ."

"I was down there yesterday, and it looks like someone's been trying to 'relocate' them already. Somebody's been destroying their nests!"

A murmur passed through the crowd, and Katz's eyebrows shot up. "Destroying them? Dear lady, I'm sure you must be mistaken. There's not even a proper walkway to the beach." He smiled at his audience. "Of course, once the Cranberry Island Premier Resort is built, there will be a path to allow everybody access to the beach."

Claudette rose from her seat, her face flushed a dangerous red. "You're a murderer!" she spat. "You murdered the terns, and now you're planning to murder the island. *You're* the one who deserves to die, not those innocent birds!" She looked as if she was ready to lunge for Katz's throat. Charlene stood up and eased her back into the pew, whispering into her ear.

Bernard Katz smoothed down his nonexistent hair and turned back toward the screen. "I can assure you that Premier Resorts will handle the terns with the utmost care and respect. Now, as I was saying, the golf course will be available to islanders at a discount." As Katz droned on, I tried to imagine the lobstermen taking up golf, and wondered how much it would cost even at a fifty percent discount, which I was sure it wouldn't be. Probably more than most islanders made in a year. I was imagining a bunch of salty-haired lobstermen wandering around the golf course in hip waders when suddenly Katz was stepping down from the pulpit to a smattering of applause, and I realized with a jolt that my turn was next.

A lump rose in my throat as I prepared to make *Save Our Terns'* case to the board. I was making my way toward the front of the church when a door banged in the narthex and Barbara Eggleby appeared, soaking wet and clutching a briefcase. Her long red hair was plastered to her face and her navy blue pants suit left a trail of drips as she strode down the main aisle.

"Am I too late?"

"No, you're just in time," I said, smiling with relief. My knees wobbled as I staggered back to my pew and wedged myself back in next to Charlene.

"Glad you could make it, Ms. Eggleby." Tom motioned toward the pulpit. "Please, go ahead. Mr. Katz has just finished his presentation."

Barbara opened her briefcase and withdrew a piece of paper. Then she pushed her wet hair behind her ears and grasped the pulpit with both hands.

"As you know," she began, "The Shoreline Conservation Association is prepared to purchase, and has made an offer on, the parcel of land on which Mr. Katz would like to build his resort. Selling the land to the association would ensure that the land would remain exactly as it is, with no future development, enabling the island to retain the character that makes it such a marvelous place and ensuring that the terns can continue to nest."

She looked around the room before she continued. "I understand that the board of selectmen must do what it believes is in the island's best interest. Of course, the association feels that conserving this beautiful piece of land for generations to come is the best possible option, but we recognize that funding is important to all communities." She took a deep breath. "And that is why we are prepared to match Mr. Katz's offer of two million dollars."

Two million dollars? Barbara must have called in every favor she'd ever been owed. I looked at Ingrid; surely she'd vote for the association to take over the land now. Her mouth twitched, but she continued to stare at the back of the church. Behind me, everybody started talking. Bernard Katz stood up, his eyes hard behind his glasses. "I'll make it $2.1 million," he called over the noise. A hush fell as a hundred pairs of eyes settled on Barbara.

Barbara shook her head sadly. "I'm afraid I am not authorized to go above two million dollars." She paused for a moment. "Mr. Katz should be aware, however, that even if the land were to be acquired by Premier Resorts, there is an excellent chance that he would be unable to develop it, as it may be designated critical tern habitat by the federal government. In fact," she continued, "representatives from the Fish and Wildlife Service should be here in a few days to begin the evaluation."

"Evaluation? What authority do you have to begin an evaluation?" Katz demanded. The room exploded with noise as everyone began talking at once. Tom stood up and called for order. When the chaos began to subside, he responded to Katz's question. "I am the one who initiated the evaluation, Bernard. Now, before we move to a vote, we need to know; is your offer still good?"

Katz was silent for a moment. Then he straightened and pushed out his chin. "The offer's good."

"Then if there are no further comments from the floor," said Tom, "I move that we take a vote." No one seemed to want to take the pulpit again, so he turned to the two other selectmen. Murray had abandoned his relaxed position and was leaning forward in his seat. Ingrid continued to stare at a point in the back of the church, her lips pulled tight. "All in favor of selling the land to Premier Resorts for $2.1 million, say aye." Murray boomed his assent immediately. Tom shook his head. All eyes turned to Ingrid.

She took a deep breath, nodded, and said, "Aye."

THREE

"I can't believe she double-crossed us." Charlene slumped in one of my kitchen chairs as I took the whistling kettle off the stove and poured hot water into the teapot. Barbara sat across from her, still shivering despite the warmth of the yellow kitchen. Fortunately, Claudette had bundled up her knitting and stormed out of the church when Ingrid voted for Katz. I appreciated her support, but I wasn't in the mood to listen to her harangues tonight.

"I can't believe you went to all of that effort to get up here and the vote went the wrong way, Barbara," I said. When her connection from Boston was canceled, Barbara had rented a car and drove eight hours up the coast, only to discover that the water taxi wasn't in service. She had run up and down the pier in a frenzy until one of the fishermen agreed to take her to the island, just in time for the meeting.

“We’ll just have to resort to other tactics,” said Barbara as I filled a plate with the few cookies that hadn’t been consumed at the town meeting. Her voice was cold. “I swore Bernard Katz wasn’t going to win this time, and I meant it.”

“But if the beach isn’t designated critical habitat, what other recourse do we have?” Charlene asked.

“And can’t he develop the rest of the property anyway?” I added through a mouthful of cookie.

“I’ll find a way to keep that resort from being built, Nat. I promise.” As I poured the tea, she stood up and stretched like a cat. “I’m bushed. Mind if I take mine up to my room?”

“Not at all. See you in the morning, Barbara. Don’t worry about getting up in time for breakfast; I’ll fix something for you whenever you come down.”

As the kitchen door swung closed behind Barbara, Charlene added liberal amounts of cream and sugar to her tea and helped herself to a cookie. “These are really good. I’d ask for the recipe, but I’d just rather you made them more often.” She took a bite of cookie and chased it with a swig of tea, then leaned forward. “By the way, I found out a little more about why the big K is staying with you instead of at Cliffside with his son."

"Oh really?"

"Apparently they had a big fight about two months ago, and since then they haven't been too chummy. Katz used to stay at Cliffside all the time, but now he never visits."

"Any word on what the argument was about?"

"Nobody knows, but my guess is that it was either about money or about Estelle." Charlene took another bite of cookie. "How do you get these to be chewy *and* cooked all the way through? Mine are always either raw in the middle or hard as hockey pucks."

"Are they having financial problems?" I felt a surge of hope. Maybe the contract for the land next door would fall through.

"I don't know, but Polly Sarkes does housecleaning for them and she says Stanley hasn't paid her in two months."

"If they can't afford to pay the housekeeper, how are they going to afford to shell out two million dollars for a hunk of land and then build a multimillion-dollar resort on top of it?"

"Just because Stanley doesn't have the dough doesn't mean his daddy doesn't."

The bank statement I had seen that morning floated back into my mind, and my wild hope deflated as I realized Charlene was right. "Okay, so maybe Stanley's in financial trouble. Why would they fight about Estelle?"

Charlene rolled her mascaraed eyes. "Nat, you've got to be kidding me. You haven't noticed Katz Sr. starting to pant the moment Estelle steps into the room?" I remembered Katz's behavior at breakfast this morning, and had to admit Charlene had a point.

"I know they've been a bit flirtatious," I said. "But Estelle's married to Stanley."

"Maybe she's discovered that Stanley's small fry and she's trying to get her hooks into a bigger fish." Charlene took another bite of cookie. "After all, *somebody's* got to fund her wardrobe."

By the time Charlene climbed into her rusty truck, it was already 11:00. I thanked her for the emergency rations — she'd brought three cartons of eggs and a gallon of milk — and called it a night. I had been planning on baking banana bread, but decided to make a batch of muffins in the morning instead.

The storm howled outside as I curled up under my fluffy down comforter, watching the lightning flicker behind the curtains. Biscuit snuggled in beside me, and the inn felt warm and solid around me. It had withstood storms stronger than this during the 150 years it had clung to the island. I tried to push the possibility that the inn's days were numbered out of my mind, and finally drifted off.

The next morning dawned clear and rosy. The kitchen's pine floors and warm yellow walls glowed in the early light, and the sea that yesterday had been leaden was flecked with peach and gold.

I put a pot of coffee on and began cutting up a watermelon, trying hard not to fantasize about it being Katz's head. I combined the crimson fruit with strawberries and blueberries and reminded myself that although Katz was odious, it was important not to let his presence undermine my professionalism. Besides, Barbara had said he might not be able to develop the preserve anyway.

As I pulled a fresh carton of eggs out of the fridge, the refrigerator's half-empty shelves reminded me that it was time to place another big grocery order. A quick mental calculation sent a wave of apprehension through me. Katz or no Katz, between the cost of food and my upcoming mortgage payment, I had to find some way to book more guests if the inn was to make it through the summer. I laid the eggs on the counter and started peeling bananas to mash for muffins. Rooms aren't like bananas. If they're not used, you can't turn them into banana bread; they're gone. I resolved to take a bunch of brochures over to Mount Desert Island that afternoon.

By 8:30, the buffet table was spread with a lavish breakfast; ramekins of shirred eggs, sausages, fruit salad, and mounds of fragrant muffins. The couple from Alabama came down five minutes later and tucked in with relish. "Storms always make me hungry," white-haired Mrs. Bittles informed me as she helped herself to three muffins and a stack of sausages. Ogden Wilson entered the dining room alone a little before nine.

"Where's Mr. Katz?" I asked as I poured him a cup of coffee.

"I haven't seen him. Maybe he went out for a morning stroll." More like a morning troll, I thought, wondering if he'd decided to do a little nest removal before the evaluation began. Barbara came down a few minutes later looking fresh and cheerful, her hair wet again, but this time from the shower. She sat down at the farthest table from Ogden and turned her back to him. I walked over with a carafe of coffee.

"Sleep well, Barbara?"

"Like a rock." She smiled. "I love being tucked in when there's a storm outside. There's nothing cozier." She took a sip of the coffee I'd just poured. "Great coffee. You run a wonderful inn, Nat."

"Thanks. I'm just hoping I can keep doing it." I told Barbara to help herself to breakfast and then headed back into the kitchen to replenish the butter. Mrs. Bittles had put quite a dent in the slab I had laid out next to the muffins.

By 10:00, the Bittles, Ogden, and Barbara had headed back to their rooms, but Katz had yet to appear. I cleared the buffet table, threw the tablecloths into the washing machine, and headed upstairs to wake up Gwen. Katz would have to forage for himself.

I knocked on my niece's door and poked my head into her room. She sat up, looking disoriented. "Wow, that storm was noisy last night. I hardly slept."

"Noisy? I didn't notice anything."

"How could you not hear the wind? It was screaming like a banshee the entire night." She shook her head as if to clear it, then rubbed her eyes.

"I've got to head down to the mainland with some brochures, but I've left breakfast on the kitchen table for you; would you mind taking care of the rooms for me?"

"No problem." She fell back against the pillow. "Is it okay if I sleep a bit more and do the rooms later? I'm wiped."

"As long as they're done by three." She grunted as the door closed behind me. Maybe I'd call from the mainland to make sure she'd gotten up.

I stuffed a stack of brochures into a backpack and headed out the door. It was wonderful to have an excuse to be out and about; the morning was gorgeous. Instead of taking the road to the pier, I had decided to walk the footpath that wound through the preserve and check the nests on my way to catch the mail boat. Even if I couldn't find the nests, I thought with a pang, I should enjoy the path while I could. As my feet negotiated the rocky, narrow trail, my eyes drifted across the water toward the mainland. Mount Cadillac and Mount Pemetic rose like craggy beasts in the distance, and white gulls soared and wheeled in the crisp air.

The waves that had crashed with such violence yesterday now caressed the rocky shoreline, and a few fishing boats chugged across the blue-green water. Like living in a postcard, I thought, clambering onto a slab of granite and turning to look back at the inn.

The Gray Whale nestled into a craggy hill, its weathered gray shingles and blue trim soft against the vivid green of the landscape. The meadow below it was awash in the pink and purple of lupines, and the magenta roses climbing up the trellis on the side of the inn blazed in the morning light. The blue window boxes overflowed with pale pink petunias and vibrant fuchsia geraniums, with little pockets of deep purple lobelia and snow-white verbena. Above them, white-curtained windows sparkled in the sunlight. I couldn't believe the inn was mine. Mine for now, anyway, I thought with a wrench as I climbed off the lichened rock and made my way back down to the path. I glanced at my watch; it was time to pick up the pace if I was going to make the noon mail boat.

The path was clearly not a major thoroughfare. Several clumps of beach roses had grown across it, and as I made my way up toward the cliffs that overlooked the terns' nests I found myself wishing I'd brought hedge clippers, or maybe a machete. The flowers were a beautiful deep pink, but the thorns were merciless; scratches soon crisscrossed my arms from pushing branches out of the way. A few broken branches dangled from some of the bushes; the leaves were wilted, but still green. It looked as if someone else had been on the path recently; someone coming to vandalize the nests? Bernard Katz? But Katz had just found out about the evaluation last night, and not even the Katzes were dumb — or desperate — enough to be out in a nor'easter.

As the path rose higher, I wondered what Barbara was planning to do if the evaluation didn't protect the preserve from development. She'd mentioned alternate tactics, but I couldn't think of any, unless she managed to come up with an extra half-million dollars. I skirted a patch of blueberry bushes in full bloom, their little white bell-shaped flowers hanging from upright branches. If Barbara did manage to keep the Katzes from flattening the area, this would be a great place to come berry picking.

I finally reached the cliff overlooking the terns' nesting area, a narrow strip of light-brown sand that stretched only a hundred yards or so along the base of an almost sheer drop-off. The terns wheeled about over the beach, their wings snowy in the sunlight, but the nests were so well camouflaged I couldn't make them out. How the heck did Claudette know they were being vandalized?

I couldn't even see them.

I eased my backpack onto the ground and edged off the path a little ways down the steep slope, hoping to get at least a glimpse of what Claudette was talking about. I fumbled for a handhold and tried to crawl crabwise down the sharp rocks. I soon gave up. How could someone destroy the nests? I couldn't even get to them.

I was scooting back up toward the path when a loose rock shifted under my left foot. My stomach lurched as I started to slide down the cliff's rocky face. My toe caught a clump of something growing out of a crack, steadying me for a moment, but whatever it was gave way, and my whole body began to slip downward. I scrabbled for a foot-hold, but my body was sliding faster now, my shirt rode up, and the lichen-covered rock scraped my stomach as I flailed for something to hold onto.

Suddenly my feet hit something solid. I flailed to keep my balance, swinging over the teeth of the rocks below; after a heart-stopping moment, my hand somehow found a tuft of grass and pulled my body back over the narrow ledge that had broken my fall. I stood frozen, afraid to move, while my ragged breath slowed. The skin on my stomach felt like it was on fire, and my knees and palms were raw. I looked back up the cliff; I had slid only fifteen feet, but it felt more like five hundred. Maybe it would be a good idea to tell the evaluators to approach the terns' nests by boat.

I looked down toward my feet. The ledge I had landed on was about five feet long and two feet wide at its broadest point. I stood on the narrowest part, at the very end; six inches farther to the right, and I would have kept sliding. I shuffled over toward the middle, then turned gingerly and eased my aching body down onto the shelf.

Great job, Nat. Not only had I gotten myself stuck hanging on a ledge halfway down a sheer cliff under an infrequently traveled path, but nobody knew I was taking the path. My battered body wasn't up to climbing back up the cliff, and I wondered how long it would be before someone figured out I was gone. With any luck it would be sometime before breakfast tomorrow.

I glanced down at the beach to see if the extra fifteen feet had improved my visibility. It hadn't. The terns were clustered a little farther down the rocky cliff, diving down and then soaring back up, not far from my narrow perch. I leaned over slightly, and caught a glimpse of something gold flashing under the flurry of wings. I craned to get a better look, then sucked in my breath.

The gold thing was a Rolex watch. I knew it was a Rolex because it was attached to Bernard Katz's arm.

Four

I closed my eyes for a moment, and then forced myself to look again. The sunlight gleamed on Katz's bald head, which hung from his body at an impossible angle. His limp arm, clad in the sleeve of a button-down shirt, was draped over a rock. He looked like an oversized doll that had been flung down by an angry child.

I leaned back against the rocks, fighting the urge to vomit. Katz looked as if he were beyond help. In a way, that was a good thing, because I couldn't see any way to get down to help him. In fact, I was in need of a little assistance myself.

A shiver passed through me. If it hadn't been for the ledge, it might have been me on the rocks next to him. I massaged my aching hands and stared out to sea, trying not to look at the body askew on the rocks. It didn't seem possible that Bernard Katz, who had been alive and boisterous and planning to ruin my inn just last night, was dead. I didn't like Katz, but I didn't wish this on him.

As the buoys bobbed up and down on the blue waves, I wondered why Katz had been out on the cliffs. Maybe Claudette had been right — he was destroying the nests, and had slipped and fallen on the rocks. That didn't seem right, though; nest removal seemed more like a task Katz would delegate. I couldn't imagine him willing to get his clothes dirty — or risk his neck — by climbing around on a cliff.

How Katz had ended up dead on a cliff was one question. What I really needed to worry about was getting *myself* off a cliff — preferably alive. Unfortunately, my perch was out of view of anything on the island, so my best hope was that a passing boat would notice me. I glanced down at my camouflaging gray T-shirt and khaki shorts. Had I known I'd end up on a cliff, I would have borrowed something a bit more colorful from Estelle. My eyes squinted down at the empty blue water, searching for a boat to flag down.

Despite the horror on the rocks below, the view was breathtaking. The waves glittered in the sunlight, and hundreds of buoys floated among the whitecaps, but no boats turned up to haul the traps that lurked under each of the brightly colored buoys. They looked like children's tops. As my eyes searched the water, I noticed that the red and green buoys that had plagued the island's lobster fleet for weeks were gone. Maybe the mainland folks had given up. On the other hand, maybe the locals had cut the long lines linking the buoys to the traps in an effort to discourage the invader.

I shifted on my narrow ledge, trying to find a more comfortable position, and avoided looking over toward where the terns were still fluttering and diving. For the first time since I'd moved to Maine, I found myself wishing for a cell phone. Since I would have stowed it in my backpack, though, the phone wouldn't have helped — my backpack lay at the top of the cliff.

As my back sagged against the rough cliff wall, the sound of a boat's engine floated to my ears. I climbed to my feet, prepared to yell and wave, but the engine's sound faded as the boat changed course. I slumped back down onto my rocky seat, trying to find a comfortable position and fighting back the panic that had begun to well in my throat. From my vantage point at the inn, boats always seemed to be coming and going.

Today, the water remained maddeningly empty.

My eyes avoided the fluttering terns, but their calls echoed in my ears, and my thoughts returned to Bernard Katz, and whether the resort would go through without him. As much as I didn't like to admit it, Katz's death, while horrible, might provide a solution to my predicament. I was mulling over options for persuading Stanley not to build the resort when the thrum of an engine reverberated below me.

The sound grew louder, and the *Island Queen* — the mail boat — inched into view. I waved my arms and yelled, gluing my eyes to the six people sitting in the back of the little ferry and willing them to look up at the cliff. Just before the gray and white boat disappeared beyond the horn of the island, a person in a white shirt waved back. I threw my arms about, hoping that the people on the boat would figure out that I was in trouble. The boat slowed for a moment — its engine thrummed lower, idling — then revved up again and kept going. I kept waving until the boat slipped out of sight, then sagged back against the wall.

It must have been twenty minutes later when my name floated down on the wind. I craned my neck toward the top of the cliff to see John's brown face grinning down at me. "Looks like you got yourself into a tight spot there, Miss Natalie." He dangled my green backpack from one finger. "Good thing you left this up here. Made it easy to find you."

My heart surged with joy and relief — and perhaps a little of something else — before I remembered the body on the cliff.

"Thank God you're here," I gushed. "But it's not just me. Katz is down here, too."

John's bushy eyebrows shot up. "Bernard Katz is down there with you?"

"Yeah." My voice caught. "I think he's dead."

John blanched beneath his summer tan. "Nat — what happened? Are you okay?"

"Get me out of here and I'll tell you everything."

"Hold on while I tie the rope to something. I'll have you up and out in a minute." He disappeared. A few moments later, a rope slithered down the rock face. I winced as my hands closed around the rough hemp, and my body screeched in protest as I worked my way up the cliff toward John. My palms were on fire by the time I reached the top. John reached out and helped me up over the edge with a warm, calloused hand. The heat of his touch ran up my arm like an electrical current.

John's eyes darted from my raw hands to my bloodied knees as I brushed myself off. "Are you sure you're okay? What happened? Where's Katz?"

I pointed back toward the cliff. "Over where the terns are." He moved toward the edge and peered down. "How did you know I was here?" I asked.

"George McLeod radioed from the *Island Queen.* Said you looked stuck."

"Thank God. I worried that he thought I was just a friendly hiker."

"Most hikers are smart enough to stay on the path." His green eyes glinted at me. "What were you doing, anyway? Trying to body-surf on the rocks?"

I shook my head. "No, I was headed to the mail boat. I decided to come this way so I could see if Claudette was right about the nests being damaged. I was trying to get a closer look when I slipped and found . . . that." I jerked a thumb toward the cliff.

John leaned over the edge, steadying himself on a rock, and I admired the play of muscles in his calves as he moved. The sun gleamed on his sand-colored hair as he turned toward me. "I see the terns, but I don't see Katz. Are you sure he's dead?"

I told him about the angle of Katz's neck,

and his eyes darkened with worry. "Can you make it back to the inn?"

I nodded.

"I need you to call the mainland police. Tell the dispatcher that we'll need both the police and the paramedics. They might want to send a helicopter, if there's one available."

"I thought you were the police."

"I am, but the state police handle homicide cases."

My heart raced. "Homicide?"

"Things have been a bit tense around here lately, and this is kind of an unusual circumstance. I don't think we can rule it out."

I nodded and had started shuffling down the path to the inn when John caught my shoulder. The hard lines of his face softened. "Don't worry, Nat. I'm sure everything will be fine; I'm just glad you're okay." I tried to smile, but the muscles of my face were frozen. Instead, I grunted and limped back down the path toward home.

When I stepped through the kitchen door, Gwen sat at the table in a fluffy blue bathrobe, starting in on the shirred eggs. Despite the fact that she had obviously just emerged from the bed covers, her ivory skin was flawless, and her hair, while wild, fell in a gorgeous tumult of curls around her shoulders.

I, on the other hand, felt — and probably looked — like the bride of Frankenstein.

Gwen looked up as the kitchen door closed behind me, and her face filled with concern as she took in my battered appearance. Her eyes darted from my skinned knees to my face. "What happened to you?" she asked.

"I fell off a cliff."

"That explains the knees. That must have been some fall. You look awful."

I grimaced. "I also found Bernard Katz. He's dead. John thinks someone might have killed him."

Gwen's brown eyes widened. "Someone murdered him?"

"It's only a theory," I said. "He could have just slipped and fallen."

I limped to the phone and dialed the police. Gwen had worked her way through two eggs and half a muffin by the time I had finished detailing the situation to the dispatcher. I hung up the phone and eased myself into a chair, helping myself to my niece's last muffin. "Well, they're sending a helicopter and the state police. I wonder if John's right; maybe Katz *was* murdered. I can't imagine him climbing around on those cliffs." I unwrapped the muffin from its little paper cup. "Then again, I can't imagine why he was out there in the first place."

My teeth sank into the muffin, the familiar sweetness of bananas and walnuts erasing some of the horror of finding Katz. My kitchen helped, too; the blue-and-white tile backsplash, the butter yellow walls, and the rich caramel-colored floor always made me feel safe and cozy. The sun streamed in through the windows, and the view of the blue ocean and the lighthouse in the distance was serene.

My niece speared a piece of watermelon. "Well, it wouldn't surprise me if someone murdered Katz. I mean, half the island hated him. Even Fernand was saying things would be a lot better if Katz just disappeared and didn't come back."

Gwen's art instructor, Fernand LaChaise, was trying to establish an art colony on the island. It was a great idea as far as the inn was concerned; in fact, my guests the Bittles were on the island for a week-long *en plein air* workshop with him. My knowledge of art was minimal, but from the easels I'd seen set up at various points on the island, I gathered that *en plein air* was a fancy term that meant "painting outside."

I looked at Gwen. "Why didn't Fernand like Katz?"

Gwen swallowed her watermelon. "Would

you come to Cranberry Island to paint a golf course?"

She had a point, but I didn't think that that was enough to warrant murder. Who else might have wanted him out of the way? Claudette, of course, had told the entire island she wished Katz were dead just last night. I wondered how she'd feel when she found out her wish had come true.

My mind touched on Barbara's comment about "alternate tactics," then dismissed it. Even if Barbara were to consider killing Bernard Katz, how would she lure him out onto a rocky cliff during a storm? And just because John had *suggested* Katz might have been murdered, it didn't mean he *had* been murdered. For all I knew, he had just slipped and fallen.

Gwen's voice snapped me out of my reverie. "You should probably go and clean those cuts up. Some of them look pretty nasty."

"You're probably right." I pried myself up from the chair and lumbered toward the stairs. I was warming up to Gwen; despite her less-than-perfect housekeeping skills, she did seem concerned about me, and about the inn. Maybe this could turn out to be a long-term relationship.

"By the way," Gwen called after me.

"Does this mean I don't have to do Katz's room?"

When I had bandaged my wounds, transferred the tablecloths to the dryer and checked the answering machine for messages (two brochure requests and six suddenly solicitous islanders, looking for news on the helicopter, but no new reservations), I started a batch of cranberry scones to take my mind off Bernard Katz. I had just finished mixing together the dry ingredients when a sharp rap sounded at the front door. I wiped my hands on a dishtowel and went to answer it.

A policeman stood on the front doorstep.

"Ms. Natalie Barnes?" the man asked in the rough voice of a pack-a-day smoker. He was a thick, short man with greasy dark hair. I caught a whiff of hair gel and stale tobacco on the breeze that eddied past him through the door.

I forced myself to smile. "That's me."

"My name is Sergeant Grimes. I understand you found Mr. Katz's body on the cliff."

"That's right." I leaned against the door. "So he is . . . dead, then?"

Grimes nodded. "Yes, he is. I have a few questions I'd like to ask you."

My body felt numb. I knew that Katz was dead, but it seemed much more official coming from a policeman. "I'm sorry to hear that. I thought he was, because of his neck . . ." I shook myself, trying to clear the vision of Katz's body from my mind. "I'm in the middle of a batch of scones, but you're welcome to come in and talk to me while I work."

Sergeant Grimes paused for a second, then said, "That would be fine." He stepped inside and followed me through the parlor and the dining room to the kitchen, his eyes taking in the antique bookshelves, the soft overstuffed couches and the pale blue and peach oriental rugs as we walked.

"Looks like you've got quite a bit invested in this inn," he said, sitting down at my big pine farm table.

I nodded. "It takes a lot to get an inn going. Can I get you some coffee?"

Sergeant Grimes declined and pulled out a small notebook. I picked up my pastry cutter and began cutting butter into the flour and sugar mixture. He watched me push the cutter down with my fingertips, trying not to aggravate my scraped and bruised hands.

"What happened to your hands?"

"I hurt them on the rocks when I fell

down the cliff."

He made a note in his book and turned his eyes back to me. They were blue, and close-set. "What were you doing on the cliff?"

"I was walking to the pier to catch the mail boat. I was going to drop some brochures off on the mainland."

Grimes raised an eyebrow. "Do you usually take the path to the pier? It seems to me that the road is a much easier walk."

"There's a strip of beach down there where black-chinned terns nest. At the board meeting last night, someone said that the nests had been disturbed. I decided to take a look myself."

"And somehow you managed to slip off the path and end up right near Mr. Katz's body."

"That's right."

I scraped the zest from an orange as Grimes made notes in his little book. He smoothed his hair with his free hand as he wrote, then fixed me with small blue eyes. "I understand that you and Mr. Katz had some . . . conflicting interests. Can you tell me about that?"

As I spoke, I stirred the orange zest into the dry mixture. "Bernard Katz wanted to develop the land next to my inn. I wanted the island to sell the land to a conservation group. Unfortunately, the board of selectmen decided to sell it to him."

"So you just threw in the towel, is that right, Miss Barnes?"

I set down the wooden spoon and sighed. "Tom Lockhart ordered an evaluation of the site, to see if it should be designated critical nesting habitat and remain undeveloped." I walked to the freezer and pulled out a bag of cranberries and a bag of walnuts. "Unfortunately, what the evaluators decide is out of my hands."

Sergeant Grimes leaned back in his chair. "If this development goes through, it won't be very good for your business, will it?"

I measured out the walnuts and added them to the bowl. "Probably not."

"You've got a lot riding on the success of this inn."

Just my life savings. "Of course." I shrugged. "All business owners are invested in their businesses." I opened the bag of cranberries and began pouring them into a measuring cup.

"Invested enough to murder someone who was threatening your livelihood?"

I started. Cranberries jumped across the counter and rolled onto the floor, bumping across the pine planks. I set down the bag and took a deep breath, fixing my eyes on Grimes. "No business is worth more than someone's life. Even someone like Katz." As soon as the second sentence slipped out of my mouth, I wanted to swallow it back.

Grimes sat up like a dog on a scent. "*Even* Katz, eh?"

"Yes. Even Katz." I began collecting berries from the counter and returning them to the cup. "Besides, who said he was murdered? I thought that was just a theory. That cliff is hazardous; I almost killed myself on it this morning."

Grimes refused to be waylaid. "So this development would have been the death knell — pardon me — of the Blue Whale Inn."

"*Gray* Whale Inn," I said, fighting to keep the irritation out of my voice. I shrugged. "Who knows? Katz told me the other day that I might even get some extra business out of the deal." Even though he was planning on eliminating my inn and replacing it with a parking lot.

Grimes' close-set eyes were calculating. "Still, it wouldn't have been quite the island retreat you had in mind when you bought the place."

"No, but hardly anything turns out like you plan." I forced a smile. "You just have to make the best of things."

Grimes' hand strayed to his hair again. No wonder it was so greasy. He couldn't stop touching it. "Yes, you seem like the type to make the best of things." He made a few more notes, then watched me add the cranberries and stir in the buttermilk before turning the batter out onto a floured wooden board.

I had coated my hands with flour and was about to roll out the dough when he snapped his notebook shut and stood up. "Where's Katz's room?"

"He's . . . I mean he was . . . in the Crow's Nest. It's on the second floor, down at the end of the hall."

"Do you have a key?"

I rinsed my hands and dried them. "I'll get it." Grimes followed me out of the kitchen to the reception desk in the front hall. I opened the cabinet behind the desk and retrieved the key to the Crow's Nest, catching another whiff of stale tobacco as I handed it to Grimes.

"Is this the only key?" he asked.

"This one and the one Katz had." I shuddered to think of where that key was now.

"If you don't mind, I'm going to go take a look," Grimes said. "We'll be treating Katz's room as evidence, so till you hear otherwise, it's off-limits to you and your staff."

Evidence? He must be pretty convinced Katz was murdered. "You're welcome to it," I said. "Is it all right if I head back to the kitchen? I'd like to finish up those scones."

"That would be fine." Grimes started up the stairs, then paused and turned around. "Oh, and one more thing, Miss Barnes." His close-set eyes were hard. "I hope you're not planning to leave the island anytime soon."

Five

I set aside half a dozen of the still-warm scones and packed the rest into a plastic container to take down to Charlene's. For the last few months, Charlene had been selling my baked goods at the store; in addition to picking up a few extra dollars a week, I hoped that the stack of brochures and the sign, "Goodies from the Gray Whale Inn," would garner me some additional guests. I wanted to take the scones down while they were fresh, but the truth was, I also needed to sit on Charlene's squashy couch and drink a cup of tea and talk.

Grimes' arrival had thwarted my plan; I didn't want to leave until he was gone. Instead, I threw a load of towels into the washer, made out my grocery list, and headed for the front desk.

I surveyed the calendar for the coming months with a sinking feeling. The long weeks of July and August, supposedly the high season, stretched before me like an empty plain, broken only by a scant four bookings. I had been counting on at least three times that number to pay the bills. Maybe it was time to talk with Fernand about setting up a series of artists' retreat weeks; we could split the advertising costs and generate more income for both of us.

I was closing the calendar and trying not to think about where the money for an advertising campaign would come from when the phone rang. My heart flared with hope. It was probably another islander who was suddenly concerned about my welfare — and any information I might happen to have about the helicopter out by the cliffs — but it might be another reservation.

"Good afternoon, Gray Whale Inn."

"Is this Natalie Barnes?" The woman spoke in a high-pitched voice.

"Speaking."

The woman cleared her throat and continued. "This is Gertrude Pickens of the *Daily Mail.* I understand you're the proprietor of the Gray Whale Inn?"

"Yes, I am."

"And you're also the person who found Bernard Katz's body this morning, on the side of a cliff, is that right?"

Goosebumps crept down my back. "Yes."

Gertrude Pickens continued in a sugary voice. "He was a guest of yours at the inn, is that correct?"

"He was."

"That must have been difficult, having a guest who was planning to replace your inn with a parking lot."

My stomach flip-flopped. How had she found that out? "Well," I said, struggling to keep my voice even, "you can't let your feelings get in the way of running your business."

"Oh, so he *was* planning to replace your inn with a parking lot?"

"I didn't say that."

"No matter, no matter." A keyboard clicked in the background. "Now, correct me if I'm wrong," she continued, "but the Cranberry Island Board of Selectmen voted to sell the property next to yours to Bernard Katz's company, Premier Resorts International, just last night. As I understand it, you were the leader of the organization — is it *Save Our Terns?* — that opposed the development. The decision must have made you very angry." Her voice was cajoling.

"Look," I said. "The police are investigating the situation. If you have questions about Bernard Katz or his business, why don't you go ask them?"

"They're investigating it then, are they? So they *do* think foul play is involved?"

"You'll have to take that up with the police. Now, if you don't mind, I'm very busy here. I'm going to have to let you go. Goodbye." The voice continued to squeak out of the receiver as I slammed it down. How had Gertrude Pickens gotten wind of Premier Resorts' plan to pave over my inn?

"Nosy neighbors?" Grimes hung over the carved wooden banister, smirking at me.

"No," I said. "Nosy newspaper reporters. I referred them to you."

Grimes swaggered down the rest of the stairs. "I think I'm finished here for today. Katz's room is still off-limits, though." He eyed me and held up the key. "You're sure this is the only key?"

"That's it," I said.

"Well, once the coroner's report comes in, I may have to have forensics out here."

I cringed. "Please tell me that doesn't mean yellow crime scene tape everywhere."

"Well, we'll see." Grimes walked past me to the front door. He turned to me with one hand on the doorknob. "I guess that's all for now," he said. Then he wagged a finger at me. "Remember what I said, though. If you've got any business off-island, you'll have to send somebody else."

"How could I forget?"

When the door closed behind him, I laid my head down, pressing my forehead against the surface of the big maple desk. My inn was in jeopardy, one of my guests had died under suspicious circumstances, the newspaper was running a story on it, and it looked as if the police had decided I might be a murderer. I was sure things could get worse. I just wasn't sure how.

Something warm pressed against my leg; it was Biscuit. I pulled her up on my lap, thankful for the company. She curled up into a ball, her green eyes half-closed as she rumbled with pleasure. "At least *you're* happy."

I was rubbing her cheeks and feeling marginally better when there was another knock at the door. Biscuit leaped off my lap as I stood up, wondering what Sergeant Grimes wanted now. To my relief, it was John.

"Thank goodness it's you," I said.

"I knocked at the kitchen door first, but I didn't see you," he said, smiling. "You look almost spooked. Who were you expecting, the bogeyman?"

"Close enough. I just had a nice little meeting with Sergeant Grimes. He seems to think Bernard Katz was murdered." I sighed. "He also thinks I might have killed him."

John's smile faded. "You're kidding me."

"Well, he told me I wasn't allowed to leave Cranberry Island, and made some pretty insinuating remarks." I realized that John was still standing on the doorstep. "I'm sorry — please, come in. Are you hungry? I just made a batch of cranberry walnut scones."

"No wonder it smells so good in here," he said, stepping through the door. "That sounds great." Biscuit sidled up to him, mewing plaintively. John scooped her up and she rumbled with pleasure as he followed me into the kitchen.

"Traitor," I muttered.

John continued to rub Biscuit as I fixed a plate of scones and filled the teakettle with water, more aware than I would have liked of John's lean limbs and the crinkle of the brown skin around his green eyes. He cooed to Biscuit, who luxuriated in the attention; with everything that had been going on, I'd neglected her for the last couple of days.

"What a day," he said, pulling out a chair and sitting down. "I think I've talked with half of the island already. For some reason, once the helicopter came, everyone was in the mood for a hike along the cliffs." Biscuit settled in contentedly on his lap, still purring.

"You're telling me," I said. "I've got half a dozen calls to return to people I've never even spoken to." I put the kettle on the stove and sat down across from him. "So," I said, "What happened?"

"They airlifted him out." John's twinkling green eyes were still, and his voice was serious. "You were right," he said. "He was beyond help."

"That's what Grimes said." I sat for a moment, thinking of what I'd seen on the cliff. "Do you still think someone killed him?"

"Well, there's still the possibility that he might have fallen. We won't be sure until the autopsy results are in." He grimaced. "I don't know, though. He looked pretty bad."

"What do you think he was doing out there?"

"It looked like he might have been going to meet someone." He paused to sink his teeth into a scone. His sandy eyebrows shot up and some of the sparkle returned to his green eyes. "These are delicious," he mumbled through a mouthful of crumbs. I resisted the urge to reach out and brush a crumb from his lower lip.

"Why do you think he was meeting someone?"

"Just something I saw. Something he had with him. Besides, he was pretty dressed up for a hike."

I snorted. "Anything less than a three-piece suit was casual for Bernard Katz." I thought for a moment. The path through the preserve ended up right next to Cliffside. Maybe Estelle had lured him out for a late-night rendezvous. "Do you think he might have been going to meet a woman?"

John looked up, startled. "What makes you say that?"

"Just a guess," I said.

John said nothing, and I guessed I had hit close to home. I wondered what Katz had had with him that pointed to a meeting with a woman. Flowers? Condoms? If he was meeting with Estelle, my guess would be something more expensive, like a forty-carat diamond bracelet. Although that might be hard to explain to Stanley. On the other hand, Stanley didn't seem to care too much what Estelle did.

"So you don't think he was out trying to destroy the terns' nests?" I asked.

"I don't imagine so, not in a sports coat and slacks."

The kettle whistled, and I got up to fix

tea. I had just poured the water into the pot when Gwen swept into the kitchen with a sketchbook under her arm, looking stunning in a red floral sleeveless dress that clung to her slim figure. I was suddenly conscious of the fact that I hadn't changed clothes or looked in a mirror since my fall on the cliff that morning.

My eyes darted to John; his eyes crinkled into a smile. "Hiya, Gwen."

"Hiya, John. Hey, Aunt Nat." Her eyes registered the plates on the table. "Ooh, scones. Can I have one?"

"Sure," I said. She grabbed two. "Where are you off to?" I asked.

"I've got a sketching class with Fernand this afternoon." Before I could ask, she said, "I'm done with all of the rooms. I didn't do Katz's, though."

"Thanks," I said. "Apparently that room's off-limits for a while, anyway. Will you be back in time for dinner?"

"Oh, don't worry about me. I'll grab a sandwich." She glanced at the table. "And maybe a scone or two, if there are any left."

"See you later, then," I said. "Have fun."

John's eyes followed her out of the room, then returned to me. I felt like an ugly stepsister in the presence of Cinderella. I hoped John didn't plan on trying out for the role of Prince Charming.

"I don't understand how she eats the way she does and stays so skinny," I said. "It's not fair."

"Ah, youth," said John. "Still, kids that young are like California fruit; they look good, but they have no flavor." He winked at me. "They need to get a few more years under their belts before they become interesting."

I felt the blood rush to my face and stood up, bumping the table with my skinned knee. "Cream or sugar?" I asked in a strangled voice.

"Neither," he said, grinning. I doctored my own tea and sat down again, still smarting.

"So," I said, "are the police considering anyone other than me as a suspect?"

"Who said they were considering you?" John said. "Just because Grimes asked some pointed questions doesn't mean you're a suspect. Besides, it's not official that Katz was murdered. We haven't gotten the coroner's report back yet, remember?"

"True. I guess I have a few days left before Grimes decides to slap me in jail."

"Nat, let's wait and see what happens, okay?" John reached across the table and grabbed my hand. Once again, my whole body warmed at his touch. Then he squeezed, and I winced.

"Sorry." He let go, and the warmth faded. "I forgot how banged up you are. Anyway," he continued, "if it *is* murder, the coroner's report may turn up some new information. It's still early going." He leaned back in his chair. Biscuit looked up and mewed for more attention.

"Maybe Grimes is just trying to make me nervous," I said. "Besides, aren't something like ninety percent of murders committed by family members?"

John laughed. "Let's find out if anyone other than Katz is to blame before we start pointing fingers."

"I guess we'll just have to wait and see."

"Yup."

By the time we had finished our scones and tea, I was feeling much better. John headed back to his cottage with Biscuit on his heels, promising to let me know as soon as he found out anything else. I checked my watch. It was almost four. I decided to clean up the kitchen and then run the scones down to the store before dinnertime.

I was just closing the dishwasher when someone knocked at the kitchen door.

"Come in!" I called.

Barbara Eggleby poked her head through

the door. "Hi, Nat. Sorry to bother you, but do you know where I can get some dinner around here?"

"Spurrell's Lobster Pound down on the wharf is good," I said. "By the way, have you heard the news?"

Barbara looked puzzled. "News? What news?"

"Bernard Katz is dead."

Barbara's face paled. For a moment, a brief flash of something like triumph flashed over her features, but it was quickly submerged.

"That's awful," she breathed. "How did it happen?"

"Apparently he fell off a cliff," I said.

"Fell off a cliff?"

"Yeah. I found him this morning. He was right above the terns' nests." I shuddered at the memory of Katz sprawled across the rocks like a discarded doll.

Barbara's eyes hardened. "Well, if he was down there messing with those nests again, he deserved it." She looked at me. "What do you think this means for Premier Resorts?"

I shrugged. "I don't know yet. We'll have to wait and see."

"I suppose you're right. Still, this may change things a bit," she said. She stood in the doorway for a moment. “Anyway, thanks for the dinner info. I don’t suppose you’d care to join me?”

“No, not tonight, I’m afraid. Too much to do.” And not enough money in my bank account. “Say hi to Connie and Ned for me, though.”

“I will. See you later, Nat.” She disappeared through the door.

Six

I strapped the box of scones onto the back of my battered blue Schwinn and started down the road toward the store. The smell of spruce and balsam wafted past me as I rode, and the only sound was the whir of the wheels and the distant crash of waves. It felt good to be outside in the cool air. The sky was robin's egg blue, with puffy clouds here and there, and the rain had intensified the deep green of the tall evergreen trees and clumps of bayberry bushes that lined the road. My worries faded under the bright Maine sun.

Before I knew it, apple trees and raspberry patches began to replace some of the towering pine trees, and the Schwinn was rolling past a cluster of painted wood-frame houses. In the winter, many of the houses had lobster traps stacked in front of them; at this time of year, though, the traps gave way to soft green grass and flowers.

The Cranberry Island Grocery looked just like a small-town grocery store should. The wooden building was painted brick red with creamy trim, and four rocking chairs decorated the wide front porch. A variety of signs and notices had been posted in the mullioned front windows, and the window boxes below them overflowed with brilliant red geraniums and trailing ivy.

As the bike nosed into the driveway, I wondered how many curious islanders were congregated inside. Charlene had converted the front of the store into what locals called the island's "parlor," a comfy little seating area filled with overstuffed armchairs and a big, saggy sofa. As I stepped onto the porch, I noticed that the line of La Marne rose bushes Charlene had pampered all winter were looking the worse for wear. Something had eaten most of their leaves, and only one feeble pink rose bloomed among the battered branches.

The bell above the door jingled as I entered the store. I glanced around the large, sunlit room. The narrow aisles were empty, and I didn't see anyone lounging on the chairs by the windows. Charlene rose from her seat behind the cash register. Her eyes were lined in dark blue to match her long denim dress, and her shellacked hair barely moved as she shook her head and wagged a plump, manicured finger at me.

"It's about time you showed up. I've been worried sick about you!"

"Why didn't you just call?" I asked. "Everyone else has."

Charlene groaned. "Phone's out of order. Again. The storm must have knocked the line down." Her eyes slid to the box I held, and her face lit up. "Ooh, goodies!" She narrowed her eyes at me. "I suppose you think because you brought food I'll have to forgive you? Hand them over."

I passed her the box and pulled up a stool at the counter. She ripped open the container and looked up, disappointed. "No cookies?"

"We ate them all, remember?"

"And you didn't bake more?"

"Maybe I'll get a batch out tomorrow."

Charlene sighed. "It's probably for the best. I like scones, but not as much as I like cookies. At least I won't eat them all before I can sell them."

"Scones?" A grizzled head popped up from the purple armchair next to the front window. It was Eleazer White, Claudette's husband and the local boat builder. He had been hunched down so far in the chair I hadn't noticed him. Eleazer was a regular at

Charlene's; today he was dressed in worn overalls and a faded plaid shirt, and as always, he looked like he'd been on the island since the dawn of time. "What kind?" he asked.

"Cranberry walnut," I said.

"I'll take two." His brown eyes were mischievous under bristly gray eyebrows. "Just promise me you won't tell Claudette."

"We promise," said Charlene, laying out two scones on a china plate. She set the plate down next to the half-full teacup on the table beside Eleazer's chair and pulled up a stool next to me, engulfing me in a wave of perfume. "Would you believe she made me eat sugarless cranberry pie last night?" Eleazer said.

"Sugarless cranberry pie?" Charlene made a face. "Another diet?"

"Ayuh," said Eleazer resignedly. "They never work, you know. If anything, she just gets fatter."

"That explains the six pounds of grapefruit she bought last week," Charlene said, fishing a nail file out of her pocket and smoothing a rough edge on one of her raspberry-painted nails.

"I'll say one thing for her, though . . . she doesn't give up." Eleazer shook his head and started in on a scone.

"By the way, Charlene, what happened to your roses?" I asked.

Charlene's face darkened. "Those damned goats again." She looked over toward Eleazer. "Sorry, Eli."

"Don't apologize to me," he said, lifting up an arm and displaying a ragged shirt cuff. "They got out while the wash was on the line the other day. Half my clothes have holes in 'em."

"At least it'll keep you cool this summer," I laughed.

"Aye, that's true," he said. "But you should see my undershorts," he continued, eyes twinkling. "I can't figure out which holes are for my legs." He shook his head again. "Claudette was out rounding them up again the other night. Came home soaked to the bone." He munched contemplatively for a minute. "I love her, I do," he said. "I just wish she didn't come with goats attached."

"Or sugarless cranberry pie," I added.

He winced. "That too." He took another huge bite of scone, smiling as he chewed. I turned to Charlene.

She examined her nails and slid the file back into her pocket. "So," she said, leaning forward on her stool. "You fell off a cliff and found Bernard Katz dead, and you're just now coming to see me."

"It's been a busy day," I said.

"You're telling me. This is the quietest the store has been since that helicopter started swooping around the island. Everyone who wasn't out investigating in person came here. They finally all had to go home and start dinner." She looked at me from the corner of her eye. "I hear your boyfriend came and saved you."

I flushed. "He's not my boyfriend. Remember? You told me he's dating a woman in Portland."

"Well, when the cat's away . . ." Charlene's glossy lips curved into an evil smile. "If you don't want him, send him my way. I could go for a man who doesn't smell like fish; it'd be a nice change."

"I'll keep that in mind."

Charlene yawned and stretched, putting some serious strain on the buttons of her denim dress. "I must have dried this dress last time I washed it," she said. "It's a bit snugger than I remember." She might not be willing to admit it, but since I'd moved to the island and started to bake cookies, she was keeping pace with me in the weight-gain department. If I didn't find some low-fat recipes soon, we were both going to have to buy new wardrobes. Large ones.

"So," Charlene said, "do you think someone offed him? Or was he just out for a little walk and slipped?"

"How come everyone assumes it's murder?"

"Nat, come *on.* Why would Mr. Namby-Pamby Katz be out on a cliff in the middle of a nor'easter?" She helped herself to a scone. "Not bad," she said. "Needs tea, though. Want some?"

"No, thanks." If I had another cup of tea at this hour, I'd be up all night. Charlene licked a bit of cranberry off her finger, then slid off her stool and walked over to the small kitchen area beside the counter.

"What did Claudette think about the whole thing, Eleazer?" I asked the back of the purple chair as Charlene poured herself a cup of Twinings English Breakfast. Eleazer's gray head popped over the back of the chair again.

"Claudette?" The crumbs in his beard bobbed up and down as he said his wife's name. "Oh, you know — she thought Katz got what he deserved." He shook his head. "There's a lot of folks she don't take to, but she *really* had it in for that fellow. If I thought she had a violent bone in her body, I might think she'd pushed him off herself."

The bell tinkled, and our eyes swiveled to

the front door as Ingrid Sorenson stepped into the store. Her eyes registered Eleazer and me; she froze for a moment, then let the door swing shut behind her with a jangle. Her pale face looked sallow against the brown of her loose cotton sweater, and her short gray-blonde hair stuck out in spikes around her head. I was surprised. Next to Charlene, Ingrid was usually the best-coiffed woman on the island. Her blue eyes darted around the room; with her sharp nose, her face resembled a wary bird's.

"Good afternoon, Ingrid," Charlene said.

"Lookin' to buy some golf balls, missy?" Eleazer piped up from his purple chair.

Ingrid thrust her chin into the air and marched across the wooden floor to the front counter. "Just here for my mail and a few groceries, thank you." Charlene set down her teacup and retrieved a large stack of mail from one of the cubbies lining the wall behind the register. She thwacked it down on the wood countertop in front of Ingrid.

"Thank you." Ingrid scooped the stack of envelopes into her mesh bag and retreated to the dairy case at the back of the store.

"Piece of work, that one," Eleazer grumbled.

I watched until Ingrid had disappeared

behind the shelves. Then I told Charlene in a low voice, "The reason I wasn't here earlier is that the police came by. They've closed up Katz's room — they'll be sending in forensics if the coroner decides it was murder." A crash sounded from the back of the store. Charlene stood up.

"Everything okay back there?"

"Fine, fine," Ingrid said. "Just dropped something. Everything's fine."

Charlene sat back down and turned to me. "So you can't even rent out your priciest room?"

"I don't have anyone to rent it to, anyway. But that's not the worst of it," I continued. "I think the police think I murdered Bernard Katz."

"You?" Charlene pshawed as she poured cream and about a half cup of sugar into her tea. "Half this island wouldn't mind seeing him dead. Why would the police pick on you?"

"Gertrude Pickens called from the *Daily Mail* this afternoon," I said. "She knew Katz was planning on replacing my inn with a parking lot."

Charlene froze with her teacup halfway to her mouth. "How did she find *that* out?"

"The only people who knew about it — except Katz's crew — were Gwen and you."

She looked affronted. "Like I'd pass that kind of information to the press!"

"Was anyone in the store when I called you and told you about it?"

Charlene's brow furrowed. "Well, there's almost always someone here, isn't there? Let me see, when was that — yesterday? Well, Tom Lockhart had come in for a mug-up with a couple of lobstermen — they'd just come from the co-op, made sure all the boats made it in okay." She tilted her head to one side. "Eli was here, of course. Other than that, though, I can't think of anybody."

"I'd really like to know who leaked that bit of information," I said.

She took a swig of tea and rolled it around in her mouth. "Are you sure it wasn't one of the Katzes?"

"They didn't include it on their presentation to the board, did they? I don't think they were ready for it to become public knowledge."

Charlene set her teacup down. "What about Gwen? Did she tell her art teacher about it? They seem pretty buddy-buddy, don't they?"

"Even if she did tell Fernand," I said, "why would he leak that to the press? From what Gwen tells me, he hated Katz every bit as much as I did." I paused for a moment. "Disliked, I mean."

Charlene's eyes narrowed. "Maybe Fernand did him in and was trying to give *you* a motive to cover his tracks."

"Well, whoever did it, I'm not too excited about having the Gray Whale linked to Katz's death in the paper."

"Don't worry about it," Charlene said, wetting her finger and picking the crumbs up off her plate. "Most of your guests don't read the local paper anyway — they're from out of town, remember?"

"I guess that's something," I said. We stopped talking as Ingrid marched up to the counter with a dozen eggs and a bottle of milk.

"You sure took your time picking those out," Charlene said. "Is that it?"

"That's it."

Charlene rang up her purchases, and Ingrid jammed them into her bag and hurried out of the store. The door slammed shut with a jangle.

"I don't know what's up with her," Charlene said, helping herself to another scone. "Used to be, she was in here every day, chowing down and chewing the fat. Now she hardly talks to anybody."

"Probably feels bad because she sold out

the island," Eleazer said.

"Why'd she do that, anyway?" Charlene asked. "A month ago, she told me she didn't think a big resort was right for the island, then she turns around and hands it to Katz on a silver platter."

Eleazer shrugged. "Maybe there was some money in it for her. A kickback, or something. People do funny things for money."

"Maybe," said Charlene, looking unconvinced. She took a bite of scone and glanced at the clock. "Almost time to close up shop. You want to go down to the lobster pound with me?"

I looked at Charlene in disbelief. I couldn't imagine she was hungry after eating two gigantic scones, but my mouth watered at the thought of succulent fresh lobster meat with sweet corn and blueberry pie. My bank account, however, was in no shape to support a lobster feed. "No thanks," I said with regret. "You might see Barbara down there, though."

Charlene perked up. "Oh, yeah?"

"She was looking for a place to eat, and I recommended the pound."

"Miss Barbara," Charlene said. "What'd *she* think of Katz's death?"

"She figured he was down there bothering the nests, and that he deserved it."

"Maybe what happened to Katz was what Barbara meant by 'alternate tactics'."

"The thought crossed my mind too," I said. "But I don't know — she doesn't seem the type. Besides, she looked surprised when I told her about it."

"Uh-huh," Charlene said. "Well, I'll see what I can dig up on Ms. Eggleby tonight. You're sure you don't want to come?"

"Maybe next week." I fished my grocery list out of my pocket. "By the way, could you add this to your next order? Let me know what I owe you."

Charlene took the list from me and pinned it up on the corkboard next to the mail cubbies. "Oh yeah," she said. "I almost forgot about your mail." She handed me a stack that included several small envelopes and a large, heavy one. "The big one's addressed to Bernard Katz. I doubt he'll be interested, but I guess you can give it to his assistant."

I thanked her and headed for the front door.

"Say hi to Claudette and the goats," I called over my shoulder to Eleazer.

"I will," he said. "Although why she doesn't just buy wool like normal folks, I'll never know," he grumbled as the door swung shut behind me.

I had just finished off a grilled cheese

sandwich and was setting up the dining room tables for breakfast when Gwen came through the kitchen door with pink cheeks and windswept hair.

"How'd the sketching go?" I asked, shaking out a bright white tablecloth.

"It's getting better every day." Gwen's eyes shone with excitement. "I've decided I want to major in art."

"Great," I said, wondering how I was going to explain that to my sister Bridget. She hadn't telephoned in about a week, and I knew another call was due soon. Bridget's idea of a proper major was business or economics, and it was a safe bet she'd consider art "a waste of time and money." I just hoped she wouldn't blame me.

Gwen disappeared back into the kitchen as I shook out another tablecloth. As the white cotton floated down over the scarred wood table, I decided to deal with it when the time came. I had enough on my plate as it was.

"Is there anything to eat?" Gwen called from the kitchen.

"I know the larder's kind of bare," I called back. "I just gave Charlene the grocery order. There's bread and cheese, though. And I left you a few scones."

I finished laying out the last tablecloths,

pulled a stack of plates out of the sideboard, and headed into the kitchen for silverware. Gwen was fixing herself a sandwich as I grabbed handfuls of forks, spoons, and knives. I paused on the way back into the dining room. "By the way, Gwen, did you mention what we found in Ogden's room to Fernand?" I asked.

"You mean the plans that showed the Gray Whale Inn being axed?" A faint line appeared between her arched eyebrows. "I don't remember saying anything about it. Why?"

"A reporter called asking about it this morning."

"That's weird. Where would they have heard about that?" She sliced a thick slab of cheddar and opened a bag of bread. "Didn't you tell Charlene about it? Maybe she said something to somebody."

"I was thinking maybe someone in the store overheard her end of the conversation, but I can't think who it could have been."

"I'm sure Charlene will find out soon enough," Gwen said as she took out a couple of slices of bread and closed the bag. "She knows everything that happens on this island."

I leaned against the kitchen door. "What was Fernand's take on Katz's death?" I asked, watching as Gwen layered a piece of bread with what must have been three-quarters of a pound of cheese.

She smiled grimly. “He said he hoped the same thing would happen to the resort.”

“He’s not the only one,” I said. “You know, I’ve been meaning to talk to him about putting together an artists’ retreat vacation package. Kind of a co-op promotion. When’s a good time to stop by the studio?”

Gwen slapped her sandwich together and took a huge bite, chewing laboriously before she swallowed. “It’s hard to say. When he doesn’t have a class, he’s usually out somewhere with his paints. You might try him around noon, though, after he’s done with the Bittles.”

“Thanks, I will.” I left her with her cheese sandwich and took the silverware out to the dining room. After arranging the last spoon, I stood back and surveyed the room. Everything was ready to go; I just needed to decide what to do for breakfast. I still had sausage and eggs, and unless Gwen fixed herself a second sandwich, I had cheese. A breakfast casserole with corn muffins on the side would fill the bill. What was I going to do for fruit, though?

I walked back through the swinging door

and opened the freezer. After a few minutes of digging, I unearthed a bag of blueberries from beneath a frozen chuck roast. With maple syrup and a dash of lemon juice, the berries would cook up into a nice compote while the casserole and the muffins were baking. I closed the freezer and glanced at the kitchen table. After polishing off her humongous sandwich, Gwen had started in on the scones. The scones might be gone, but at least I'd have cheese for the casserole. I gazed at her full mouth and slim body with envy.

The golden light that had poured through the kitchen window most of the day had faded; the sun had disappeared behind Cadillac Mountain, leaving a glowing band of red on the horizon. Fatigue swept through me as my eyes swept across the last dregs of sunset. I had planned to dust and vacuum the parlor this evening, but it could wait until tomorrow. Bidding Gwen goodnight, I headed upstairs to draw myself a hot bath, and after a good long soak with a candle and a book, I climbed into bed.

Despite my exhaustion, the day's events kept running through my mind like a looped film. When I realized my eyes had been glued to the same page for twenty minutes, I put on my slippers and a robe and padded down the stairs, figuring if I was wide-awake and fidgety, I might as well get something done.

I grabbed a dust rag and a bottle of furniture polish from the utility room and tackled the parlor. Dusting was generally my least favorite task, but tonight the rhythmic rub of the cloth against the antique furniture soothed my overactive brain. I was polishing the mantel above the river-stone fireplace when a loud clunk sounded from above. I glanced at my watch — it was midnight. A little late to be moving furniture around. I listened for a moment, and when nothing further happened, I gave the mantel a final swipe with the rag and moved on to the coffee table.

I was just replacing the basket of silk flowers in the center of the table when there was a second clunk, louder than the first. I told myself it was probably just Ogden, but my heart began thumping against my ribcage as I set the rag down next to the flowers and climbed the stairs to investigate.

The upstairs hall was dark, except for the faint light from the parlor downstairs. I crept down the hall, pausing at Ogden's door. Unless Ogden was moving furniture around in the dark, the noises were coming from somewhere else; no light shone through the narrow gap at the bottom of his door. A chill ran down my spine. Both the Bittles and Barbara Eggleby were on the first floor. The only other occupied room on the second floor belonged to Bernard Katz, and he was dead.

As I padded slowly toward the door at the end of the hall, the floor groaned beneath me. I froze. After a very long moment, another clunk sounded; it was definitely coming from the room at the end of the hall. Whoever was in Katz's room was still going about his or her business.

My heart thundered so loudly that it seemed impossible that whoever else — or whatever else — was up here couldn't hear it. I wiped my clammy hands on my robe and tiptoed to the end of the hall. I stood for a long moment outside of Bernard Katz's door, listening to the creak of footsteps. Adrenaline coursed through me as I grasped the cold brass doorknob and turned it.

The door was locked.

Of course. Grimes must have locked it that morning. Which meant that whoever was in the room had entered through the window. Unless . . .

I crept back down the hall as quickly as possible and ran down the stairs on tiptoe. I raced to the reception desk and opened the key cabinet. A small brass door key dangled on its own hook at the end of the second row: the skeleton key. Gwen and I used it when we were cleaning the rooms. As my hand closed around it, I realized that I'd forgotten to tell Grimes about it.

I clutched the cold key in my hand and started back up the stairs. Halfway up, I paused. Did I really want to walk in on an intruder unarmed? I hurried back down to the parlor and slid the poker out of the rack of fireplace tools, giving it an experimental swing with a shaky arm before tackling the stairs again.

As I reached the top landing, I realized I hadn't heard anything for a few minutes. Maybe the intruder was gone. A wave of relief and frustration swept over me at the thought that I might arrive too late. When I took a step toward Katz's room, another bump sounded from behind the wood door. Sheer terror prevailed once again.

I reached the end of the hall and checked my grip on the poker. I would have been happier with something a little more long-range, like a shotgun, but it would have to do. My hand trembled as I struggled to fit the key into the lock without tipping off the intruder. I was afraid I was going to have to put down the poker and try it with both hands when the key finally slid home. I rotated the key in the lock. Then I wiped a sweaty hand, said a little prayer, and turned the knob.

I had a brief glimpse of a profile reflected in the light of a flashlight. Then the flashlight hurtled toward me. I swung the poker wildly, but before it could connect, a bright red pain exploded on the side of my head and everything went black.

Seven

I was trapped under black water, gasping for breath. Something was clawing at my head, pushing me down . . .

I opened my eyes to darkness. As I raised my head from the floor, a stabbing pain shot through my left temple, and my stomach turned over as my eyes searched the inky blackness. Panic had begun to constrict my throat when I caught a glimpse of the crescent moon through the window.

I relaxed slightly — I could still see — and then a chill passed through me when I remembered where I was.

I remained still, my head throbbing, listening for the sound of my attacker, but Katz's room was empty. As my eyes adjusted to the darkness, they registered the shadowy curtains fluttering in the breeze. My attacker had come — and presumably gone — through the window.

I climbed to my feet, gripping the footboard of the bed for support. As my body straightened, a sharp pain swelled behind my temple, and my knees buckled. I groped my way to where I knew the night table was and fumbled for the switch of the reading light. I winced as bright light flooded the room. The place had been ransacked.

The clunks I had heard must have been the hasty removal of drawers from the antique dresser; they lay overturned on the pine floor, their contents strewn across the room. The white counterpane and sheets had been torn from the king-sized bed, and the mattress lay askew on the box spring. I didn't know what my attacker had been looking for, but whoever it was had been very thorough.

I stepped over piles of clothes to reach the long walnut desk next to the window. Piles of paper were heaped randomly on the desktop. A breeze from the open window sent a few receipts fluttering to the floor, and I bent over reflexively to pick them up. My head began to pulse again as I gathered them up: a restaurant receipt from New York, an airport parking ticket receipt, and a handwritten receipt from Seaglass Jewelers, a store down on the Cranberry Island wharf. I glanced at it — it was for $600 — and tucked it into the pocket of my robe.

The papers on the desk were primarily bank statements. I riffled through them. The accounts the statements represented were not empty, but they certainly weren't as substantial as I would have expected for a corporation like Premier Resorts International. One of them was almost as low as my own checking account.

I replaced the papers and looked around the room. The desk drawers had been emptied, too — they lay tumbled beneath the window in an untidy heap. The twin night tables, however, appeared to have been left untouched. Whatever my attacker had been looking for, he — or she — hadn't found it. I'd interrupted the search.

The bump on my head yowled for attention, but I ignored it. If whatever the intruder had wanted was still here, this might be my only opportunity to find it. If Katz *had* been murdered — and I was starting to believe he had — the clue to his killer's identity might be hidden here.

I skirted the upturned drawers and walked to the nearest night table. I slid open the drawer, but it was empty. I felt around underneath it, and bent carefully to peer behind it, but found nothing. An identical search of the table's twin yielded only a pair of reading glasses. I replaced them in the drawer and slid it shut.

I stepped over piles of clothes and walked into the large tiled bathroom. The intruder hadn't made it this far — the white towels were still neatly folded, and the only thing out of place was a scum of whiskers and shaving cream in the bowl of the marble sink and a glob of toothpaste on the vanity top. I was thinking I'd have to tell Gwen to double-check the sinks when she cleaned when something caught my eye. A piece of paper stuck out from where it had been wedged behind the bathroom mirror.

I pulled it out gently and examined it. The envelope was made of thick, creamy paper and labeled, simply, "Oh." I opened the heavy flap and withdrew a single sheet of the same heavy paper.

Oh,
How about Thursday . . . same time, same place?

XO
Ess

The handwriting was cramped, and the crabbed letters slanted backward. As I read it a second time, I wondered if this was what the searcher was looking for. There was always the chance that the note had been left by a previous guest, but my gut instinct told me that Katz had put it here for a reason. Did "Ess" stand for Estelle? Maybe "Oh" was her pet name for Bernard . . . or maybe he'd discovered she'd had a rendezvous with someone else, and was using the letter for leverage. If so, I imagined the discovery was recent. Bernard and Estelle had seemed pretty friendly two days ago.

I slipped the letter into my pocket and continued sifting through the room. Forty-five minutes of searching turned up nothing else of interest, other than the fact that Katz wore a 42 waist and favored brightly colored silk boxers.

My head was throbbing by the time I decided to call it a night. My watch read half past one when I shut and locked the window, turned out the light, and used the skeleton key to relock the door behind me. I'd let John know what happened in the morning; the police could sort through the mess when they got here.

It seemed that I'd only been asleep for ten minutes when the alarm buzzed like a hornet's nest. I slammed my hand down on it and groaned. Why did breakfast have to come so early?

My temple pulsed angrily as I swung my

legs over the side of the bed and stood up. Biscuit had come to join me at some point; she stretched and glanced at me before burrowing back into the covers as I shuffled over to the mirror.

What had been a pink bump last night had swelled to an angry purplish-blue knot above my left eye. More than anything, I wanted to take a handful of aspirin and go back to bed, but I limited myself to two, wrapped myself in my flannel robe, and trudged downstairs.

As I dumped frozen blueberries into a pot, I wondered again who had broken into Bernard Katz's room the night before. Could it have been one of the guests? Just because the intruder had come in through the window didn't mean he or she wasn't staying at the inn.

My head continued to throb as I opened the door to the pantry. I was glad the menu wasn't complicated this morning; I could whip up corn muffins in ten minutes, and the sausage and egg casserole would be done in another twenty. When my hand reached for the cornmeal bag, my plan evaporated; it was almost empty. So much for corn muffins. I leaned my head against the doorframe, my mind scrambling for an alternative.

Finally, inspiration hit. I pulled down the flour and sugar canisters and flipped through a cookbook until my fingers found my favorite pancake recipe. It was a bit more time-intensive — I'd have to stand over the griddle — but it wasn't too difficult, and pancakes would go well with the blueberry compote. Maybe I'd forget about the casserole and just cook up a few sausages instead. If anyone wanted eggs, I'd make them to order.

As I was measuring out the flour, a knock sounded at the kitchen door. It was John, looking rumpled. A comforting whiff of fresh-cut wood blew in on the cool morning breeze as I opened the door to let my neighbor in. John hadn't shaved yet, and his hair was disheveled, as if he'd just gotten out of bed. Meeting him like this felt strangely intimate. When my hands moved to brush stray flour off my clothes, I realized why. I was still wearing my bathrobe.

John hadn't noticed the bathrobe; his eyes zeroed in on the knot on my head. "My God, Nat! What happened to you?"

My hand flew to my temple. "Somebody bashed me over the head last night."

"Where? When?"

"First come in and have a cup of coffee." Just thinking about last night made my head ache. I needed caffeine. John sat down at the table as I scooped beans into the coffee grinder and filled the pot with fresh water, recounting the night's events as I worked.

When I turned around, his expression was grim. "Why didn't you come and find me?"

"By the time I came to, whoever it was was long gone," I said. "Came *to?*" His green eyes were filled with disbelief. "You mean they knocked you *out* and you didn't come and find me?"

I shrugged sheepishly. "I didn't want to wake you."

"Not good," he said. "Not good." He sighed and leaned forward, cupping his chin in his hands as his elbows slid across the table. "I've got some more bad news," he said. "Grimes just called."

"A little early for a business call, isn't it?"

"The coroner's filed the report. Katz was murdered." I slumped against the counter. The lines around John's eyes and mouth looked deeper than usual as he continued. "I hope you didn't touch anything while you were up there. They're sending forensics over to go through Katz's room today."

My stomach fluttered. "Katz's room is part of my inn. My prints are going to be all over the place."

"Yeah, but not on his personal belongings." His green eyes studied me. "Right?"

"Right," I said feebly. I sat down at the table across from him and took a big swig of coffee, wondering how many more aspirin I could take without doing myself irreparable damage. "Just what I need for the business. Rooms festooned in yellow crime-scene tape."

"I'll ask them to be discreet."

Being discreet on an island of five hundred curious inhabitants was like asking an elephant to walk on tiptoe, but I thanked him anyway.

"You know, I didn't believe you yesterday," John said, "but I think you may be right. Grimes seems to think you're involved in this." I already knew that, but hearing it from John turned the blood in my veins to ice.

"Well, he hasn't had much time to ask around yet, has he?" I said with false brightness. "I think he'll find I wasn't the only one who wasn't on spectacular terms with Bernard Katz. Besides," I continued, "the intruder should be a good lead to follow."

John looked at me. "How did this person get in, anyway? Was the door unlocked?"

"Through the window," I said. "I haven't been out to look, but I'm guessing whoever it was climbed the rose trellis. The window was open when I got there."

"Well, maybe they left footprints. If you were planning on doing any gardening, I'd recommend you wait till the police have taken a look out there."

"Don't worry. I've got enough to occupy me without worrying about the perennial beds. I'll probably just do errands this afternoon."

"Errands?" He cocked one eyebrow at me. "Just try to keep out of trouble, okay?" He reached across the table and brushed the hair away from my temple. His voice was gentle. "You might want to get that looked at."

"I can't, remember? I'm not allowed to leave the island."

He dropped his hand and sighed. "I'll talk to Grimes, see if you can go into town to see a doctor." Then he smiled. "Maybe I'll promise to come with you and try to keep you out of trouble." His eyes twinkled, and for the first time, he grinned. "Although that might be a tough job. Trouble seems to come looking for you."

I smiled back at him, confused. I was attracted to John, and it seemed as if he might be attracted to me, but Charlene had it on good authority that he was dating a woman in Portland. I was also a suspect in a murder case that he was involved in investigating. Besides, things were complicated enough already. Adding a romantic relationship with my neighbor was not what I needed right now.

John finished his coffee and headed for the door. "I'm guessing the next few days are going to be pretty busy. I'm going to head down to the workshop and churn out a few more boats while I can. Tourist season is short." *Don't I know it,* I thought. I thanked him for letting me know about the coroner's report and gave him the last scone to take with him.

When the door closed behind him, I sank into one of the kitchen chairs, dazed. Bernard Katz really had been murdered. I sat warming my hands on the coffee cup until a popping sound from the stove reminded me that there was cooking to be done. My head twinged as I stirred the blueberries, which had started to bubble around the edges, and added some cornstarch. I took another sip of coffee before retrieving the baking powder and salt from the pantry and plugging in the griddle for pancakes.

As my hands measured out the ingredients, my thoughts turned to Katz's murder. Grimes might be too lazy to dig up other suspects, but if someone didn't find out who had killed Katz, a cloud would remain over me — and the inn. If I didn't end up in jail, that was.

I closed up the baking powder and poured a small hill of salt into a measuring spoon. My head throbbed as the possibilities reeled through my mind. Who might have wanted Katz dead? Estelle was a good candidate. After all, John had indicated that Katz might have been going to meet a woman when he died. A flirtation had obviously existed between them, and the cliff path did pass right under Cliffside. I dumped the salt into the bowl and looked out the window at the dark blue water. Why would she have killed him, though? So that Stanley could inherit his money?

I stirred the dry ingredients together with a fork and walked over to the fridge. Stanley might have been interested in an early inheritance, too. I pulled out the eggs and butter and closed the door with my foot. Maybe he was in financial straits; Charlene certainly thought so. Had he been desperate enough to kill for money?

After cracking three eggs into a bowl and whisking them together, I unwrapped the butter and put it in the microwave to melt. Maybe Stanley had gotten fed up with the flirtation between Estelle and his father.

Maybe he'd discovered that it was more than flirtation. He didn't seem to care too much about what his wife did, I mused, but maybe the knowledge that she'd cuckolded him with his own father would be enough to push him over the edge. Then again, I had no way of knowing what the relationship between Bernard Katz and Estelle was; it was all speculation.

The bell on the microwave dinged and I poured the melted butter into the eggs, whisking them together. Who else might have wanted Katz dead? Claudette, of course, had practically threatened to kill him in front of the entire island. I remembered the look of blind rage on her square-jawed face at the board meeting and shivered. Eleazer might not think she was capable of violence, but I wasn't so sure.

Barbara was another possibility. She'd managed to get the association to pony up an extra million dollars. The purchase of the preserve was pretty important to her. Important enough to kill for? If so, why wouldn't she have killed him before the meeting? Because she hadn't had the opportunity, I realized as I poured the flour mixture into the eggs and butter. She didn't get to the island until the meeting was already under way.

I gave the batter a few turns with a wooden spoon and covered it with a dishtowel, then poured myself a second cup of coffee. The throbbing in my head seemed to be abating slightly; the aspirin must be kicking in. As I sipped my coffee, I heard the pipes whine as a shower went on overhead. Gwen was up early this morning. Maybe she could help me with the pancakes so that I could lie down. Her culinary skills were less than extensive, but she might be able to manage pancakes if the batter was already done.

I sat down at the kitchen table and turned the problem of Bernard Katz's murder over in my head. Who else was close to Katz? An image of Ogden's greasy hair and Coke-bottle glasses floated into my mind, but I couldn't see how he'd benefit from killing Katz. If anything, Katz's death would put him out of a job.

The clock above the stove read eight o'clock. I adjusted the heat on the pancake griddle and tasted the berries — they needed just a touch more maple syrup — before pulling a package of sausage from the freezer and plunking a block of frozen links into a pan.

My hand slid into my pocket, and I fingered the receipt I'd found in Katz's room last night. Maybe Berta could tell me what

Katz had in mind for the jewelry he'd bought. Talking to Berta was easy; I would stop by Seaglass Jewelers and drop off some brochures that afternoon. What I really needed to do, though, was talk to Estelle and Stanley. Unfortunately, chances were pretty slim that they'd roll out the red carpet for me at Cliffside.

The sausage was beginning to sizzle when the phone rang.

"It's Charlene."

"What's up?"

"I hate to always be the bearer of bad tidings, but you haven't seen the paper yet, have you?"

"Of course not." Like everyone else on the island, I had to go down to the store to pick it up. "Why?"

"Apparently Grimes isn't the only one who thinks you did in Bernard Katz. Get a load of today's headlines: 'Local Inn Guest Dies after Squabble with Innkeeper'."

I tried to look on the bright side. "At least they didn't name the inn."

"Oh, yes they did," she said. "About four times. You were in there a lot, too."

"How? I only spoke with Gertrude Pickens for two minutes yesterday."

I heard the sound of chewing. "She knew all about Katz's plans to bulldoze your inn.

The way the article reads, you did too. There's even a partial picture of the blueprint." She paused, and a slurping noise traveled down the phone line: probably coffee. "She talks all about your 'crusade' against the resort," she continued, "and how the board vote went against you anyway. The whole article is about why you didn't like Bernard Katz, followed by a paragraph about how the police may suspect foul play." She took another bite of whatever she was eating.

"Wait till they find out he was murdered," I said.

The chewing stopped. "What?"

"I just found out this morning."

"Lovely. I can only imagine what tomorrow's headlines will be." She slurped again. "By the way, if you ever need work, I'm always looking for an extra cashier."

EIGHT

I hung up the phone and turned the sausages. As there was no sign of Gwen, I sprayed the griddle with cooking spray and ladled six circles of batter onto the hot surface, then stirred the blueberry compote.

I thought about the newspaper article as tiny bubbles appeared on top of the batter. Even if Grimes wasn't eyeing me as Bernard Katz's murderer, it was obvious that I needed to clear my name — fast. And to do that, I needed to talk with Estelle and Stanley.

How was I going to get into Cliffside? As the spatula slid under the pale circles and turned them over, the smell of pancakes filled the room, soothing me. Food was always a comfort. I paused with my spatula in midair. *That* was how I was going to get into Cliffside. With a big batch of cookies to comfort the bereaved family.

I flipped the last pancake with renewed

energy and transferred the sausages to the oven to stay warm. I'd figured out how to get across the threshold. The only problem was, Estelle turned her nose up at my kind of cooking; she avoided fat like the plague, but most of my recipes called for substantial amounts of butter or oil. Could I come up with something she would actually eat?

I tucked the finished pancakes into the oven next to the sausages and poured six more circles; then I headed to the hutch and pulled out a stack of cookbooks. For the next fifteen minutes, I shuttled back and forth between the griddle and the books. The last six pancakes were sizzling on the griddle when Gwen sailed down the stairs, looking radiant in a ruffled blue sundress and carrying a portable easel. It looked like I was on my own for breakfast again.

"Hi, Aunt Nat." A cloud of perfume engulfed me as she swept by. "What smells so heavenly in here?"

"Pancakes and sausages. Where are you off to?"

"Fernand said I should try catching some of the morning light." Her brown eyes rested on my temple. "What happened to you?"

I gave her a brief rundown of last night, ending with an admonition to lock her door at night and be careful walking around the island after dark.

"Sure, Aunt Nat," she said, her oval face solemn under a mass of dark ringlets. Then she peeked into the oven, and all thoughts of late-night intruders vanished. "Mind if I have some of that?"

"Go ahead." There was plenty for everyone this morning, particularly since the inn was short one guest. She piled a plate high as I turned the last pancakes and ran upstairs to throw on a pair of jeans. Five minutes later, I started shuttling food out to the warming plates in the dining room.

I was setting out the butter next to a pitcher of maple syrup when the Bittles walked in.

Mrs. Bittles eyed me critically from beneath an oversized purple beret. "Whatever did you do to yourself, dear?"

I paused with the pitcher in my hand, baffled by the question. Then I followed her eyes to my temple and remembered what had happened last night. The aspirin must be working; I'd forgotten all about it. "Oh, I tripped and hit a door frame," I said in a casual tone. No need to broadcast the fact that I'd been hit over the head by an intruder. Whoever had broken in last night was interested in Katz's room, not the Bittles.

I filled both of the Bittles' coffee cups as they investigated their breakfast options. Mrs. Bittles was retreating from the buffet table with a stack of pancakes that wobbled as much as her beret when Barbara walked into the room. As she sat down at a table next to the window, I poured her a cup of coffee.

"Wow, Natalie. You're a mess. What happened to you?"

"Somebody whacked me over the head last night," I said quietly, studying Barbara's face. "An intruder broke into Katz's room last night; whoever it was, I interrupted them."

Her thin eyebrows squinched together in a look of concern. "What do you think they were looking for?"

"I don't know. But I don't think they found it."

"Yikes." Barbara stirred sugar and cream into her coffee. "You should let the police know about that. I'm glad you're okay." She took a sip of coffee. "By the way, I ran into your friend Charlene last night. She's kind of nosy, isn't she?"

I laughed. "Don't be offended. She's that way with everyone."

Barbara looked relieved. "Good. For a little while there, I was wondering if she thought *I'd* killed Bernard Katz."

Killed? As far as I knew, nobody but John and me knew he had been murdered. The coroner's report had just come back that morning.

"I expect she'll be grilling half the island," I said lightly. "We've got pancakes and sausage with blueberry compote this morning, but if you'd like eggs, I'd be happy to fix them for you. Oh — and by the way — the police will be here again today, doing some work in Bernard Katz's room."

I watched her narrow face, but it registered no visible emotion. Instead, she eyed the mounds of pancakes and sausage. "Well, then, I guess I'll get started." She got up and headed for the buffet table, and I returned to the kitchen to refill the coffeepot. Gwen, of course, was already gone, but her empty plate and half-full coffee cup lay on the table where she'd sat. So much for help with breakfast.

The Bittles and Barbara had wandered out of the dining room by the time Ogden showed up. He barely glanced at the knot on my head before serving himself two pancakes and two sausages. He laid his white napkin across his lap and began cutting his pancakes into tidy squares.

I came over to his table to fill his coffee cup. His pale skin looked pasty; I wondered if he'd even left his room since he checked in.

As I finished pouring, Ogden looked at me from behind his thick glasses. "By the way, Mr. Katz will be joining me for breakfast tomorrow morning."

I almost dropped the coffeepot. Then I realized he meant Stanley, not Bernard. "That'll be fine," I said. "During normal hours, I presume?"

"At nine o'clock," he said, and dabbed a square of pancake into a neat puddle of syrup.

"If you'd like eggs this morning, let me know; I'll make them to order." He nodded curtly, and I retreated to the kitchen.

I sat back down at the kitchen table, relieved to have made it through the morning without scaring away any guests. I picked up another cookbook and flipped to a recipe for chocolate meringues. Perfect: the comfort of chocolate without the fat. I rummaged through the fridge and the pantry and laid out the ingredients on the kitchen counter, and soon I was separating eggs and measuring flour and cocoa, slipping out to the dining room from time to time to see if Ogden needed more coffee. By 10:00, a mound of billowing chocolate filled the bowl and the aroma of chocolate suffused the kitchen.

I had to bake the meringues in shifts, so by the time the buzzer went off for the last time I had cleaned up after breakfast and set up the dining room for the next morning. It was early afternoon when I headed out from the inn on my blue Schwinn. The police hadn't shown up yet, but John had promised me he'd let them in if they arrived before I got back.

The winding road up to Cliffside was almost more than my legs could take. Just as I was about to give up and walk, the bike crested the hill and I glimpsed an imposing gray structure between the trees. Parked in the driveway was the late-model, cream-colored BMW the Katzes kept for tooling around the island. Most islanders' cars looked like rejects from the dump; since they never left the island, they were all unregistered, and most were missing doors, trunk lids, and sometimes even roofs. Not the Katzes, though; they'd had the car shipped over specially.

I leaned my bike up against a craggy old spruce tree and unstrapped the plastic box of meringues from the back. It wasn't the most attractive container, but it was the only thing I could think of that would get them up the big hill intact.

My eyes probed the house as I walked up the flagstone path to the massive front door. No pesky rocks to interfere with Estelle's stilettos here. Like the Gray Whale Inn, the building was sheathed in weathered gray shingles; where the Gray Whale was welcoming and cozy, however, Cliffside was imposing and formal. The shrubbery was pruned into a rigid geometry, and instead of starched cotton curtains, heavy brocaded fabrics shrouded the windows. The turret I had often seen from the water was hidden from the front of the house.

I pushed a glowing button to the left of the heavy walnut and leaded-glass door, and the doorbell chimed solemnly. I was wondering whether anyone was home when a bright blue form materialized behind the wavy glass. Estelle.

She opened the door and eyed me with suspicion. "What are you doing here?" Although it was 12:30 in the afternoon, she hadn't gotten dressed yet. She wore only a bright blue silk kimono, but had taken the time to do her face. I was surprised; her makeup was usually flawless, but today the blue eyeliner rimming her icy eyes was so thick that she looked almost clownish, and her frosted lipstick only approximately followed the lines of her mouth. Her blond pouf was flattened on one side, as if she had slept on it.

"I came to tell you how sorry I am about your father-in-law's death," I said, holding out the container of meringues. "I brought you some cookies."

Estelle's garishly painted eyes narrowed as she looked at the plastic box.

"Don't worry," I said, "they're low-fat."

She reached out a manicured hand and took the box, then stood in the doorway staring at me. I wasn't sure she was going to invite me in, so I invited myself.

"Would you mind if I had a glass of water?" I asked. "That hill is murder." I felt my face redden as I realized what I had said.

Estelle looked annoyed. "Oh, all right." She opened the door wider, and I followed her fluffy mules through the ornate marbled entry hall into the cavernous living room. She disappeared through a door off the side of the room with the box. I wasn't sure if I was supposed to follow, so I lowered myself onto a couch upholstered in mauve- and cream-striped satin and scanned the room. It was tastefully and expensively furnished, with a rich lilac and blue oriental rug and heavy silk curtains framing a million-dollar view of the water and Mount Desert Island beyond. The furnishings were all dark wood with ornate carving, and polished to a high sheen. It looked as if Polly Sarkes had been continuing to clean despite the lack of pay-checks.

I could see what looked like Stanley's study through one of the arched side door-ways; the room's centerpiece was an over-sized mahogany desk flanked by bookshelves loaded with antique-looking books. Prob-ably bought by the yard by a designer; Es-telle and Stanley didn't strike me as lovers of classic literature.

Estelle lurched back into the room a minute later holding a juice glass filled with tepid water and no ice. I caught a strong whiff of gin as she thrust it at me. She tot-tered across the broad expanse of plush rug and flopped onto a couch opposite me, reaching for what looked like a thirty-two-ounce tumbler of ice water. Probably a gin-and-tonic. It was already half gone.

"How is Stanley holding up?" I asked.

"Stanley?" She took a long sip of her drink. "Oh, I imagine he's surviving."

"His father's death must have been quite a shock."

"Yeah, you're telling me. He's got the

worst timing . . ." She ran a lacquered finger around the rim of her glass.

I was confused. "Stanley?"

She looked at me as if I were an imbecile. "Bad timing for you, too, isn't it? I mean, if Bernard had kicked off the day before, you'd have your stupid little nests all to yourself. And the Moby Dick, or whatever it is you call it."

"The Gray Whale Inn."

"Right. Whatever." She poked at an ice cube. "I don't know *why* he was so hell-bent on getting this god-forsaken island. There's nothing to *do* here." She took another sip and looked out the huge picture windows at the stunning vista. "I'd almost convinced him to do one in the Bahamas, instead, but then *she* got involved . . ." She stared dreamily into the distance, and it seemed for a moment that she had forgotten I was in the room. "Once that happened, there was no way he was going to back down . . ."

"Who?"

She blinked, and turned to look at me. "Oh, *you* know." She reached over to the side table and picked up a pack of Ultra Slims and a silver lighter. She slid a cigarette out, lit it with a wobbly hand, and inhaled. "The bitch," she hissed through the thin stream of smoke that issued from her painted lips.

The air was heavy with the scent of gin and cigarettes. On an impulse, I said, "He was murdered, you know."

Estelle's heavily lined eyes grew big. "Murdered?" She let out an explosive laugh. "You're kidding me, right?"

"The coroner's report came back this morning."

"How was he killed?"

"I don't know. I didn't get the details."

Estelle looked at me closely for the first time, blinking as she tried to focus. "Maybe I'd better get those cookies tested before I eat them." She looked out the window again, then lurched to her feet and teetered out of the room.

I was confused for a moment, but when I heard a door close and the tap of her mules on tile, I decided she must have visited the bathroom. My eyes strayed to the mahogany desk in the next room. After a moment's internal debate, I scurried over to the office overlooking the water and darted behind the massive desk.

While the rest of the room was spotless, the top of the desk was awash in stacks of paper. The inbox was overflowing, and I leafed through the pages quickly. Overdue notices for credit cards and utilities. It looked like Charlene was right about Stanley's financial situation.

I slid open the drawers and glanced through them — nothing but office supplies, except for the bottom drawers, which were locked. A quick search failed to reveal the key; Stanley must have hidden it. A rush of water sounded from somewhere in the house, and I quickly closed the drawers. As the top drawer slid shut, I caught a glimpse of a stack of creamy envelopes. The same heavy linen, the same tapered flap . . . the letter in Katz's room had come from here.

A door opened somewhere as I shut the last drawer and raced back to the candy-cane striped couch. I had just perched on the edge again when Estelle wobbled back into the room.

She threw herself back into the sofa and took another swig of her gin and tonic.

"Where's your husband today?" I asked.

"Oh, off moping somewhere. He's always wandering around this stupid island."

I was silent for a moment, debating how far to push my luck. I decided my chances of getting a second interview with Estelle were slim, so I forged ahead. "I hope you don't mind my being forward, but you have such a beautiful house . . . why didn't your father-in-law stay here?"

Her gaudy face hardened. "That's none of your business. I'd say it's because he liked your cooking, but that can't be it." Anger rose in my throat, but I quelled it. Estelle shot a pointed look at my untouched glass. "Are you done with your drink?"

I took a hasty sip of the tepid water. "Can I take this back to the kitchen for you?"

"No, just put it on the table. The maid will take care of it." She took an exaggerated look at the jeweled watch on her slender arm. I decided the interview must be over, and stood up.

"Well, I've got to be off," I said. "I'm headed down to drop some brochures off at Berta's shop." I watched Estelle's painted face closely. "She makes such beautiful jewelry, don't you think?"

"If you can't afford the real stuff," she said with a toss of her head.

"I'll just walk myself out," I said. "Don't bother getting up." Estelle didn't look as if she were going to anyway.

The fresh air felt like a tonic as the door to Cliffside closed behind me. As I headed down the smooth front walk toward my bike, I saw Stanley approaching up the driveway. "Hi," I said.

Stanley looked up, startled. "I was just dropping off some cookies," I said. "I'm so sorry about your father."

"Thanks." He ducked his head. Dark circles ringed his eyes, and his clothes were rumpled; he looked as if he hadn't slept in days.

"Have the police been in touch with you yet?" I asked gently.

"The police?" Stanley looked around nervously. "No. Why?"

"Apparently your father was murdered."

All of the blood drained out of Stanley's face. His voice was so low it was almost a whisper. "No . . . you must be wrong."

"The coroner's report was filed this morning." Stanley looked as if he were about to be sick.

"I've . . . I've got to go," he said. Before I could say another word he had disappeared around the house. I stood on the path for a moment, then heard a door close somewhere behind me.

Nine

The pungent smell of seaweed and fish wafted over me as the pier came into view. It must be low tide. I hoped Berta would be in her store, rather than beachcombing in search of more raw material. All of her jewelry — or so the advertisements said — was made of unpolished sea glass from the shores of Cranberry Island. Since a national style magazine had recently featured Berta's pieces, business had apparently skyrocketed, and I wondered how she was keeping up with the demand. Maybe she'd started dumping buckets of broken bottles overboard herself.

My bike bumped over the weathered boards as I rode past Spurrell's Lobster Pound, my mouth watering at the smell of boiled lobster and corn. I promised myself I would have dinner there soon, regardless of the state of my bank account. A little farther down the pier was Island Artists' mullioned front window, which featured a bright line of John's boats. I smiled as a curly haired little boy picked up one of the gaily colored sailboats and tugged at his mother's shirt. John had told me Claudette's sweaters and hats were for sale there as well, but they hung on the racks in the back.

Berta's store was the last one on the pier. I leaned my bike up against the weathered wood wall and glanced at the display in the big glass window, where three sea glass mobiles twirled in the afternoon light and glowed like living pearls. My eyes were drawn to the smallest of the three, which was an iridescent mix of milky blue and green glass. It would be perfect in the window over my kitchen sink. Maybe if business turned around I'd buy it.

When I walked into the small store, Berta sat behind the counter, peering through jeweled reading glasses as she helped a middle-aged woman select a pair of earrings. Berta didn't look much like a fashion maven in her flowing blue-green dress and gray bouffant; she looked more like somebody's wacky maiden aunt. The customer she was helping wore a fanny pack strapped to her ample waist, and I guessed she had come over on the mail boat to wander around Cranberry Island for the afternoon.

She'd probably read about Berta's store and had made the trip just to buy her own genuine Berta Simmons earrings from the artist herself.

While Berta helped her customer, I checked the price tag on the mobile that had caught my eye — $500. If I wanted a mobile, I would have to find my own sea glass and figure out how to string it myself. As the price tag slipped from my fingers, I glanced outside. On the next wharf over, a police launch bobbed beside two lobster boats. It looked as if I'd have company when I got home.

The cash register dinged, and Berta handed the woman a bag and a receipt. When the door swung shut, I walked up to the register and smiled.

"Business is booming, eh?"

Berta took off her glasses, which hung around her neck from a chunky silver chain. "Ever since that article hit the stands, I've been taking as many orders as I can fill. I'm glad we had that storm the other day," she said. "I was just about out of materials, but it washed plenty more up on the beach." She ran her ringed fingers through a big porcelain bowl filled with shards of blue, green and milky white glass, then looked at me with shrewd brown eyes. She might look dreamy, but underneath the gauzy trappings, Berta Simmons was all business. "So, what brings you down to the pier?"

"I was just stopping by to drop off a few brochures," I said. "I was also hoping to pick up a few of yours to display at the inn." Berta's eyes darted to the newspaper rolled up next to the cash register.

I sighed. "I see you've been reading the *Daily Mail.*"

She pursed her lips. "Well . . ."

"Don't believe everything you read." Despite my effort to control it, my voice wavered. "As far as I know, Gertrude Pickens hasn't even spoken to the police yet. And they've just started investigating the case." Berta opened and closed her reading glasses and stared at the mobiles in the window. I tried a new tack.

"Look, Berta. I want to know as much as you do what happened to Bernard Katz. Trust me, I had nothing to do with what happened out there on the cliff. Do you think I'd jeopardize my livelihood — or my life — on Bernard Katz's account?"

Berta put down her reading glasses and gave me a small smile. "I'm sorry, Natalie. It's just . . . that article seemed so *sure.*"

"So I've heard," I said. "I don't know how, though, since the police have just started the investigation."

"You're right. It's just so sad, isn't it? I mean, he was in here just three days ago, picking out a necklace for his lady friend, and now . . ." she trailed off.

"He was picking out jewelry? I didn't realize he had a girlfriend."

"His wife died years ago, he was telling me, but he'd recently started seeing a woman — a very stylish dresser, he said — and wanted something special for her." She sighed. "He probably never even got a chance to give it to her. Poor man."

I gazed at the array of jewelry in the display case. "All of your pieces are so beautiful," I said, looking at the necklaces and bracelets arranged among sand dollars and dried sea stars. They were made of sea glass pieces rimmed in gold, connected by tiny gold links. "Which one did he pick?"

"Well, no two pieces are exactly alike — each one is unique, of course — but he selected a necklace that looked very much like this one." She withdrew a string of pale blue glass and laid it on top of the glass case. "He chose blue because he said it matched her eyes." I looked at the necklace for a moment before she replaced it in the case, thinking that Estelle's eyes were blue. A little darker than that necklace, perhaps, but definitely blue.

"Was his lady friend back in New York?" I asked.

"He didn't say," Berta answered as she relocked the case. "He just said she was ending a bad relationship, but that he hoped she'd be interested in marrying him when it all got sorted out."

Was Bernard Katz trying to break up his own son's marriage so he could marry his daughter-in-law? I didn't think much of Katz, but that seemed beyond even him. I made a sympathetic noise. "That *is* tragic, isn't it? I had no idea Bernard Katz was involved romantically. I hope she wasn't too deeply in love with him; if so, what a horrible loss."

"Well, hearts do mend," Berta said. "But still, you're right. It is a terrible way to lose a loved one."

"I hope the police get it all sorted out soon," I said. Berta composed her thin lips into a polite smile. "Anyway," I said, "I should probably head back to the inn. You must be swamped with orders to fill." I unzipped my backpack and laid a stack of brochures on the counter.

"Thank you," Berta said. "Let me just get a few for you to take back with you." She disappeared into the back room and returned with a half-dozen brochures of her own. "I have to get more printed," she said sheepishly.

"Thanks, Berta. And thanks for having faith in me. I'm sure this will all be cleared up before we know it."

"I hope so," she said as I headed for the door. As I got onto my bike, I peered back through the glass. Berta had disappeared into the back room again. And so had my stack of brochures.

The gray-shingled building looked as tranquil as ever as I rode up to the inn. Pale pink and blue sweet peas climbed the columns next to the blue front door, and brilliant magenta roses spilled from the front beds. I noticed a few stray clumps of grass poking out from among the flowers as I wheeled my bike around to the side of the inn; it was time to get out and do some weeding. I stowed the Schwinn in the shed and touched a hand to my temple, which had begun to throb again during the ride home. No weeding right now, though. Right now, I needed more aspirin, and maybe a nap.

A blast of cigarette smoke hit me as I opened the door to my kitchen. Sergeant Grimes sat at my kitchen table next to a saucer full of cigarette butts and several half-empty cups of coffee, looking like he owned the place.

"Ah, Miss Barnes. I hope you don't mind — I made some coffee for the forensics crew."

"No problem," I said, forcing my face into an approximation of a smile. "But do you mind smoking outside? Some of my guests are sensitive to smoke."

Grimes' jowly face registered surprise. "I'll just finish this one up then," he said, and took a long drag of the half-smoked cigarette dangling between his yellowed fingers. I looked at the butt-filled saucer — my saucer — with fury. It would be days before I got the smell of smoke out of my kitchen.

"The guys are up working in Katz's room," he said.

"Did John tell you about the intruder?"

"Oh yeah. He mentioned you hit your head." He glanced at the knot on my temple. "Nasty. You should get that looked at. What'd you do, trip and whack into something?"

"Someone broke into Katz's room last night. They were looking for something. I heard them doing it, and interrupted the search. Whoever it was hit me over the head and knocked me out, then took off."

"You went into Mr. Katz's room and found someone?" He smoothed his hair with his free hand; the cigarette smoldered in the other. He reminded me of a big, greasy toad. I imagined him blowing up with cigarette smoke and floating through the window, then exploding in the clear Maine air like an overfilled balloon.

"That's right."

He leaned back and put his feet up on one of my chairs, making his belt disappear between his paunch and his heavy legs. "What I'd like to know is how exactly you got *into* Mr. Katz's room. I locked that door before I left yesterday, and you told me I had all the keys."

I swallowed. "I forgot about the skeleton key. My niece uses it when she cleans the rooms."

"The skeleton key, eh? You 'forgot' about it. How convenient." Grimes took his feet off the chair and pulled a small notebook out of his pocket. "And how did this — *intruder* — get into Mr. Katz's room if *you* had the skeleton key?"

"Through the window."

"Through the window. What, did he fly?" He flapped his arms, sending ash flying onto my pine floor. I restrained myself from hurrying over to scoop up the ashes.

"The window was open," I said evenly. "I imagine whoever it was climbed the rose trellis. Have you taken a look at the ground below the window? There might be footprints."

Grimes took another drag of his cigarette and made a few notes in his little book. He exhaled a thick stream of smoke and said, "No, haven't sent anyone out there yet. We'll get there — let the professionals handle this." Well, that leaves you out of it, I thought.

He took a last puff and ground out his cigarette on my saucer. I looked at the pile of butts with distaste. "Do you mind if I take that outside?"

He shrugged. "Be my guest." I grabbed the saucer and walked out the kitchen door with it. After emptying it into the trashcan at the side of the inn, I leaned against the wall and stared at the waves crashing against the rocks, trying to relax. Between the image of Grimes smoking in my kitchen and my ruminations on the culinary expertise of state penitentiary cooks, however, it didn't work too well.

After a few futile minutes, I returned to the kitchen. Grimes stood in the middle of the room, smoothing his hair again. He hitched his belt up over his paunch and looked at me with those too-close blue eyes.

"Well, that'll do it for now. I'm going to head upstairs."

"Don't forget to look out by the rose trellis."

"Just let the police do their job, okay, Miss Barnes?"

I raised my hands in surrender and watched as he waddled through the swinging door. Then I scooped up the coffee cups and put them into the dishwasher, opened the windows, and sprayed the kitchen with orange spray. The stench of smoke would take days to dissipate.

My eyes slid to the clock: it was already 2:30. I suddenly realized I hadn't asked Gwen to do the rooms that afternoon; I needed to make sure she had cleaned them. If she hadn't, I'd have to do it myself — and fast.

I jogged to the front desk, grabbed the skeleton key, and headed down the first-story hall. Ogden's room was the first door on the left. I knocked, and when no one answered, I let myself in.

The blue and white counterpane was tucked in tidily, and a stack of fresh white towels lay folded in the bathroom. I smiled. Gwen had taken care of the rooms without my asking. My eyes strayed to the rolltop desk; it was open, but both the blueprints and the stack of statements were gone. They hadn't been in Katz's room the other night, either. Where was Ogden keeping them? I was tempted to check the drawers, but decided I'd done enough snooping for the day. Besides, the inn was crawling with police.

I closed Ogden's door behind me and returned the skeleton key to the cabinet by the front desk. As the cabinet door clicked shut, my eyes fell upon the stack of mail Charlene had handed me. It lay unopened on the blotter.

I pulled the large manila envelope addressed to Bernard Katz out from the bottom of the stack, weighing it in my hands. The return address was Downeast Investigations in Bangor. I turned it over and examined it, wondering what the penalty was for opening someone else's mail. I knew it was a federal offense, but did it mean jail time? Then again, if *someone* didn't find out who had killed Bernard Katz, jail time was probably in my future anyway.

The envelope was latched and taped. I lifted a corner of the tape experimentally; it came off easily. I looked around to make sure I was alone, and then removed the rest of the tape and slid the contents out onto the desk.

Downeast Investigations
540 East River St.
Bangor, Maine 04401

Dear Mr. Katz:
Per your request, enclosed is a copy of the report on Claudette White. We have also enclosed a bill for our previous services. Our records show that your account is past due; please remit payment at your earliest convenience.
If you have any questions, please contact us at (207) 532-8978.

Sincerely,
Jacob Smiley

A report on Claudette White? I flipped through the pages to the computer-generated report and reviewed it quickly. Born Claudette Rose Kean in 1946, married to Eleazer White in 1968, resided on Cranberry Island ever since. Nothing new here. I turned the page.

According to this report, Claudette had had a child when she was sixteen. My eyes scanned the typed page. A search of Maine records had turned up the birth of a son at the Bangor hospital to Claudette Kean in

1962; father's name not recorded. According to the report, she had moved in with an aunt in Bangor while she was pregnant, then put the child up for adoption and returned to Cranberry Island. Nobody on the island knew about it.

I set down the sheaf of paper and stared out the window at the dark pine trees cloaking the hill in front of the inn. So Claudette had had a child. I felt a wave of pity for her; I could only imagine how horrible it must have been first to discover she was pregnant, then to leave the island in secret and have to give up the child, without breathing a word of it to anyone. Had she told Eleazer about it?

I flipped through the rest of the report, but there was nothing else unusual. Was Bernard Katz trying to blackmail her with this information? I pulled the bill out of the stack and looked at it; there were four account numbers listed, but no names. Had he had four islanders investigated? If so, who?

I turned back to the cover letter. Call for assistance, the letter said. Was it a crime to do what the letter told me to do? Then again, I wasn't the person the letter was addressing. Still, desperate times called for desperate measures. I'd already opened somebody else's mail. Was calling the sender for more information any worse?

I glanced around. I was alone; the guests were either out of the inn or in their rooms, and Grimes was upstairs with the forensics team. If anyone were coming, I'd hear him or her from down the hall. I picked up the phone and dialed.

After three rings, a woman's voice answered, "Downeast Investigations."

"Jacob Smiley, please."

"One moment." My palms began to sweat as I waited on hold, hoping that Grimes would stay upstairs for a while. Finally, the phone clicked again as the call transferred.

"This is Jacob Smiley."

"Mr. Smiley? This is Bernard Katz's assistant. I just received your last report. I was wondering, though, could you send us duplicates of the other reports? The originals are at the office, and we're still on Cranberry Island."

"Where's Mr. Wilson?"

Mr. Wilson? Oh, Ogden. "Oh, he's here . . . it's just that everything's been so busy lately, I'm helping out with the administrative details."

"What's your name?"

"Natalie Barnes- . . . ton." I hit my left temple with my palm, then winced. Great alias, Nat. No one would be able to decipher that one.

"Shall I send it to you, then, Miss Barneston?"

"No, you can address it to Mr. Wilson or Mr. Katz, but at the same Gray Whale Inn address. And could you send that express mail?"

"Of course. You received the bill, as well?" he asked.

"Oh, yes. I'm sending it right over to accounting."

"Excellent."

"Do you think you could get those reports out today?"

"I'll see what I can do."

As I thanked him and hung up the phone, footsteps approached from the upstairs hall. I shoved the paperwork back into its envelope and jammed it into a drawer. By the time the heavy tread of Grimes' boots had started down the stairs, I was opening my own mail.

Ten

"Where can you get lunch around here?" Grimes asked, hanging over the banister. Even though he was more than ten feet away from me, I could smell stale cigarette smoke.

"There's always Spurrell's Lobster Pound," I said. "But the Cranberry Island Store has great sandwiches." I hoped he'd decide on the store; after all, it was my tax dollars he'd be spending, and I didn't feel like funding a lobster lunch for Grimes, no matter how indirectly. Besides, Charlene might be able to pry some information out of him that would be useful — like how Katz had died, for example.

As Grimes receded down the hall, I opened the rest of the stack of mail, logging the bills with a heavy heart and setting the brochure requests aside in a small stack. "You need a Web site," one of the letters said. I'd add it to the list.

I glanced at the answering machine; its red light was flashing. I jabbed anxiously at the play button, hoping for a reservation. As the voices burbled out of the machine, my hopes deflated; two potential guests had called asking for information on rates and availability, but there were no new bookings for my empty calendar.

As I began stuffing envelopes with brochures, I wondered how long Ogden and Barbara would be staying. From a financial perspective, the longer they stayed, the better. Ogden wasn't my favorite person, but the money was a big help, and at least he was low-maintenance. Since both of them were connected to Bernard Katz, I reflected, maybe the police would insist that they stay until the case was cleared. Then again, since I appeared to be the prime suspect, Grimes would probably let them leave early.

My stomach rumbled as I licked the last envelope. I got up and started into the kitchen, then doubled back and locked the drawer with Katz's mail in it, slipping the key into my pocket. I might not be the only person snooping around in other people's desks. It wouldn't surprise me if Grimes decided to do a little investigating while I was out.

As the kitchen door swung shut behind

me, I wrinkled my nose; the smoke smell still lingered, despite the ocean breeze pouring in through the windows. I opened the fridge and gazed at the barren shelves, then grabbed a half-empty jar of strawberry jam and picked up the phone.

"When are those groceries expected in?" I asked when Charlene answered. I fished two stale slices of bread out of a bag and arranged them on a plate. "I'm down to peanut butter and jelly here."

"They should be in on the 4:00 mail boat. Want me to swing by with them when I close the store? I'll bring up some frozen chowder and we can have it for dinner."

"That would be fantastic." My old Toyota Celica resided in a parking lot over on the mainland. If it weren't for Charlene's old rusted-out pick-up truck, I'd be hauling groceries with a wheelbarrow. "I'll pull some bread dough out of the freezer, and you can tell me all about dinner with Barbara."

"And *you* can tell me what *you've* been up to. From what I hear, you've been all over the island today."

"We'll talk about it when you get here. 6:30, then?"

"I'll be there with bells on."

I hung up and bit into my peanut butter and jelly sandwich. It was coming close to

3:00, and I wanted to get to Claudette's and back before dinnertime.

A few dark clouds loomed on the horizon as my bike rolled up in front of Claudette's house a half hour later. The goats grazed in the meadow behind the little wood-frame house, chained to an old tire and bleating as they devoured everything in sight. Claudette's sweet peas were bare stems below the six-foot mark, and only one petunia peeked out among the stumps of geranium and ivy in the whiskey barrels that lined the front porch. It gave me comfort to know that Claudette's garden suffered, too.

The barn that housed Eleazer's boat-building shop was set back a bit behind the house. Both buildings were painted white with aquamarine trim, but while the house's paint was fresh and clean and the porch neatly swept, the barn was starting to peel in places, and the yard next to it was cluttered with boats in various stages of decomposition. As I looked at the rotting hulls, I decided to ask Eleazer if he could find me a cheap skiff; it would be much easier than relying on the mail boat.

The wooden steps creaked beneath me as I climbed to the front porch. I knocked on the aquamarine door with trepidation; I didn't know how to broach the subject of blackmail, and was more than a little afraid of what Claudette's reaction would be.

The aroma of browning beef and onions wafted over me as Claudette opened the door, dressed in a long floral housedress and a white apron spattered with cooking oil. Her hair was pulled back into a tight gray bun, accentuating her heavy jaw, and her cool gray eyes registered surprise.

"Smells great in there," I said. Despite the peanut butter and jelly, my mouth had begun to water.

"I'm making stew for dinner." Claudette wiped her hands on her white apron. "Come in."

I followed her through the small entryway and into the cramped kitchen. The floor was covered in brown linoleum, and the small kitchen table was draped with a red-and-white checked cloth. An assortment of pots and pans with the dull shine of many scrubbings hung from a pot-rack over the porcelain sink, and a line of antique canisters stood next to a thirty-year-old gas stove. An old-fashioned wood-burning stove appeared to be the source of heat for the kitchen; although a teakettle rested on one of its black burners, I was guessing it wouldn't be lit again until September. A basket full of wool with an assortment of knitting needles sticking out of it sat next to the back door.

I slid into one of the two kitchen chairs as Claudette stood at the stove and stirred the onions and beef in a pan. Something about her looked different. My eyes strayed to the basket of wool, and I realized that it was one of the few times I'd seen her without a pair of knitting needles.

"So, what brings you here?" Claudette asked. "Any news on the preserve?" Her raspy voice was guarded, and reminded me of why I had come.

"Nothing yet. The evaluators should be out there any day now. I assume nothing's changed with Premier Resorts, though."

Claudette grimaced. "I thought not. It's too bad Bernard Katz didn't die a day earlier. Could have saved us all a lot of trouble." She added salt to the pan with a sharp jerk of her wrist. "I hear he was murdered."

"That's what they're saying. The police came out to look at Katz's room today." Claudette replaced the saltshaker on the ledge behind the stove. I leaned forward in my chair. "Have the police been out to talk to you yet?" Claudette's gray eyes darted from the pan to me for a moment. She thrust out her jaw.

"No. Why would they?"

"Well, they've been all over me," I said lightly. "You'd think I was the only one on the island who didn't like Bernard Katz."

Claudette took a deep breath and then launched into the beginning of one of her trademark tirades. "He's just like the rest of the greedmongers, wanting to take nature and pervert it to their own uses." She thrust the spoon into the pan. "There's no room for nature anymore. It's all plastic cartons, plastic wrappers, trash everywhere. No one is interested in the natural rhythm of things, in conservation."

If I didn't head her off now, it would be hours before I got a word in edgewise. She paused for a breath and I jumped into the gap. "I agree with you, Claudette, and I'd love to discuss it sometime, but I came by this afternoon because I have a question for you." She fell silent. Her gray eyes flicked to me, then returned to the pan in front of her. "I ran across something the other day that made me think Bernard Katz was trying to blackmail some folks here on the island."

Claudette's jaw jutted out even farther, and the intensity of her stirring increased. She fixed her eyes on the contents of the pan.

"I was wondering if he'd ever approached you," I said. "Tried to convince you to back off *Save Our Terns.*"

Claudette's knuckles whitened as she gripped the wooden spoon. She spoke through clenched teeth. "What exactly did you find that would make you ask me that, Natalie?"

I shifted in the hard chair. "He sicced a private investigator on you, didn't he?" I asked gently. "Tried to blackmail you into backing down by threatening to tell everyone about the child you had to give up." Claudette stopped stirring. "But you didn't give in, did you?"

Claudette stood motionless at the stove. Her gray eyes shone, and as I watched, a tiny drop trickled down her thick cheek. She was silent for a long moment, and the hard lines of her face seemed to soften. "I was young," she whispered. "He was a fisherman from the mainland, promised me he'd marry me." She made a strange sobbing noise. "When I told him I was pregnant, he signed on with a ship. Left port the next day." She sniffled and wiped her eyes. I got up from my chair and retrieved the tissue box next to the sink. She took it from my hand without looking at me.

"What a terrible thing to do to a young girl," I said softly.

She pulled a tissue from the box and

dabbed at her eyes, then stood silent for a long moment. "I went to stay with an aunt in Bangor," she continued in a voice so low it was almost a whisper. "My mother insisted, said no one could know. Told everyone I was taking a course in etiquette." She gazed out the window. "I never saw my baby. I never even saw him."

I sat silent as she wiped her eyes with the tissue. "And then later," she continued, "with Eleazer, when we wanted children . . ." she trailed off. Her thick body convulsed. I rose and patted her soft back. "I couldn't have another child. That's why I have Muffin, and Gretel, and Pudge." For a moment I was confused. Then I realized she was talking about her goats.

"What an awful experience," I murmured. "I can't imagine what it must have been like for you. Does Eleazer know?"

"No." Her voice was venomous. "But Bernard Katz was threatening to tell him about it."

"You know, you and Eleazer might be able to adopt."

She sighed. "It's too late for that. Look at me. I'm fifty-eight, and Eleazer's almost seventy. Who would give a child to us?" The smell of singed onion began to fill the room, recalling Claudette's attention to the stove;

she turned the gas down and stirred wildly, scattering bits of meat and blackened onion across the clean white surface.

"Bernard Katz came and threatened to tell Eleazer. And the whole island." Her voice was edged with bitterness. "I told him he could shout it from Cadillac Mountain if he wanted to. It doesn't make a whit of difference to me now."

"Do you know where your son is now?"

"They gave him to a family in Bangor. He's grown now, has a family of his own. A girl and a boy. I've never met him — I didn't want to upset his life — but I keep tabs on what he's doing. And his kids — my grandkids, really," she said wistfully.

"Maybe you should try to get in touch with him. You'd make a wonderful grandmother. And I'm sure he'd understand — you were so young, and things were very different then."

"Maybe. I just have to get through this thing with the police first."

"What thing?"

She gave me a curious look. "Everyone on the island saw how angry I was at Bernard Katz the night he died. I just about threatened to kill him myself, didn't I? I'm surprised they haven't been beating down the door already."

"But surely Eleazer could vouch for you. I mean, you went home right after the meeting, didn't you?"

Claudette's eyes flicked out the window, to where Muffin and her friends were tearing up part of the backyard. "Yes," she said, "of course."

The sky was just starting to spit fat drops of rain as I pulled up beside the inn, stowed my bike in the shed, and dashed to the kitchen door. The lacy white kitchen curtains billowed in the wind as the door slammed shut behind me, and I rushed to close the windows before the rain turned into a downpour. My eyes swept the room, looking for more cigarette butt-laden saucers. To my relief, although the acrid smell of smoke still lingered in the air, it looked as if Grimes had taken any further cigarettes outside. I peeked at the bread dough, which had started to puff up beneath its blue and white towel, and headed to the front desk to check for messages.

The red light was blinking again. I hit the play button.

"Hello, Natalie? This is Gertrude Pickens of the *Daily Mail* again. If you could give me a call, I would appreciate it." Her saccharine voice made my head begin to ache again.

My finger jabbed at the erase button halfway through the phone number; I wasn't about to provide her with more ammunition for tomorrow's edition.

A clunk from upstairs reminded me that the police were still at the inn. Although I was tempted to go upstairs and ask questions, the safer course would probably be to stay busy in the kitchen. I glanced at my watch; there was enough time to start getting things ready for breakfast tomorrow before Charlene arrived. Then again, I was short on groceries until she showed up. Still, maybe there would be something I could start working on.

As I headed into the kitchen to take inventory, thunder boomed. I froze. Had the police been out to the rose trellis yet? If not, all the evidence would be washed away.

I tore up the staircase and pounded on Katz's door. Grimes opened it and eyed me quizzically. The room was still a shambles, only now it was a shambles dusted with powder. Fingerprint powder, I presumed.

"Did you check the bottom of the rose trellis?" I gasped. "It's starting to rain."

The two men behind Grimes looked up. "Rose trellis?" asked the smaller of the two, a thin dark man with round wire glasses.

"Somebody broke into the room last

night. I think they climbed up the rose trellis and came in through the window." He gave me a blank look from behind his glasses. The other man, a plump redhead, raised his eyebrows at Grimes.

"You didn't tell us that."

Grimes shifted from foot to foot. "That's what she *says* happened. Looks to me like she was coming up with an excuse for having her prints all over the room. Probably whacked herself in the head getting out of the shower or something, and thought it would be a good cover story." He smirked at me. "By the way, we'll need a full set of prints from you before we leave for the day."

"Does this mean you're not going to look at the ground beneath the trellis?"

The short dark-haired man looked outside at the now pouring rain and grimaced. "Any evidence out there has probably washed away by now. We'll go out and take a look, but . . ." He shot Grimes a hard look. "I'm sorry we didn't know about this earlier." Grimes ran a finger around his collar and cleared his throat.

"I think that will be all, Miss Barnes. We'll come find you if we need anything further." He started to close the door on me.

I stuck my foot between the door and the frame. "One more thing."

"What?"

I pushed the door open far enough to address the two men. "Would you mind not using crime scene tape? I'm afraid it will frighten away my guests."

The dark-haired man's eyes crinkled into a smile. "Of course not. That won't be necessary at all. In fact, I think we're almost finished up here, don't you?" His red-haired partner nodded.

I withdrew my foot, and the door shut with a bang. As I made my way down the stairs, I heard voices coming down the hall. At least they'd look at it. I cursed myself for not thinking to point it out to them earlier. Clearly Grimes thought he had an open-and-shut case, and was not interested in gumming up the works with information that might lead to the real killer. For a moment, I regretted taking the letter out of Katz's room last night; maybe the investigators could have made something out of that. That was water under the bridge, though. I couldn't exactly go up and give it back to them.

The sound of the front door slamming shut reverberated through the house as I dug through the freezer, sorting through bags of frozen pork chops and chicken until I found a bag of raspberries. The rain was sheeting down the windows as I tossed the bag onto the counter; I hoped the policemen had brought raincoats. I opened the fridge to see what I could find. There was no sour cream and only a quarter of a pound of butter, but a container of dehydrated buttermilk lurked in the corner of the fridge. I pulled it out and leafed through my cookbooks until I found a recipe for raspberry coffee cake that involved minimal butter and called for buttermilk instead of sour cream. I'd make the batter this evening and keep it in the fridge; in the morning, I'd add a streusel topping and pop the cake into the oven.

I was just washing up the bowl when Charlene's truck clattered down the road. I threw on my rain slicker and raced out to help her unload the groceries.

"What are those guys doing on the side of your house?" she yelled as we ran in through the kitchen door, our arms filled with wet plastic bags.

"Looking for clues," I called back as I headed out for another load of groceries. "I'll tell you all about it when we get this stuff inside." Within ten minutes, the kitchen counters were covered with dripping white bags and we were soaked. "I'm glad you used plastic instead of paper," I said.

"It didn't help me much," she said, peeling off her bright yellow rain slicker. Charlene's silky magenta blouse clung to her skin, and the hem of her denim skirt was splattered with mud. Her usually immaculate hair stuck to her face, and mascara oozed down her cheeks. I put on a teakettle and tossed her a clean towel from a stack in the laundry room. She dabbed at her face and hair with it as I put the groceries away and told her about my day.

"Someone broke into Katz's room and hit you over the head?" she asked, raccoon eyes wide.

"Yeah, but Grimes didn't tell the forensic guys about it. When it started to rain, I went up and asked if they'd had a chance to look outside yet. Grimes hadn't even told them about it."

Her eyes narrowed. "What a jerk. Can't you call and have someone else put on the investigation?"

"That would look good. The primary suspect calling to complain because she doesn't like the investigating officer." The teakettle began to whistle. I threw a tea bag into the teapot and poured hot water over it, then turned the oven to 400 degrees for the bread.

"I see your point," Charlene said. "Maybe I should call."

"Thanks, but I really don't think it would make any difference. I did find out something else about Katz today, though."

"What?"

"I think he was blackmailing some of the islanders. Or trying to."

Charlene stopped dabbing at her mascara. "You're kidding me. Who?"

"I'll let you know when I'm sure." What Claudette had told me today was between her and me. I wasn't going to divulge that information to anyone, even Charlene. I changed the subject. "So, what did you find out about Barbara?"

Charlene sighed and resumed dabbing at her face. "Not much. Apparently she's spending most of her time at the Somesville library doing 'research', but she wouldn't tell me anything more about it."

"Did you find out anything about what she meant by 'alternate tactics'?"

Charlene was glum. "Not a word. I must be losing my touch. Barbara sure can pack it away, can't she? She ate a two-pound lobster, half a dozen rolls and two huge slices of pie."

"I know. It's not fair, is it? Gwen's the same way." I unveiled the bread dough and popped the pale loaf into the oven. "Where's that chowder, by the way?"

"I think I left it in the truck." She rose to get her raincoat again, but I was already at the door.

"I'll get it. You were nice enough to bring me my groceries — and the chowder. Besides, you just got yourself cleaned up." She sank down into her chair as I slipped back out into the rain.

When I returned with the Tupperware container, Charlene was looking around the kitchen. "By the way, where *is* your niece?"

"Out painting, I presume. She's off with her sketchbook and easel whenever she gets the chance."

Charlene's lips curved into a smile. "Have you seen her work?"

"No, I haven't. I've been meaning to head over to Fernand's, but I haven't had the chance. Why?"

"It's pouring out there. Do you really think Gwen's outside painting right now?"

I glanced out the window at the sheeting rain. The last time I had seen her, Gwen was wearing a light sundress, and her raincoat still hung on the peg by the door. "I see your point." I looked at Charlene, who was still smirking. "So, where is she?"

Charlene examined her pink nails. "The way I hear it, she's been spending a good bit of time with Adam Thrackton."

"The kid who threw all his books off the pier and decided to become a lobsterman?"

"Yup. Apparently Gwen's been spending a lot of time out on his boat." She bent down to examine a miniscule snag on a pinky nail. "Do you have a file?"

"No, I don't. So, is she going out with this guy?"

"Well, he's not hauling too many traps lately, the way I hear it."

I looked out at the whitecaps on the water. "You don't think she's out with him in this weather, do you?"

"I think he'll take care of her. They all say he's a natural on a boat."

I groaned. "How am I going to tell my sister about this?" I narrowed my eyes at Charlene. "Are you absolutely sure?"

"Trust me." Charlene rubbed at her nail for a moment, then looked up at me. "At least he has a degree from an Ivy League school."

"Had," I said. "Didn't he pitch that into the drink as well?"

"Well, yeah."

As if on cue, the kitchen door banged

open. My niece appeared in the doorway with her mass of brown hair plastered to her pink cheeks, wearing a heavy orange rain jacket and a starry-eyed smile.

ELEVEN

"How's the painting going?" I asked.

Gwen pushed a strand of wet hair away from her face. "The painting? Oh, great — really great." Charlene gave me a nasty look; I ignored it.

"I'm looking forward to seeing your work. I've got to get over to Fernand's someday soon to take a look at it."

"That'd be cool." She peeled off the orange raincoat. "Mind if I run upstairs and change? I'm drenched."

"If you're hungry, I've got bread in the oven, and Charlene brought over some chowder."

"Sounds good," she said, kicking off her mud-covered sandals and heading for the stairs. As she disappeared, Charlene cocked an eyebrow at me.

"So, you think that glow comes from art?"

"I concede the point. As usual, I'm the last to know."

Charlene pointed at the orange raincoat dripping on the hook next to the door. "At least he's enough of a gentleman to lend her his coat. He can't be all bad."

"Unfortunately, I don't think her mother will see it that way." I grimaced. "I never dreamed I'd see her in a fisherman's jacket."

"She's nineteen. She can't be under her mother's thumb forever. Didn't you have a few flings when you were young? Or were you always this averse to anything romantic?"

"Of course," I said. "It's just that I'm responsible for her . . ."

"Responsible for giving her a place to live and feeding her and making sure she doesn't do herself bodily harm. She's getting her work done here, isn't she?"

"I suppose so."

"So let her deal with her mother. Stay out of it." Clearly she didn't know Bridget very well, but I just nodded and said nothing. I got up and peeked into the oven; the bread was close to being done, so I popped the chowder into the microwave. As I turned around, a knock sounded at the kitchen door, and three very wet policemen crowded into the kitchen. Grimes hung close to the door, a sour look on his face.

"You guys are soaked!" I said. "Do you

need towels?"

"No, we're just going to head back to the launch," the dark-haired forensics investigator told me. "We're done for today."

"Did you have any luck outside?"

The plump redhead grimaced. "Some of the vines were torn away from the trellis, and the wood was broken in a few places, but if there were any footprints or fingerprints, they got washed away in the rain. I'm sorry."

My heart sank. On the plus side, they did seem to believe that someone had climbed the trellis. Grimes stood sullenly, his wet uniform dripping on my pine floor. His hand strayed to his pocket, and then retreated. Reaching for a cigarette.

"Do you need a ride back to the town dock?" Charlene asked, trying to puff up her flattened hair.

"No, thanks. We called the launch — if you don't mind, we're going to board at your dock."

"Be my guest. Are you sure you don't want a cup of tea to warm you up?"

They declined, and filed out the doorway. Grimes hung back to deliver a parting shot. "I'll be back to take prints tomorrow," he said, then shut the door behind him with a bang.

Charlene looked at me. "Prints?"

"I know. Not good."

"Well, at least the other two policemen were nice," she said. "The guy with the glasses was kind of cute."

"It's just the investigating officer I've got a problem with."

Charlene and I were on our second bowls of chowder when Gwen swept down the stairs in her fluffy blue bathrobe. She tore off a big hunk of bread and began filling a bowl with steaming chowder. I spooned up some more of the creamy soup and waited until she sat down at the table before I asked the question.

"Did Adam lend you that jacket?"

Gwen froze with her spoon in midair. "How did you know?"

"I'm best friends with Charlene, remember?" Gwen blushed. Charlene leaned forward and patted her hand.

"Adam's a fine boy, sweetheart. You don't need to hide him from us."

"Are you going to tell your mother about him?" I persisted.

Gwen shifted in her chair. "I don't really think he's mother's type," she said in a faint voice.

I sighed. "Gwen, I'm responsible for you this summer. From what Charlene tells me,

Adam is a good person. I'm afraid your mother's going to be less than thrilled, though. I'm not going to call her and report your every movement, but if she asks me if you're seeing anyone, I'll have to tell her."

Gwen toyed with her spoon and stared at the table. "I know."

"Good lord, Nat, lighten up!" Charlene paused between bites of chowder to wag her spoon at me. "You'd think Gwen was dating a convicted murderer." She gave me a funny look. "Sorry. Bad choice of words." She licked her spoon. "But Gwen's a young woman now, not a child. She can choose who she wants to see."

"I know," I said. "I just don't want to get in the middle of things."

"Then don't."

Gwen shot Charlene an appreciative look and took a tentative taste of chowder. "This is really good." She was right. Charlene's chowder was a masterpiece of potatoes and clams cloaked in a velvety sauce. I scooped up a little with a crust of bread and made a mental note to get the recipe.

Charlene smiled proudly. "New England style. None of that tomato-y Manhattan stuff." She dabbed at her mouth with a napkin. "At any rate, sweetheart, how is

Adam doing? Is he involved in the gear war?"

I was baffled, but Gwen seemed to know just what she was talking about. "I don't think he's cutting any traps himself," she said, "but he's all for taking measures to protect our traditional fishing grounds." I looked up from my bowl. *Our* traditional fishing grounds? She'd been on Cranberry Island a sum total of six weeks.

"What gear war?" I asked. Charlene and Gwen gave me a pitying look. "You do know that some mainlanders have been moving in on Cranberry Island's fishing grounds?" I nodded. "Well," Charlene continued, "somebody's been cutting buoys loose from the traps. You know, the red and green buoys that keep popping up like bad pennies? They belong to mainlanders. The lobster co-op has been moving them back over the line into mainland territory, but whoever's fishing them keeps moving them back onto Cranberry Island's turf. So someone started cutting their gear. It's been the talk of the island," she said. "That and what happened to Bernard Katz, of course."

She turned to Gwen. "So, how's the haul been?"

"A lot of shorts, and Adam says he's been changing a lot of water."

"Changing water?" I asked.

"That's what they call it when the traps come up empty," Gwen said in an authoritative voice. "But Adam says the hauls don't really start picking up until the beginning of July, so he's not worried." I raised my eyebrows. In less than two months, my California niece had started talking like a Maine lobsterman.

"What are shorts?"

"Lobsters that are two small to keep. Conservation measures."

"Ah." Clearly I had a lot to learn about lobstering. "Gwen, have you done *any* painting since you've been here?"

Gwen's face lit up. "Oh, yeah, Aunt Nat — I did a great watercolor of the Gray Whale the other day. I sketched it while I was out on the boat."

"I could use one of those for a new brochure," I said.

Gwen's eyes sparkled. "Really? You'd use it on your brochure? I could do a series, you know."

"Well, the next printing is a ways away," I said, not wanting her to get too excited — I hadn't even seen one of her sketches, after all — "but it's a definite possibility." If there *was* a second printing.

Gwen beamed at me. "Thanks, Aunt Nat.

That'd be great in my portfolio." She started buttering her bread and I turned back to Charlene.

"Gertrude Pickens called me again this afternoon."

Charlene spoke through a mouthful of clam and potato. "What did you tell her this time? I can hardly wait to read about it in tomorrow's paper."

"I didn't tell her anything. She left a message; I didn't call her back."

"She'll still make you sound like an ax murderer."

I stared at the fat raindrops dashing themselves against the kitchen window. "I wonder how he *did* die? It might help to know that."

"Help what?" Charlene sounded skeptical.

"Well, if Grimes isn't going to investigate, I figure *someone* should."

"Planning on adding a little breaking and entering to your dossier? Grimes would like that." Charlene took another bite of chowder before she continued. "What I want to know is, how are you planning on getting into the police station unnoticed? Particularly since you're not supposed to leave the island."

"I'm not planning on breaking or entering

anything," I said, wondering if going through Stanley Katz's desk qualified as breaking or entering. "Maybe John knows."

"I know he likes you, but I don't think he's allowed to share that information with you. He probably doesn't know anything, anyway." She licked a bit of chowder off her spoon. "Grimes seems like the type who would keep that sort of information close to his chest."

"He was there when they lifted Katz out, and saw something that made him think Katz was murdered. Even if he didn't see the autopsy report, he could at least give me something to go on."

"I don't know," Charlene said. "Grimes may not be the best investigator in the world, but I don't think you should go trying to get yourself into more trouble than you're already in."

I couldn't keep the frustration out of my voice. "So I should just sit back and let Grimes convict me of murder?"

"Calm down, calm down. All I'm saying is, there are other ways to go about things. Let me ask around, see if anyone saw anything that night. Besides, you were telling me earlier you had a good lead."

"What lead?" Gwen asked.

"Your aunt thinks Bernard Katz was

blackmailing some islanders."

Gwen wiped the last of the chowder from her bowl with a crust of bread. "Maybe that's why Ingrid changed her vote." The thought had occurred to me, too, but I said nothing.

"Good point," Charlene said. "But who else would he blackmail? I'd say your Aunt Nat would be a good candidate, but she's too much of a goody-two-shoes." She narrowed her blue eyes at me; without mascara, they seemed strangely naked. "Unless there's some deep dark past you've been hiding from us."

I laughed. "Not unless I have a second personality I'm not aware of." I wondered if Katz had considered trying to blackmail me. I'd find out soon enough if he'd tried; copies of the investigative reports should be here any day.

"What makes you think he was blackmailing people?" Gwen asked.

"I can't talk about it right now, but I'll know more soon," I said. "Please don't say anything to anyone about it yet, though. I want to be sure."

Charlene smiled wryly. "Your aunt is considering going into private investigation as a sideline."

"She's just kidding," I said as Gwen

looked at me questioningly.

We finished our chowder, and Charlene headed home, promising to ask around and see if anyone was out the night Katz died. Gwen helped me set up the dining room, and we both headed upstairs at the same time.

"I'm glad you've found someone who makes you happy," I said as we climbed the creaky staircase.

Gwen smiled. "Thanks, Aunt Nat."

"Just don't do anything I wouldn't do, okay?"

Gwen groaned. "Do you have to be so limiting?" We both laughed.

"Have a good night, Gwen. And thanks for taking care of the rooms today."

"No problem."

I could hear the shower running in the bathroom next door as I filled the claw-foot tub with hot, bubbly water and lit a candle. One nice thing about living in an inn was that you never ran out of hot water.

I lowered myself into the hot fragrant bubbles with a sigh of pleasure, luxuriating in the tingle of heat on my chilled legs and feet. In Texas, it rarely got chilly enough to appreciate a good hot bath. Here in Maine, though, evenings were always nippy enough to make baths a real pleasure. And I hadn't even spent a winter up here yet.

I picked up my book and soon lost myself in the pages, enjoying the flicker of the candles and the scent of the bubbles. The shower had gone off next door, and I could hear the rain patter against the windowpane, and below that the soft rush of the waves as they lapped against the rocks outside.

I had just turned a page and was sinking deeper into the fragrant water when a crash of breaking glass sounded from somewhere in the inn.

TWELVE

I leaped out of the bathtub and grabbed a towel. Within seconds, I had wrapped a robe around myself and was running down the stairs. I hit the kitchen light and scanned the room, but nothing was out of place; the sound must have come from elsewhere. My hand trembled as I slid a carving knife from the block and approached the swinging door to the dining room on tiptoe, gripping the knife. The droplets of water falling to the floor from my wet hair sounded like hammer blows as I shouldered through the door into the dark room and fumbled for the switch.

The lights went on with a click. I stood squinting into the glare, holding the knife out before me like a talisman. The dining room was empty, but someone had thrown a rock through the window. It was perched on the corner of one of the dining room tables, surrounded by shards of twinkling glass.

I tiptoed over to the glass to take a closer look. It was a chunk of granite almost as big as my head, and the glass window it had evidently come through was shattered. As I bent down to examine it, something crashed behind me. I whirled around, stabbing the air — but it was only a chunk of glass falling out of the window frame.

My breath shuddered out of my chest as I looked back at the rock. A folded piece of lined notebook paper had been tied to it with a piece of rough twine. I laid the knife down where I could retrieve it quickly and slid the paper out from beneath the twine.

I peeled the paper open with shaking fingers. It was wet with rain, and the ink had begun to run, but the message, which had been written firmly with a black marker, was clear: *GET OFF OUR ISLAND.*

I stood staring at the angry block letters when the sound of someone hammering at the kitchen door made my heart start thudding all over again. Blood thundered through my veins as I grabbed the knife, and it occurred to me that it might be a good idea to consult a cardiologist soon. Island life hadn't been nearly as relaxing as I'd hoped. As I crept toward the kitchen, a sharp pain lanced through my foot. I yelped — I must have stepped on a shard of glass — and hobbled the rest of the way, my heart racing as I pushed open the swinging door.

A wave of relief swept over me at the sight of John standing outside in the rain. I limped over to the door and unlocked it, leaving a trail of blood on the wood floor. His hair was rumpled, and he was dressed in a holey T-shirt and plaid flannel pajama pants. As the door opened, I became acutely conscious of my threadbare bathrobe, and pulled it tighter around myself.

"We have to stop meeting like this," I said as he stepped into the kitchen.

"I heard a crash. What happened?" His green eyes leapt to the blood on the floor. "Are you okay?"

"Someone delivered a message through the dining room window. I'm fine; I just stepped on a piece of glass."

"Someone broke the window?"

"Threw a rock through it, actually. I'm surprised half the inn isn't up. The rain must have masked the noise."

"The only reason I heard it is that I have a window open." I raised my eyebrows at him. "Kitchen mishap," he said sheepishly. I didn't probe further. "Are you okay in here?" he asked. "I'm going to see if I can track down whoever did this."

"Go ahead," I said. "I'm fine."

"I'll be back as soon as I can." The door shut behind him, and I limped over to a chair to inspect my foot.

The piece of glass embedded in my foot was a quarter of an inch long, but fortunately it had slid in sideways, and hadn't penetrated too deeply. I eased it out between my thumb and forefinger; it looked like a crystal tooth. Blood welled in the wound, and after staunching it with a paper towel, I hopped up the stairs to the bathroom.

As I cleaned and bandaged the cut, I caught a glimpse of myself in the mirror. The knot on my forehead was beginning to turn an interesting shade of purplish green, my hands and forearms were scabbed from my slide down the cliff, and the thumb I had caught in Ogden's roll-top desk had turned dark purple. My gray-streaked brown hair was wild around my wan face, and dark circles ringed my eyes. I was hardly the ravishing creature I hoped John would see. In fact, I was beginning to look like a poster child for the Battered Women's Shelter. There was nothing I could do about my bumps and bruises, but I did throw on a pair of jeans and a clean T-shirt before I headed back downstairs. I might not look like Aphrodite incarnate, but that didn't mean I had to meet John in my threadbare bathrobe again.

I had finished sweeping up the glass and was examining the jagged hole in the window when John came through the swinging door from the kitchen.

"Your foot okay?"

"Yeah, it was just a sliver. Did you see anyone?"

"Whoever it was took off in a hurry." He walked over to the table and picked up the soggy paper. "Looks like you've got a secret admirer."

"Next time I hope they'll send flowers instead." My eyes returned to the shattered window. Water dripped from the broken glass, and had started to pool on wood floor. There was no way to hide that from the guests tomorrow morning. Maybe I could blame it on a renegade seagull. "Is there any way to get this covered up for the night?"

"I've got a plastic drop cloth I could tape up for now. It won't be perfect, but at least it will keep the rain out." He looked at me thoughtfully. "I'd be happier with something a little less flimsy, though. Do you have a lock on your bedroom door?"

"Yes."

"Use it. And make sure Gwen locks her door, too. I'm glad you're both on the second story. I'll head over to the mainland and pick up some glass tomorrow."

"I wonder if Grimes will think I did this, too."

"Throw a rock with a nasty note tied to it through your own dining room window?"

"Well, he didn't believe anyone had broken into Katz's room and knocked me out. He didn't tell the forensics investigators about it until the rain washed away all the evidence."

John looked up at me, his face drawn. "They didn't get any evidence?"

"By the time they got around to it, it was pouring. If I hadn't gone up and said something to them myself, I don't think Grimes would have mentioned it. He told me he thinks I fell and hit my head and concocted the whole story."

"I didn't realize that."

We were silent for a moment, staring at the window. The lines around John's mouth looked deeper than usual, and his usually sparkling eyes were dull. I said, "I've been meaning to ask you — do you have any idea how Katz was killed?"

John's head jerked up sharply. "Why do you want to know?"

"I thought it might give me an idea of who might have done it."

His mouth twisted into a frown. "I didn't see the autopsy report, but it looked to me as if someone hit him on the side of the head with something heavy, then pushed him over the cliff."

I shuddered. "I'm glad I didn't see that side of him." I thought for a moment. "Do you think a woman could have done it?"

John shrugged. "If she was angry enough, I imagine so." He shot me a warning look from beneath his thick, sandy eyebrows. "You didn't hear any of this from me, though."

"Of course not."

John ran his hand through his hair and looked back at the shattered window. "Why don't you put some towels down and I'll see what I can do to get this window covered up." His shoulders looked bowed as he closed the kitchen door behind him. I took a look at the blood, water and mud on the floor and retreated to the laundry room for a stack of towels. As I mopped up the floor, he knocked out the rest of the glass and taped up a big piece of cloudy plastic. We worked together in silence, our minds on other things.

By the time I made it back to my bathtub,

the bubbles had deflated and the water was cold. I blew out the candle and headed for bed. The clock read 12:45. I groaned. I had only six hours to go before it was time to be up and in the kitchen.

I lay awake for a long while, listening to the patter of rain on the roof, before I finally drifted into a dream in which Estelle and Bernard Katz were throwing huge chunks of sea glass at me and laughing. Bernard Katz was saying something to me that I couldn't understand, and he kept pointing to the side of his head. Bits of skull poked from a jagged hole gaping above his ear, and a long trickle of blood ran down over his starched white collar onto his pin-striped suit.

The next morning dawned gray and cool. The rain had slowed to a drizzle, but it was still coming down steadily as I headed downstairs, afraid of what I'd find on the dining room floor. Fortunately, John's quick fix had held for the night, and the old pine planks hadn't been damaged by the rain. I laid a new tablecloth and place settings on the table the rock had landed on, frowning at the plastic and hoping John could get the window repaired today. Then I sighed and headed into the kitchen to start breakfast.

Twenty minutes later, I was sliding a raspberry coffee cake into the oven and pulling down a coffee cup for a much-needed hit of caffeine. My head was better, but the knot on my temple still ached, and the cut in my foot stung with every step.

I had started stirring chunks of cheddar cheese into a bowl of eggs when the phone rang. I picked it up and cradled it on my shoulder. "Gray Whale Inn."

"It's just me," Charlene said. "I thought you'd want to know; the paper just came in."

"More good news?"

"Developer Murdered on Cranberry Island: Investigator says innkeeper 'person of interest'."

"Sounds better than suspect, anyway." I glanced over at the oven and checked the timer: ten minutes to go. Cooking was usually balm to my soul, but this morning the rich smell of coffeecake filling the kitchen did nothing to dispel the sick feeling in the pit of my stomach.

Charlene said, "Between Pickens and Grimes, you've got yourself an anti-fan club going."

I sighed. "I'll head down later to pick up a copy of the paper. Do you have any good news for me?"

"Well, the evaluators are due in today."

"I'm not sure that qualifies as good news." I shifted the phone to the other shoulder. "Someone threw a rock through the dining room window last night with a note attached."

"You're kidding me. What did it say?" When I told her, she said, "You're the Bermuda Triangle of the Maine coast, you know that?"

"I know. Any idea who could have done it?"

"Well, there are a few islanders who want the development to go through so they can sell out at high prices. Maybe they're worried you'll interfere with the resort."

I gazed out the window at the dark gray ocean. The surface was dulled by the spatter of raindrops, but a few lobster boats chugged across the sullen water. I wondered if Adam's was one of them. As my eyes followed the progress of the nearest boat, I remembered that I wanted a boat of my own. "By the way," I said, "when you see Eleazer, could you tell him I'm looking for a cheap skiff?"

"I thought you were supposed to stay on the island."

"I didn't say I was going anywhere," I snapped. "I just said I needed a skiff." I gave the bowl of eggs and cheese a final stir and put it into the refrigerator. "Whose side are you on, anyway?"

"Relax, Nat. I'm just trying to keep you out of trouble."

I rummaged through the freezer and pulled out a package of bacon. "It hasn't worked out too well so far."

"True. But you can't blame me for trying. By the way, when are you going to send another batch of cookies my way?"

I promised her I'd try to get some made after breakfast and hung up the phone with a heavy heart.

Ogden appeared just before nine in slacks and a beige sport coat. His thick glasses were the same as always, but this morning his lank hair was slicked back, and he reeked of Polo. Although he had clearly made an effort, he was not exactly GQ material; his brown slacks were short enough to expose more than I liked of his wildly patterned socks, and both the pants and the socks clashed with his scuffed black leather shoes. His eyes looked huge behind the convex lenses as he inspected the window. "What happened?"

"The window broke." I decided it would be best not to give the details. "It will be fixed today. Can I get you some coffee?"

Ogden looked as if he wanted to ask something else, but changed his mind and nodded curtly. "You do recall that Mr. Katz will be joining me this morning?"

I didn't recall, but I nodded anyway. "Of course. I'll have coffee out in a moment."

I went into the kitchen and grabbed the coffee pot. When I stepped back into the dining room, Stanley Katz had materialized, looking as haggard as he had at Cliffside. His shirt was half-tucked into wrinkled brown trousers, and his eyes were bloodshot. He deposited a sheaf of papers on the table as I filled Ogden's cup.

"Would you like some coffee?" I asked. He nodded without looking at me. I glanced down at the stack of papers and caught a glimpse of letterhead, "Brown and Watson P.C.", before his hand moved over to cover the paper. I poured the coffee and retreated to the kitchen. "I'll be back shortly with cream and sugar."

When I came out a few minutes later, Ogden and Stanley stood at the buffet. I glided over to the table with a pitcher of cream and a sugar bowl and glanced over my shoulder; both Ogden and Stanley had their backs turned to me as they filled their plates. I set down the cream and sugar and took a closer look at the top sheet of paper.

The lawyers' address was in New York City, and the letter was dated May 18.

> Dear Mr. Katz:
> Per our conversation yesterday, attached please find a copy of the new will and testament you requested. As we discussed, we have changed the beneficiary to reflect your wishes. Please review the enclosed documents. If everything is in order, contact my secretary to arrange a date and time to come in and sign the amended will. Please call me if you have any further questions.
>
> Best regards,
> James Watson

New beneficiary? I was tempted to flip through and find out who that might be, but decided not to push my luck. I glanced back at the buffet; Stanley and Ogden were at the end of the line and about to return to the table. Stanley seemed to sense my gaze, and turned around suddenly. His eyes widened when he saw me at the table, and he stumbled in my direction, his lank hair falling into his face as he jerked the stack of papers off the table.

I made a show of arranging the cream and sugar as he clutched the stack of papers to his sunken chest. "Let me know if you need anything else," I said, and walked back into the kitchen. Stanley's eyes followed me the whole way.

The rest of breakfast was uneventful. The Bittles were the last ones down, but even so, everybody had been served by 9:30, and I cleaned up from breakfast and started on a batch of chocolate chip cookies to take to Charlene's. As I folded chocolate chips into the buttery golden batter, my thoughts turned to the papers Ogden had clutched to his chest at breakfast. I wondered how and why Bernard Katz had changed his will. I also wondered if he had had a chance to sign it.

The first batch of cookies was ready for the oven when Gwen came downstairs, dressed to kill as usual in white Capri pants and a low-cut blue T-shirt. Her mass of hair had been captured in a loose bun, accentuating her slender neck and long-lashed brown eyes. She looked strangely vulnerable. "How's your foot?" she asked.

"Much better." I had woken her up and told her to lock her door after the rock came through the window last night. "Did you sleep okay?"

"Just fine." She opened the refrigerator. "What's for breakfast?"

"Cheese eggs, raspberry coffee cake, bacon, and fruit salad. There's still coffee, too."

"Great." She pulled out Tupperware containers and started loading up a plate. "When are you heading down to Fernand's?"

"I don't know. I have to drop cookies off at Charlene's this afternoon; maybe I'll swing by then." I wanted to ask Fernand a few questions, anyway. "Can I count on you to take care of the rooms? You've been doing a great job the last week."

"No problem." She glanced out the window at the leaden sky. "The light isn't too good today, anyway." She beamed at me through a mouthful of coffee cake. "I'm glad you'll be going down to the studio; I can't wait for you to see my work."

"I'll head over as soon as the cookies are done."

It was almost 11:30 when I strapped the container of warm cookies onto the back of my Schwinn and headed up the hill. I had decided to drop the cookies off at Charlene's store first; then, if it didn't start raining again, I'd head over to Fernand's.

The normally vibrant landscape was subdued today. The towering evergreens formed a dark corridor, and the weather-stained humps of granite rearing up among the ferns and bayberry bushes mirrored the leaden sky. The rain had let up, but the pavement was still wet. I took the turn up the hill from the inn carefully; my poor body was banged up enough already without adding a spill from my bike.

Despite the foreboding atmosphere, it felt good to be out in the sea air and pumping my legs up the hill. The smell of rain was sweet, and the silvery droplets of water dangling from the blossoms in the clumps of blueberry bushes made them look as if they had been touched with fairy dew. The sound of the waves grew fainter as I puffed to the top of the hill, and I sat back with relief as the Schwinn crested it and started the steep descent through the pine trees.

The wind was whipping through my hair by the time I was halfway down, and my hands squeezed the brakes lightly. The brake levers clacked against the handlebars. I squeezed again; they clacked louder, but the bike didn't slow; in fact, it kept picking up speed. My stomach filled with ice water as the pine trees receded into a blur of green. Soon I became conscious only of the wet blacktop hurtling toward me. My mind raced, trying to come up with a way to stop the bike. A sharp turn was coming up; if I could make it around that, the rest of the road was relatively straight, and the bike would be able to run its speed down gradually. I braced myself and leaned into the curve as hard as I could, struggling to stay upright.

I hung tightly onto the handlebars, shifting all of my weight to the left, and was just about through the tightest part of the curve when the Schwinn hit a slick spot and began to skid. As the bike careened sideways, I hung suspended in midair over the wet blacktop. I fought to regain control, but the bike slipped farther, slamming me hard against the wet pavement. For a long, searing moment the Schwinn and I skidded across the asphalt; then we crashed to a halt in a tangle of bushes on the side of the road.

Thirteen

I lay in the bushes for a moment with my eyes closed, reflecting on what a great idea it had been to move to Maine to escape the stresses and worries of day-to-day life. As the blood pounding through my veins began to subside, I could feel cold metal pressed against my leg. The rest of my body, however, was numb. For a moment, I wondered if I would be running the inn as a quadriplegic, but a few cautious movements assured me that I still had use of my limbs. The smell of leaf mold and bayberry was mixed with the warm scent of chocolate; I guessed that the cookies hadn't survived the crash.

When I opened my eyes, I saw that I was sprawled sideways atop a clump of bayberry bushes, with several chunks of cookie and the Schwinn beside me. The cold metal I'd felt against my thigh was a contorted handlebar. My hip flared with pain as I shifted, but everything seemed intact.

I wriggled out from under the handlebar and stood up shakily. My heavy jeans had protected me from the worst of the road. Gravel had penetrated in one or two spots, but aside from what felt like some major bruises, my leg was in working order. My left arm stung as I straightened it; I'd lost a bit of skin on my left forearm, and a few dark pebbles clung to the abraded skin, but it looked as if it would heal quickly. I brushed myself off and glanced back at the massive hunks of granite lining the steep turn. If the bike had gone down a few seconds earlier, I would have smashed head-first into a boulder.

I had survived the fall without major damage, but the Schwinn had not been so lucky. The powder-blue metal frame was bent in several places, and the handlebars resembled chrome antlers. Broken chocolate chip cookies lay scattered across the damp forest floor next to the smashed plastic container. At least the raccoons would enjoy some home-baked snacks. I bent down and took a close look at the brakes, wondering what had gone wrong with them. What I saw made my heart skip a beat.

The cables had been snipped.

I fingered the blunt ends for a moment

and stood up. Had the same person who had thrown a rock through my window cut my brake lines? I looked at the fragments of chocolate chip cookies scattered across the ground with a sick feeling in my stomach; it could easily have been me lying there in pieces instead. As my eyes returned to the severed brake lines, fear gave way to a smoldering anger. Vandalizing my inn to scare me off was one thing, but I could have been killed by this little prank. Suddenly an image of Bernard Katz sprawled across the rocks flashed through my mind, and a chill ran down my spine as I realized that perhaps that had been the point.

I bent down to collect the shards of plastic and then pulled the bike upright. The front wheel was warped, but the bike still rolled, so I strapped what was left of the container to the back and limped up the road toward the inn.

The phone jangled as I opened the kitchen door. I walked over to it, but my hand hesitated over the receiver. I wasn't up for a call from Gertrude Pickens right now. On the other hand, if it was a guest calling to make a reservation, I needed to book it before they had a chance to call elsewhere.

Survival instincts won out.

"Gray Whale Inn."

"Natalie? It's Bridget." I stifled a groan, and the pain in my hip twanged as I leaned up against the counter. My sister wasn't Gertrude Pickens, but she still wasn't high on the list of people I wanted to be talking to right now.

"Hi, Bridget," I said with as much brightness as I could muster. "How's California?"

"Wonderful. How are things out on Cranberry Island?"

"Doing fine," I said in what I viewed as a massive overstatement. I stared out the window at a lobster boat plowing through the leaden water, and wondered if my niece was aboard it. "Gwen seems to be enjoying herself."

Bridget's tone became guarded. "Oh? How so?"

"She's been taking an art class on the island," I said, watching as the white boat moved from buoy to buoy, like a bee collecting nectar from flowers. "Apparently it's going very well."

"She's not . . . seeing anyone, is she?"

Was my sister psychic? "Well," I began, "there is someone . . ."

"Does he at least have a college degree?" she interrupted. "Yes," I said. "From Princeton, I believe."

"Princeton?" The relief in her voice was

palpable. "Well, that can't be too bad. What does he do for a living?"

"Oh, he's involved with boats," I said. The boat I had been watching picked up steam and moved farther out. How nice it would be to spend the day out on the water, breathing salt air and feeling the swell of the waves. Then again, Charlene had told me the salted herring in the bait bags could get pretty smelly. Maybe I was better off watching from a distance.

Bridget's voice jerked me back to my kitchen. "Boats? What do you mean? Does he have a yacht?"

Not exactly. "No, not a yacht. Boats are more of, well, a *career* for him."

She pounced on my words. "A career. Shipping? That's a good, solid line of work. Lucrative, too. It sounds like my daughter's judgment is improving. Is she keeping up with things at the inn?"

I closed and opened my mouth a few times, feeling like a fish caught on dry land, before responding. "It was a bit rough at the start, but she's been a real help."

"I'm glad to hear it," Bridget said. "Maybe the break will help her apply herself when she gets back to UCLA in the fall. She can get this art thing out of her system over the summer and be ready to get back to business."

"I thought she was majoring in economics."

"You know what I mean," Bridget huffed. "Something practical. Real life. How's business going, by the way? Surviving your first season?"

"Oh, things are chugging along," I said, walking over to the sink and wincing as I held my battered arm under the rush of water. I decided to leave out the parts about a guest being killed, the cops being interested in me as a suspect, and vandalism with potentially murderous intent. "I'd put Gwen on to talk to you herself, but I don't think she's here right now. Shall I have her call you?"

"Please do. I'm relieved to hear that everything's going so well." She chuckled. "Knowing Gwen, I half expected her to take up with a fisherman."

I choked out a laugh. "Well, I'll tell her you called."

"Thanks, Nat. Take care."

I hung up with the distinct feeling that I had just made things worse, not better. I finished taking care of my arm and had started to wonder how I was going to explain the conversation to Gwen when

Eleazer's gnarled face appeared at the kitchen door.

"Heard you were in the market for a boat," he said as I opened the door.

"News travels fast."

"Well, if you're going to be an islander, you need a boat. When Charlene told me you were looking for a skiff, I knew I had just the boat for you." He motioned for me to follow him, and we walked across the back deck and down the sloping meadow behind the inn to a small weathered dock. Normally, only John's skiff, *Mooncatcher,* was moored there, but this afternoon it had been joined by a second small wooden boat, painted bright white. It looked to be about twelve feet long, and bobbed cheerily among the waves.

"Just put a fresh coat of paint on her yesterday," Eleazer said, patting the bow fondly. "She's got great lines, this one does." He looked like a gnome in his dark brown cap and red jacket.

"It's beautiful," I said, "but how much is it? Things are kind of tight right now."

He waved me away with a gnarled hand. "You can pay me when business gets going. Right now I'm just glad to get this girl into the water where she belongs. Her name's the *Little Marian.* I got her off of one of the summer folks — they wanted something fancier, and let her go for a song." He hopped into the small boat like a mountain goat and looked up at me expectantly. "What are you waiting for? Let's take her for a spin!"

I eyed the sky warily. "What if it rains?"

Eleazer glanced up at the low gray ceiling. "Nah," he said. "It won't rain for a while yet. I can always tell. Now, come on. Hop in."

I clambered aboard the *Little Marian* awkwardly, bumping my sore hip against the side. I winced, but Eleazer didn't notice; he was busy untying the ropes from the cleats and lowering the outboard motor into the water. He pulled the cord and the engine roared to life, and moments later we were moving away from the dock. I looked down through the glassy water, mesmerized by the green sea grasses floating among rocks and pearly mussel shells, and the hundreds of greenish-brown sea urchins that clung to the rocky bottom.

The water quickly grew deep, and the urchins faded from view. "Here are your oars," Eleazer said, "and the anchor's up here. And life jackets, of course." He patted two weathered orange life vests. "Not that you'd last more than fifteen minutes in this water anyway, but best to be safe. And here's a bucket to bail with — just an old coffee can, nothing fancy — you might want to get a plastic one, though, one that don't rust." He scooted forward in the boat and motioned me toward the motor. "Why don't you come and take the rudder, get a feel for her."

A surge of excitement coursed through me as my hand closed on the thrumming rudder. My own boat. I looked up at the Gray Whale Inn receding across the water and grinned. The island was no longer an enclosed world; it was a point of departure. I pushed the rudder experimentally to the right, and we started moving toward the preserve. "Why don't we see if the evaluators are out?" I said, enjoying the smell of salt water and the fresh white paint, which was still tacky under my fingertips.

The scents brought back a rush of memories, of sitting in a similar boat among whales and icebergs, fishing with my grandfather one distant summer off the coast of Newfoundland. The boat's wake was a string of pearls on the dark glass of the water, and as we turned toward the tree-covered cliffs, I said impulsively, "Would you teach me how to fish?"

Eleazer's blue eyes crinkled into a smile.

"Next thing you know you'll be wanting to go out lobstering with your niece." I smiled, thinking of Gwen in that huge orange raincoat. The water might be magic for her, too, but I suspected her interest was influenced by a more human element. As we rounded the bend and the narrow strip of beach came into view, Eleazer pointed at what looked like a small indentation at the base of the cliff. "See that little cove in there?"

"Sort of," I said, straining my eyes. It looked more like a dent than a cove.

"Rum runners used to keep their stash in there, back in the days of Prohibition."

"Smugglers?"

"Ayuh. It's a great place to hide things; you can only get in and out when the tide's out. When it comes back in, the cove disappears. They'd store the liquor out here on Cranberry Island and sneak it out into Somesville. Some say it was used by pirates before, but I think that's just talk."

My curiosity was piqued. "Can we go take a look?"

He shook his grizzled head. "Nope. Tide's not right. Besides, it's tricky getting in and out of there. Not enough room to swing a cat. Got to get you more practice first." He pointed over at the beach, where two people in green windbreakers knelt in the sand. A small boat lay on the brown sand of the beach. The evaluators had wisely elected not to clamber down the cliff. "Looks like your friends are working hard," Eleazer said.

"Let's hope the terns' nests haven't been destroyed beyond repair."

"Ayuh. I don't care much for the terns, not like Claudette, but I sure would hate to see this island turned into a playground for those folks up there." He pointed at Cliffside, which loomed high above on top of the cliffs.

"How did the Katzes end up moving here, anyway?" I asked Eleazer. "Estelle just doesn't seem like the island type."

"She ain't," Eleazer said with a twinkle in his eye. "No designer stores up here. Stanley Katz bought Cliffside a while back as a summer cottage — some cottage, eh? They just came down here in May. I hear they've got a place up in New York, too. Seems more her style, wouldn't you say?"

"Yeah," I said. "It does. Why did they buy here at all, I wonder?"

"Young Stanley came up here once or twice as a kid. His gram had a place up here."

"He had a grandmother living here?"

"She was just summer people. Had a little

house out in the village, near the store. Nothing much. I guess the salt water gets into your blood, though."

"Yeah, I guess it does," I said, thinking of my own childhood summers. I gazed up at Cliffside's tall turret. "I wonder why they decided to build a resort here?"

"Trying to make another Bar Harbor, I guess. Or Kennebunkport." He shrugged. "Why build one anywhere?"

I laughed. "Good point." We sat listening to the hum of the engine and the slap of the waves for a few minutes. Something gray and pointy poked out of the water in front of the boat, then disappeared. "What's that?"

"A harbor seal, looks like. They haul up on the rocks over by the lighthouse." I looked toward the red and white spire out at the far tip of the island. "Haven't you seen them?" Eleazer asked.

"I guess I haven't gotten out of the inn much." I grinned. "That'll change now, though." I felt like a teenager who had just been handed the car keys for the first time. "I can't thank you enough, Eleazer. The *Little Marian* is wonderful. You're going to have to teach me how to tie her up, though."

Eleazer adjusted his cap and grinned back at me. I noticed for the first time that he was missing a few teeth, but it didn't detract from his mischievous smile. "First you have to get her up to the dock, missy. Don't go putting the cart before the horse."

As he showed me how to make the ropes fast, I asked, "How's Claudette doing, by the way?"

His bright eyes dimmed. "A little off," he said. "This resort thing's got her in a tizzy." He stepped back from the ropes and looked at the boat with satisfaction. "You might want to get your neighbor to go out with you the first few times, just till you get the hang of it. You can get gas at the town dock; you'll want to get a spare gas can, too."

I laughed. "I'm going to need to write all this down."

"It'll come," he said. "It'll come."

As I walked back up to the house, I waved at Eleazer, and he tipped his cap at me. I had told him I'd stop by and pick up the boat later, but he insisted on walking home and leaving the boat with me. I couldn't even convince him to have a cup of tea. "I'll be making another batch of chocolate chip cookies," I told him, "and I'll leave some down at the store for you."

"I'd better get there early, then, or there won't be any left. You know Charlene."

I opened the kitchen door in a far better

mood than I had left it in, only to have it dissipate instantly. Grimes was back, and once again he was lolling with his feet up in one of my kitchen chairs. His hair was as greasy as ever, and his eyes, if possible, seemed even closer to the narrow bridge of his nose. He looked at me as if I were something that had washed up on a beach at low tide. The feeling was mutual. At least he wasn't smoking.

I forced myself to smile. "Hello, Sergeant Grimes. What can I do for you?"

He nodded toward the inkpad lying in the middle of the table next to what looked like two index cards. "I came to get prints."

"Let me just wash my hands and I'll be right with you." As I squeezed a dollop of dish soap into my palm, I said, "Somebody threw a rock with a note attached to it through my dining room window last night. Did John tell you about it?"

"No, haven't seen him today. What'd it say?"

"You can read it for yourself." I nodded toward the counter next to the phone, where the rock lay in a large Ziploc bag. "John sealed it up for you to take to the lab." Grimes made no move to retrieve it as I rinsed my hands and toweled them off. "Also," I said, "I went for a bike ride this morning, and almost crashed into a boulder. It looks like someone cut my brake lines."

"You're not too popular around here, are you?" Grimes asked. For once, I had to agree with him.

I was scrubbing at the black ink on my fingertips when the phone rang again. The kitchen, thankfully, was empty of Grimes; after he had taken my finger prints, he had grudgingly taken the rock and promised to take a look at the bike.

I dried my hands and picked up the receiver. "Good afternoon, Gray Whale Inn."

"Hello. May I speak with Barbara Eggleby?"

"I'll check her room. May I say who's calling?"

"Yes. This is Ermalinda Waggoner of the Conservation Association."

"Could you hold on for a minute?" I jogged down the hall and knocked on Barbara's door, then hurried back to the kitchen. "Sorry . . . she's not here. Can I leave her a message?"

"Is this Natalie Barnes?"

"Yes."

"I want to thank you for trying so hard to help us win the bid on the preserve. Barbara's said wonderful things about you." She sighed. "I understand Katz swept it out from under us again."

"He's done this before?"

"Oh, yes," Ermalinda said. "Didn't Barbara tell you? Out on Fawkes Point, in North Carolina. Barbara was furious. She said she'd see him dead before she'd let him win another one."

Goosebumps prickled along my arms. "Funny you should say that," I said. "Because Bernard Katz was murdered the day before yesterday."

FOURTEEN

As I stepped into Charlene's store, the crowd that had gathered in the front parlor fell silent. The bell above the door hadn't stopped jangling before Marge O'Leary lowered her newspaper and stared at me with hatred and distrust in her beady brown eyes. Marge was the informal leader of the group of women who congregated there regularly for tea and gossip. She was also the type of person I imagined was responsible for starting the Salem Witch Hunts. I gave her a polite smile, and one of her compatriots, a skinny, washed-out blonde, leaned over and whispered something into her ear. Ingrid was still missing from her normal spot at the counter.

After the call from the Conservation Association, I had whipped up another batch of cookies and borrowed one of the inn's spare bikes to take them down to Charlene's. The seat was less comfortable than the Schwinn's, but at least the frame was intact, and as an added bonus, the brakes worked. I had imagined heading down to the store and settling in for a comfy chat with Charlene; I had forgotten about the afternoon regulars, and about the article that had appeared in that morning's paper. Gertrude Pickens of the *Daily Mail,* I decided, was not my friend.

"Good afternoon, ladies," I said cheerily. They stared at me suspiciously, and Marge harrumphed, sending a jiggle through her jowls. Her dark reddish-brown hair hung lank around her doughy face, and I resisted the urge to recommend she find out the name of Charlene's hairdresser. I was one to talk, I thought, reaching up to smooth my own unkempt hair. A roomful of eyes bored into my back as I marched past the couches and pulled up a stool at the counter. Charlene ambled over with a cup of tea and sat down next to me, picking a speck of lint from her sweater.

"Shouldn't be serving that type, she shouldn't," Marge O'Leary grumbled loudly as I put the cup to my lips.

Charlene looked up from her sweater. "I'll serve who I like, Marge." Her voice was steely. "And if you don't like it, you can find somewhere else to spend your afternoons."

Marge's pasty face reddened, but her scowl deepened. "Don't you read the paper, Charlene?"

"I thought you were smarter than that, Marge," Charlene scoffed. "You should know better than to believe everything you read in the *Daily Mail.*" A few of the women drew in their breath, and the room was dangerously silent. I looked at Charlene with raised eyebrows, trying to communicate to her that she didn't need to alienate her customers on my account, but she ignored me and continued directing blue laser beams at Marge. Finally, Marge mumbled something about outsiders on the island and had a sip of tea, and after a few minutes, the hum of gossip filled the store again. I mouthed "thank you" to Charlene and took a big sip of my own cup of sweet, hot tea. Once the noise level in the store had returned to normal, I filled her in on my morning.

"Somebody threw a rock through your window and cut the brake lines on your bike?" Charlene shook her caramel-colored locks in wonder.

"Not necessarily the same person, but yes, that's what happened."

"How did you stop your bike?"

"The hard way," I answered. I might look

like death warmed over, but Charlene, as usual, was radiant. Today she wore an emerald green cashmere sweater with hot pink sequined flowers on the front and tight-fitting jeans. She closed her eyes — green frosted shadow, a perfect match with her sweater — and bit into a warm chocolate chip cookie. "Mmmmm," she groaned, flicking away a crumb with a fingernail the exact color of the sequined flowers.

"Don't forget to save some for Eleazer."

"He brought you the *Little Marian,* then?" I nodded. "Don't worry," she said, "I'll save him at least a couple." She licked her fingers and reached for another cookie. "So, did Sergeant Grimes have anything to say about what happened last night?"

"Well, he took the rock and the note with him." I reached over for a cookie of my own. "He promised to take a look at my bike, too, but we'll see. Oh — and someone from the Conservation Association called." I leaned forward and spoke in a low voice. Not that I needed to; the group on the couches had reverted to their normal loud chatter. "Apparently Bernard Katz and Barbara have met before."

Charlene opened her green-rimmed eyes wide. "Really? Where?"

"They fought over a piece of land in

North Carolina. Katz ended up building the development, and Barbara swore she'd kill him before she let him win again."

Charlene let out a long, slow whistle. "Maybe she was the one Tom saw out on Seal Point Road the night Katz died."

"He saw someone?"

"Yeah. He went out to check the porch light, and saw a flashlight bobbing along down the road. He called out, but whoever it was didn't answer." I bit into a cookie and let the dark chocolate and buttery crumbs melt in my mouth. Lots of people lived down Seal Point Road. Ingrid, Fernand, and Claudette were among them.

I washed my mouthful of cookie down with a swig of milky sweet tea. "Which way was the light going?"

"Toward the main road," Charlene answered. "Could have been heading out toward the preserve." I'd have to ask Fernand if he'd seen anything when I stopped by. I thought of Gwen's excitement when I told her I might use her watercolor for my brochure, and remembered the conversation I'd had with my sister earlier.

"Gwen's mother called this afternoon."

Charlene arched a penciled eyebrow. "What did you tell her?"

"She asked if Gwen is seeing someone,

and I said yes. I told her he has a degree from Princeton and a career in boats."

"A career in boats?" Charlene studied my face, which I tried to keep blank. "Nat, what did you tell her?"

"Nothing, really. She kind of leapt to conclusions."

"What kind of conclusions?"

Now Charlene's blue laser beams were directed at me. I shifted on my stool. "Well, she seems to think he's a shipping magnate or something."

Charlene's eyebrows shot up. "A *shipping* magnate? What exactly did you *say* to her?"

I blushed. "Weren't you the one who told me to stay out of it?"

"I said stay out of it, not jump in with both feet and make it worse." She shook her head at me and groaned. "I hope Gwen will be able to handle it better than you. What'd she say about all of the goings-on here on the island?"

"It didn't come up." An image of my sister's black hair and sharp chin floated in front of my mind's eye. I was very glad she and I lived on opposite coasts.

"It didn't come up? You've got to be kidding me." She rolled her eyes. "Well, maybe Gwen will make less of a hash of it than you did. Although how she could do worse,

I don't know." She reached for another cookie and bit into it delicately, careful not to mar her bright pink lipstick.

"So," I said, changing the subject, "where's today's paper?"

Charlene reached back and grabbed it from the counter behind her. "Read it and weep." I unfolded the front page and spread it out on the counter next to my tea. The headline blared DEVELOPER MURDERED ON CRANBERRY ISLAND in what looked like sixty-point type.

My stomach turned over as I scanned the article. Charlene was right; the article went into Katz's pavement plan for the Gray Whale Inn in some detail, and my connection with *Save Our Terns* received multiple mentions. I was described by islanders (unnamed) as "kind of stand-offish" and "a bit odd." The inn didn't come off sounding any better.

I folded it up and shoved it aside. "She's really even-handed about the coverage, isn't she?"

Charlene chuckled. "Anything to sell papers. On the plus side, I hear Grimes has been interrogating people other than you for a change."

"I wondered where he was going when he wasn't at the inn."

"He's been making the rounds," Charlene said. "He was out to Eleazer and Claudette's, and I hear he's talked to Tom Lockhart, too. Word is, he even made it out to Cliffside."

"I hope Tom told him about the flashlight." I took a sip of tea. "I wonder if he's really looking for other suspects, or if he's just trying to tighten the noose around my neck."

Charlene gave me an encouraging smile. "I think it's a good sign, Nat."

"Maybe you're right. At any rate, at least he's not smoking up my inn anymore."

The rain had started again when I walked across Charlene's front porch to my bike. I hadn't taken the newspaper with me — no use torturing myself with it at home.

I glanced at the sky, and decided today was not the day to ride out to Fernand's. The clouds had deepened to dark gray, and ominous black thunderheads were rolling in from the sea. I pedaled toward the inn as fast as I safely could, giving the brakes a compulsive squeeze every few minutes.

At the top of the big hill, a short gray body skittered across the road. One of Claudette's goats had gotten loose again. I debated going back to tell her, or even trying to collar this one, but Claudette's goats had a reputation for being ornery with everyone except Claudette. I slowed the bike, thinking of turning back, but when the rain started coming down even harder, I decided to call her from home. I didn't envy her chasing them down in the rain. As the goat — was it Muffin, or Pudge? — disappeared into the bushes, I realized with a flash what it was about my visit to Claudette's that had struck me as not quite right.

Water was gushing off the roof when I ran in through the kitchen door. The one message on the machine was from Gertrude Pickens, and once again I deleted it halfway through. My eyes drifted to the black water beyond the sheeting rain, and a shiver of apprehension ran through me. I hoped Gwen was not out in the storm.

Charlene might think Gwen was old enough to date without oversight, but I didn't feel comfortable with the amount of time she was spending with Adam. Guilt pricked at me as I realized I hadn't even met him. But would it matter if I had? Gwen had reached the age of majority, and I wasn't her mother. As the roses outside the window swayed wildly in the wind, their blowsy blossoms shredded by the onslaught of raindrops, I resolved to have a long conversation with Gwen when she came in this evening. I would also invite Adam over to dinner soon so that I could meet him myself.

Thunder rumbled ominously as I checked the guest rooms; everything was neatly tucked in, the floors shone, and the towels had been restocked, so Gwen must have stopped in long enough to clean up. Only Ogden was in his room; he opened his door just a crack and told me everything was "satisfactory." I was sitting down with a cookbook planning tomorrow's breakfast when John knocked at the door. He'd evidently come from his workshop; a few wood shavings clung to his sandy hair, and his pine-colored shirt was speckled with sawdust. Despite the dusting of wood scraps, he still looked as if he had just stepped out of an L. L. Bean catalog.

"Everything okay?" I asked as the door closed behind him. The warm smell of freshly sawed wood filled the kitchen, and I noticed a fleck of blue paint on his cheek.

"Yeah," he said, fixing me with those mesmerizing green eyes, "everything's fine. I've been meaning to ask you something, though."

My heart rate picked up. Did he want to know if I'd snooped in Bernard Katz's room that night? Had he found out I'd been poking around at Cliffside?

"What?"

He ran his hand through his hair, dislodging a few pine shavings. "Would you be interested in coming over for dinner tomorrow night?"

"Dinner?" I laughed, relieved and more thrilled than I liked to admit. "I'd love to. That'd be wonderful."

He smiled, looking relieved himself.

"Can I bring anything?"

"No. You cook all the time. Let me take care of it — you deserve a night off."

"Not even dessert?"

"Nope." He smiled a slow, dazzling smile, his teeth bright white against his brown skin. "I've got it all under control." My mind flashed to the kitchen mishap of the previous night as I smiled back.

"By the way," he said, "I got the glass for the dining room window today, but it doesn't look like I'll be able to install it until tomorrow."

"Thanks a million for picking it up. I don't know how I could have gotten it taken care of without you." My happiness faded slightly as I remembered why I wouldn't have been able to pick up the glass myself; I was a suspect in a murder case, and wasn't allowed off the island. Although now that I had my own boat . . . "Tell me how much it was, and I'll pay you back." I fixed him with a stern look. "And that includes labor, mister."

"Consider coming to dinner tomorrow payment in full."

I laughed. "Somehow that doesn't seem quite fair."

As the door closed behind him, a smile spread across my face, and I resisted the urge to do a little jig. I had a date with John! I was tempted to call Charlene, but decided instead to tell her about it afterward. I glanced at the phone and realized I had forgotten to call Claudette. I hurried over to lift the handset. No dial tone. The storm must have knocked the line down. I hung up, slid into a kitchen chair, and picked up a cookbook. Claudette would figure out that her goats were gone soon enough; there was nothing more I could do.

As I leafed through recipes, the front door slammed. I poked my nose through the kitchen door, but it was only the Bittles, just back from Spurrell's Lobster Pound. They left their giant striped umbrellas next to the door and bid me good night, and a few minutes later, Barbara came in, the door blowing shut behind her with a bang. As the guests returned to their rooms, I flipped through a stack of cookbooks and decided on a recipe for blueberry tea bread with a sweet lemon glaze. After double-checking to make sure all the ingredients were in the fridge or the pantry, I decided to whip it up after dinner. It would be great with an egg dish and some sausage or bacon and a little fresh fruit. With that decided, I turned my attention to dinner.

I put a pot of water on for spaghetti and pulled a bag of meatballs out of the freezer. One nice thing about cooking for Gwen was that she wasn't a picky eater. As the frozen meatballs tumbled out onto a cookie sheet, I glanced at the clock — it was coming up on six — and wondered again when she'd be home. The rain was still pouring down, and the thunder and lightning had increased in intensity.

The lights flickered as a particularly loud crack of thunder sounded overhead, and for the first time, I felt a twinge of unease. Gwen was usually home by now. Maybe she was just waiting for a ride, or waiting for the rain to let up to walk home. Surely she wouldn't be out on a boat with Adam in this storm. I glanced out at the dark, icy water, which had whipped itself into a frenzy and was lashing itself against the rocks. There were no boats out, or at least none that I could see.

Gwen didn't show up for dinner. I picked at my spaghetti and meatballs for a half hour, but my stomach was twisted into knots, so I shoved my plate into the fridge. My eyes scanned the dark water outside as I rinsed the pots, wondering who to call to find out about my niece. I set the last pot in the dish dryer and picked up the phone to call Charlene, realizing the flaw in my plan as soon as the handset touched my ear. The phone was still dead. As I stood trying to decide what to do next, thunder cracked again. The lights flickered twice and went out.

I fumbled through the kitchen drawers for a flashlight, then dug out my box of emergency candles and matches. Then I did the rounds of the rooms, delivering candles and matches to Ogden, Barbara, and the Bittles and hoping that the inn wouldn't burn down before the night was through.

After reassuring everyone that the lights would doubtless be back on soon, I returned to the kitchen and lit a candle of my own, then sat down at the kitchen table. There was no getting around it; I was worried about Gwen. Normally, I'd cook to keep my hands and mind busy, but with the power out, the oven wasn't available. The water that earlier today had been glassy now looked black as night, and Eleazer's words came back to me: "That water's so cold you wouldn't last more than fifteen minutes." The last time I saw her, Gwen was dressed for a beach party, not a wild night at sea.

Don't be stupid, I told myself. *She's probably holed up at Adam's house, waiting for the storm to blow over.* Still, I knew I wouldn't sleep until I was sure she was safe and on land. As I stared out the window into the night, my eyes searching for the green and red lights of a boat, I understood why the houses of fishermen all looked out to sea.

I sat peering anxiously out into the darkness when a car engine rumbled down the drive. A surge of relief passed through me; Gwen had found a ride home.

A minute later Charlene burst through the doorway. "You've got to come down to the store." Her face was ashen. "The whole fleet's back, but Adam didn't make it in. He's still out there somewhere, and Gwen's with him."

FIFTEEN

"Is anybody out looking for them?" I asked as we bumped up the road toward the co-op. Charlene had told me that all of the island's lobstermen were there, huddled around the radio and waiting for news.

"Coast Guard's out looking," she said, "but I'm not sure if anyone else has headed out. It's pretty rough out there." As she spoke, a vein of lightning lit up the sky, followed by a crack that sounded as if the earth were splitting in two. As the rain pounded on the truck's rusted metal roof, I was thankful that Charlene's pickup was one of the few island cars in full possession of all its doors and windows. Judging from the mildewy smell emanating from the worn seats, though, it still wasn't completely watertight. My mind flitted to Adam's boat; did Gwen have a dry place to ride out the storm?

"Someone must have some idea where

they are. Hasn't he radioed in?"

"The problem," Charlene continued, "is that no one can get them on the radio."

My stomach turned over. "My God," I whispered. "Do you mean they might have gone down?"

Charlene's pink lips were a thin line. "Don't go jumping to conclusions. It could mean lots of things. Radio broken, generator down. Who knows?" She spoke lightly, but her expression was grim in the greenish light from the dashboard. "The thing is, with no communications, the Coast Guard doesn't know where to look. It's like finding a needle in a haystack." Another flash put her worried features in sharp relief, and we both flinched at the boom that followed it.

"Watch out for goats," I cautioned her as we rounded a curve.

"They're on the loose again?" I was comforted by the trace of the old Charlene in her exasperated voice. "What do they do, eat through their chains?"

The pine trees, lovely in the daylight, were menacing in the glare of the headlights. I was relieved when they fell away and were replaced by the warm glow of porch lights and windows.

"You've got power?" I asked.

"Lights, but no phone. I figured we'd stop

by the co-op and find out what's going on, then wait it out at the store."

"Why at the store?"

"There's nothing to eat at the co-op, unless you like salted herring."

"You've got a radio at the store?"

"How else do you think I keep on top of things?" Charlene asked as we pulled in next to a worn clapboard building on the pier.

The waves roared against the rough planks as we dashed into the small wooden building. The smell of fish and wet wood and sweat enveloped me as I closed the door behind me. The only light in the building came from a single lightbulb dangling from the middle of the ceiling. The walls were covered in peeling buoys, mildewed ropes, and an assortment of fishing gear. Benches and rickety chairs had been pulled up in a rough circle around the radio, and seated on them was a motley crew of fishermen, some still in their foul weather gear. Eleazer was stationed right next to the radio, and rose to his feet and tipped his cap when he saw me. His weather-beaten features sagged, and there was no trace of the gnomish grin I'd seen that afternoon.

"Any word?" Charlene asked anxiously. I could read the answer in the downcast faces gazing at the rough wooden floor.

"Nothing yet," Eleazer replied. "Murph Hoyle just went out looking for them, though. His nephew, Jake, is Adam's sternman."

"Clyde White went out too," piped up a tall, thin man with a shiny, bald head.

"Are you sure Gwen was with Adam?" I asked.

"Ayuh," a grizzled man with wild gray hair and orange waders growled. I recognized Eddie O'Leary, Marge's other half. "I allus told him, bad luck to have a woman aboard, but them college boys are too smart for us old-timers."

"Now, now, Eddie. It's too late to worry about that." Tom Lockhart's voice was calm and controlled. I hadn't noticed him before, but when he spoke, he radiated strength and calm, and I was surprised I had missed him. "What we've got to do now is find him, and Jake, and Nat's niece." His blue eyes swept the room with cool confidence, and I could see why he had been president of the Cranberry Island Lobster Co-op and Chair of the Board of Selectmen for six years running. "I know he had traps down near Sutton Island and East Bunker Ledge. Anybody seen them anywhere else?"

"Well, he ain't been hauling too many lately, if you know what I mean." A few men chuckled. “But I did see a couple of his over by Shag Rock.”

“Anywhere else?”

“I saw a few out north, by the Flats,” said another man.

Tom picked up the radio and relayed the information to the searchers, then asked for a status report.

“Nothing at Shag Rock or the Flats,” a crackly voice replied. “I checked over by Sutton, and I’m headed out northward now. I just saw the coast guard liner — it’s cruising toward open water.”

“Thanks, Murph. Keep us posted,” Tom said. “And be careful. We don’t want to send search parties out after the search party.”

The crackling of the radio subsided, and the lobstermen lapsed into grim silence. Charlene tugged at my arm. “I’m taking this lady over to the store for some tea,” she announced to the solemn crowd. “I’ve got fresh cookies, too. You’re welcome to join us there.”

A few men grunted and shook their heads; they would finish their vigil together, in the dim light of the co-op.

The wind tore at my jacket as we sprinted back to the truck. Both Charlene and I were quiet as we bumped along the road to the store. I couldn’t tear my eyes away from the cold, dark sea.

I collapsed into one of the armchairs at the front of the store as Charlene flipped the radio on and busied herself filling the teakettle. "How often does this happen?" I asked.

"What? That someone doesn't come back?"

"Yeah." My mouth felt dry as paper.

Charlene turned the gas on and lit a burner. "Once or twice a year, I'd say. They almost always turn up, though, of course."

Almost always. "How inexperienced is Adam?"

Charlene turned and looked at me. "He's experienced enough to have his own boat and a native islander as his sternman," she said levelly. "So don't you worry about that." She popped the container of cookies open and piled them onto a plate. "Here," she said, sliding them onto the table in front of me. "Tea will be ready shortly. Get your jaws working on these. Then you can't ask any more silly questions."

She disappeared into the back of the store, and the only sounds were the drumming of the rain and the lonely howl of the wind through the eaves, punctuated by sharp cracks of thunder. The radio crackled whenever lightning flooded the sky, as if translating the forked fingers of light into some strange language. I picked up a cookie and turned it around in my hand, but my stomach was too queasy to eat. I set it back on the plate and shifted on the couch, tensing every time the radio crackled.

A few minutes later, Charlene bustled over with a teapot, two cups, and cream and sugar. She busied herself fixing us both cups of tea, and settled herself into the flowery cushions of the couch across from me, grabbing a cookie from the overloaded plate. "Try not to worry about Gwen," she said. "They know where to look now. Adam was laying his traps not too far offshore. They'll find them."

I blew air through my lips and closed my eyes. Every time there was a change in the hiss of the radio, I sat up straight. Beneath the static, I thought I could make out the threads of whispery voices across the airwaves, like ghosts from the sea.

"Marge sure was in fine form today, wasn't she?" Charlene said, pulling me back from the lonely sea to the couch in the front of her store.

"I don't know how those women can stand her."

Charlene shrugged. "She overpowers them."

"Thanks for backing me up today. You could have lost a lot of business over that."

Charlene waved a hand at me. "Nah. I'm the only store on the island."

"But they come here for tea, too."

"Where else are they going to go? Marge's house?" She shivered. "I think Ronald Reagan was in office the last time somebody lifted a mop in Marge's kitchen."

"Marge was complaining about off-islanders today. Do you think she might have thrown that rock through my window?"

Charlene considered this for a moment. "Were all the words spelled right?" Despite the pit in my stomach, I laughed. "Honestly, though," she continued. "I can see the rock, but I'm not sure she's smart enough to think of the brakes." She sighed. "It's a good thing all the islanders aren't like her, or I'd be out recruiting mainlanders to move here. She doesn't know what to do about the group Murray Selfridge is trying to put together. If she joins it, she's encouraging people to come over from the mainland, and if she doesn't, she's helping you."

"What group?"

"Oh, Murray's got a lawyer to make sure the Shoreline Conservation Association can't get the land even if the evaluators say the beach is critical nesting habitat. He's been out drumming up supporters."

"I didn't realize it was that important to him."

"He's been buying up land for years, and I think he's scared he won't get a return on his investment."

"I wonder why he didn't organize the group when Katz was alive?"

Charlene shrugged. "I don't know. Maybe he thought it was in the bag."

The lights flickered, and thunder crashed almost directly overhead. We both flinched and glanced at the radio. It flared for a moment, then continued its eerie hiss.

I shifted on the couch. "I noticed Ingrid wasn't around. Is she still making herself scarce?"

"Yup. She's been back and forth to the mainland a lot, though. I don't know what she's been up to." She munched on a cookie. "Or Barbara. How much research can you really do in the Somesville library?"

"If they have an Internet connection, probably more than you'd think," I said. "So Barbara's still back and forth too?"

"She's on the ten AM mail boat, every day."

Suddenly the radio crackled, and a rough voice spilled out of it. "I'm headed up to Shag Rock."

"Murph Hoyle," Charlene murmured.

"No sign yet, but I'm still looking," the voice continued. "It's pretty rough out here."

"Aye," another voice answered. "Just had a fifteen-footer. Almost flipped us."

"Watch out there," the rough voice answered. "Don't want two boats lost." Charlene and I stared at the radio, listening to the ghostly whine of radio silence. After a long moment, Charlene turned back to me.

"I forgot to tell you something earlier today. Now that you've got a boat, there's something you might want to check out."

"I thought you told me to leave the investigating to the police."

"Well," she said, "the problem is, the person who saw something was in a bit of a compromising position when he saw it."

"What are you talking about?"

Charlene pursed her lipsticked lips for a moment. "Natalie, did you notice how those red and green buoys disappeared the night of the storm?"

I hadn't thought about it, but she was right. "Somebody was out cutting gear the night of the storm?"

Charlene eyed me sideways. "That's one way to phrase it. I might put it a little differently if I were talking to the police."

"What did they see?"

Lightning flashed again, and Charlene waited for the long roll of thunder to fade before she answered. "Somebody was in Smuggler's Cove that night."

"The night Katz died?"

Charlene nodded.

"Why didn't you tell me earlier?"

"What could you have done about it? You didn't have a boat. Besides," she said, "Gwen was going to tell you."

"Gwen?" I put two and two together. "You mean Adam was out there that night? I thought you said he had good judgment."

Charlene turned pink under her Mary Kay pressed powder. "I stand by my statement. He's a good seaman."

"But a risk-taker." I stood up, furious. "And now he's out there God-knows-where with my niece." I glared at Charlene. "Don't tell me she was out with him that night, too?"

"Oh, no." Charlene looked stricken. "Nat, I'm so sorry. No, she wasn't with him that night. I should have told you about it earlier, though." She swallowed hard. "I really did trust him on the water. Do trust him, I mean. He thinks so much of Gwen — I didn't think he'd ever dream of putting her in harm's way."

"Well, she's there now." I buried my head in my hands. Charlene said nothing, and we sat in silence as the rain lashed the windows.

Finally, I looked up. "I never thought anything like this would happen, Nat," she whispered. "I should have told you. I just never thought . . ."

My anger ebbed, and I moved to sit next to her on the flowery couch. This was my friend, my friend who had put her business at risk defending me that very afternoon. "Listen," I said, "I'm sorry. I overreacted. Even if you had told me, what could I have done about it? It's not your fault. Gwen is old enough to make her own decisions, good or bad." Charlene bowed her head and made a snuffling noise. I patted the soft green cashmere stretched across her back. "Besides," I said, "They could turn up at any moment now." An image of Gwen floating among the waves, long hair streaming through the water like seaweed, came to my mind unbidden. I banished it with a shudder.

As Charlene hunched beside me, wiping her eyes, my stomach clenched. Seeing Charlene so upset made me realize how grave the situation was. We sat together for a long time, listening to the rain and the thunder and the hiss of the radio.

As the night progressed, the searchers continued to comb the dark waters and come up empty-handed. We would sit up straight, craning our ears at every explosion of sound from the radio, only to sink back into the cushions in disappointment, struggling to hold onto the fraying edges of hope.

Finally, just before 2:00, a voice crackled out of the radio. “We got something!”

Charlene and I leapt from the couch as another boat responded. “What is it?”

“There’s a light buoy out by Flower’s Island. Hang on a minute.” The silence stretched out into what seemed like hours before the radio crackled back to life. “We got it! We found the *Carpe Diem*!” My body tingled with relief, and I sank back into the cushions.

“Anyone on it?”

“They’re not on the boat,” he said. My throat seized up. They were gone, lost at sea. Then the voice crackled out of the radio again. “They’re all on the island.” On the island?

“Everyone okay?”

“Looks like it. We’ll bring ’em on in.” Charlene and I let out a huge whoop and hugged each other.

As we dashed through the rain to Charlene’s truck, I couldn’t help but laugh. The

Carpe Diem? You can take the boy out of college, but you can't take the college out of the boy. I had a hunch Adam's was the only lobster boat on the entire Maine coast with a Latin name.

It was a bedraggled threesome that staggered through the doors of the co-op a half hour later, accompanied by Murph Hoyle and Clyde White. Gwen's hair looked like limp seaweed, and her face was waxen.

"Gwen!" I rushed over and gave my niece a huge hug. She was still shivering despite the layers of blankets wrapped around her.

Gwen's voice was faint. "Hi, Aunt Nat."

I turned to the young man standing close behind her. He was pale under his mop of brown hair, and his young face looked haggard. I opened my mouth to tell him what I thought of him, but before I had a chance, he reached out and hugged Gwen fiercely, as if he were afraid to let go of her. "You're not coming out with me anymore, Gwen. Not after tonight." Well, at least we agreed on that point.

"You must be Adam," I said. He released Gwen and held out his hand; it was ice cold, and trembled as I shook it. "I'm so glad you made it back in okay," I said. "What happened? We've been worried to death."

"We were out hauling traps, and the radio wasn't working. I thought we'd just pull a few more up, then head back in, but the storm came up too quickly. Then I was having trouble with the motor, so I anchored in the lee of Flower's Island." He glanced at Gwen, who carried on from there.

"To make a long story short, Aunt Nat, we dragged anchor and ran aground on Flower's Island. We couldn't radio for help, so Adam put out a distress buoy and we waited it out on the island. We figured they'd come out looking when Adam didn't show up at the co-op." Adam had stayed out at sea with a broken radio, and he didn't know how to fix the engine when the storm came up? So much for being a stellar seaman. I glanced at Charlene. She was studying her nails.

I turned to Murph. "Thank you so much for finding them, and bringing them back in. I don't know how I can repay you."

Murph's dark eyes twinkled. "Well, first get these kids into some hot water." He eyed Adam. "The bath kind, I mean, not the clinging to a rock kind." Adam's lips twitched into an embarrassed smile, and Gwen laughed. "But I wouldn't say no to a pan of your brownies," Murph continued. "And maybe the recipe, if you don't mind."

"I'll make a pan of brownies for you every day of the week if you like!"

"Don't start offering — I might just have to take you up on it!" he replied.

I laughed and hugged Gwen again. "Well," Murph continued, "all's well, that ends well. I guess we'll be headed home."

I felt I could float through the rusted roof of the truck as Charlene and I jounced back down the road to the inn, my shivering niece wedged between us. Gwen didn't say much, and I didn't either; I was just happy she was back. We could talk about Adam tomorrow.

The power was still out when we got back to the inn, but fortunately my hot water heater ran on propane. I lit candles and drew a hot bath for Gwen, then left her with a plate of cookies and a glass of milk. I wished her good night, and for the first time in a week, curled up under the covers and slept without waking up once.

Sixteen

Until the alarm went off three hours later, that is. I pried open an eyelid and slammed my hand down on the alarm clock, praying that the power was restored. I flicked the switch of my bedside light.

It wasn't.

I staggered down the stairs in a daze, racking my brain for a way to cook breakfast without the benefit of my stovetop or oven. I fumbled for the coffee scoop, realizing the magnitude of the problem only when my finger pressed the button of the coffee grinder and nothing happened.

No power meant no coffee. Short of building a fire out in the backyard, there was no way to cook anything. I glanced outside. The rain had abated, but the world still looked pretty soggy.

I sat down at the kitchen table and stared at the freezer. Was there anything in there that I could use for breakfast? I knew I had tossed some extra blueberry muffins in a few weeks ago, and there were a few dozen bagels and some smoked salmon from Charlene. I could lay out lox and bagels with blueberry muffins, and maybe make a fruit salad with fresh whipped cream. The absence of coffee or tea would be a problem — at least for me — but there was plenty of milk and orange juice. It wouldn't be perfect, but it would be passable. If the power came on, I could whip up eggs and sausage or bacon.

I dug what I needed out of the freezer and set to work cutting up melon and strawberries. I'd whip the cream later; maybe the power would be back on and I wouldn't have to whisk it by hand.

I was no more awake when 8:30 rolled around. The power wasn't back yet, and neither was the phone. My bleary eyes turned to the kitchen window. The waves had calmed, and the clouds were breaking up; now that the storm had passed, with any luck they'd get the repair crews out fast. I remembered the fierce waters of last night and said a quick prayer of thanks that Gwen was safe, sleeping upstairs in her bed.

As I laid out a cold buffet, I reflected that if power outages were going to be a regular occurrence, I'd have to either switch the appliances to gas or invest in a camp stove. Fortunately, all of my guests — even Ogden — were understanding. "Lox and bagels?" Mrs. Bittles exclaimed when she came into the dining room. "How lovely! I haven't had that in ages!" The Bittles were leaving the next day, and as I stopped by their table to see how they'd fared last night, Mrs. Bittles asked if I'd been by to see her paintings.

"No," I said, "but since you're leaving tomorrow, I'll have to get down there today!"

Fernand's studio was at the end of Seal Point Road, in a yellow wood-frame house with lavender shutters and pale blue trim. Lots of people on the island painted their houses bright colors, but Fernand was the only person to include lavender in his palette. The first floor of the two-story house had been converted into a studio with a commanding view of the lighthouse and the ocean. I glanced at the beach beyond Fernand's house; the ground was littered with egg-shaped granite rocks. I wondered if the rock that had come through my window had originated on this part of the island.

When I rapped at the pale purple door, I was relieved to hear movement from inside the house. I had walked instead of riding my bike, and didn't relish the thought of making the long trek home without having seen Fernand.

The door swung open to reveal a short, trim man with a neatly kept brown beard and small, wire-rimmed glasses. His eyes were a piercing blue behind the glass lenses.

"Natalie Barnes," he said in a clipped Canadian accent. "Come in, come in." I walked into his studio, which was empty of furniture save for an easel set up by the wall of windows overlooking the ocean. The walls were hung with canvases, mostly oils of boats and houses, with neon blue and pink skies, and stacks of canvases leaned up against the walls. I walked closer to inspect a huge oil of a purple-orange sunset, and noticed the flourish of Fernand's signature on the bottom right-hand corner. I looked at Fernand in his creased khakis and button-down blue plaid shirt, amazed that someone so neat and tidy was the creator of such wild explosions of color.

"What brings you to this part of the island?" Fernand asked.

"Gwen and the Bittles asked me to come by and have a look at their work."

He nodded. "Your niece is a talented artist. Come on back, I'll show you some of her paintings."

"What about the Bittles?" I asked as we walked toward the back corner of the studio.

Fernand looked at me for a moment, then gave me a brittle smile. "They're having a good time."

I laughed. "That bad?"

"You can see for yourself," he said, pointing to a group of blotchy watercolors featuring crudely rendered boats and some grayish blobs that might or might not have been birds.

I bent down to inspect them, wincing as I flipped through the paintings to a particularly painful rendering of the Gray Whale Inn. "I was going to ask you if you'd be interested in putting together an artists' retreat package with me, but I'm afraid the Bittles might have put you off the idea."

He laughed. "They're very nice people, and they're having a good time. Anything I can do to help fund my life here on the island, I'm happy to do. And besides," he said, pointing to a small but exquisite watercolor of a lobster boat, "students like Gwen make dealing with the Bittles worthwhile." I walked over to the painting and squatted down for a closer look. The green-gray humps of the mountains on the mainland framed a solitary lobster boat steaming across the deep blue water. A gull wheeled behind the boat, tipping its wings in the breeze, and the man at the wheel wore a jaunty red cap. I'd seen many paintings of similar subjects, but this one was so crisp I could almost hear the slap of the water on the bow of the boat.

"Wow," I breathed. "She *is* good. I had no idea."

Fernand leafed through a folder and pulled out another one. "She did this one of your inn," he said, and I sucked in my breath at the golden light reflected from the windows, and the vibrant spill of the roses against the weathered gray shingles. I could definitely put that on a brochure. The drawing I had commissioned for the first one was child's play compared to this. He handed me the folder, and I leafed through scene after vivid scene of Cranberry Island. "If she's interested in staying on, I'd love to have her," Fernand said as I picked up a watercolor of one of the island's lupine fields. It looked like the one near the cranberry bog, but I wasn't sure; wherever it was, she had captured the beautiful blues and purples of the majestic spikes perfectly, as well as the tender green of their leaves. "She's mainly done watercolors," Fernand continued, "but she's interested in trying out oil and acrylic."

"It's fine with me; I'd love it if she stayed. It's up to her, though . . . and to her mother." I handed him the folder. "She really is an artist."

"I hear she had a close call last night," Fernand said, his clear eyes clouded with concern. "Is she going to be all right?"

"She did, but thank God she's okay. I'm not sure the same can be said for Adam's boat, though."

"I ran into Tom down the road this morning." Fernand smoothed his beard with his hand. "He said they'll tow her in today, and that she'll probably be back in the water in no time."

"I hope so. As long as Gwen isn't with him." Fernand's mention of running into Tom reminded me of something. "Tom saw somebody out with a flashlight the night Bernard Katz was killed," I said. "I've been meaning to ask you; did you notice anything unusual that night?"

His face remained expressionless as he shook his head. "No, I didn't, but then I wasn't really paying attention; I was touching up one of my canvases. Besides," he said, "I'm at the end of the road."

I decided to push a little further. "What do you think of the whole business with

Bernard Katz?"

He paused for a moment before answering. "Well, they say things like this are usually family affairs."

"I've thought about that. I wonder if maybe Stanley was jealous of Estelle and his father? They seemed pretty chummy."

Fernand snorted. "I don't think *that* was the motivation."

"What do you mean?"

Fernand cocked an eyebrow at me. "You mean it isn't obvious?" I shook my head, and he sighed. "Let's just say that I don't think Stanley would be jealous of any woman."

It took a moment for it to dawn on me what Fernand meant. "Wait a second. Do you mean Stanley is gay?"

Fernand put up his hands. "You didn't hear it from me."

"Why do you think he's gay?"

"I visit the mainland from time to time," Fernand said, "and I've run into him in the company of someone other than Estelle."

"Who?"

"Let's just say it wasn't a woman." He looked at me over rims of his glasses. "And they were awfully friendly for just friends."

I stood with my mouth hanging open. Who could it have been? Unfortunately, it looked like Fernand wasn't going to tell me. I looked at his startling blue eyes and pressed blue shirt. He was an attractive man. Was this his way of telling me that Stanley had been with him?

I dismissed the thought as soon as it came to me; a man as good-looking as Fernand couldn't possibly be attracted to Stanley. "Well," I said, "that would explain why when every other man in the room has his tongue hanging out when Estelle walks in, he hardly notices her. I just put it down to being married for a long time."

Fernand rolled his eyes. "Oh, please. They haven't been married *that* long."

"If Stanley's gay, why would he have gotten married in the first place?"

Fernand shrugged. "Lots of gay men do. They do it thinking it'll 'cure' them, or to appease their families."

I thought about that for a moment. Had Stanley married Estelle to ensure his inheritance? "That's a terrible reason to get married," I said.

"Isn't it?" Fernand smiled at me. "Well, I hate to run, but I've got to get out before the light changes. Let me think about that retreat program; we probably can't get it going until all of this stuff with the development blows over, but it's a good idea."

"Do you think the resort will go through?"

Fernand grimaced. "If Murray Selfridge has anything to say about it, it will. Do you think the Gray Whale Inn would survive a big resort next door?"

"I don't know. I'm still hoping the evaluators will decide it can't be built. How about you?"

Fernand gazed out the wall of windows at the sweeping view of the open ocean. "Of course I don't want it to be built. As for the studio . . . I don't know either." He sighed. "I guess we'll just have to wait and see."

The clouds continued to break apart into clots as I walked back toward the inn, and I wondered if the evaluators were back on the island. When I came to the path that led off the main road up to the cliffs, on an impulse I decided to take the rough way home. Maybe I could catch a glimpse of the evaluators.

As the rocky path wound around Cliffside, I glanced up at the blank windows and the copper-clad turret that rose like a lighthouse from the back of the imposing house, and my mind turned over the conversation at the studio. I wondered if Fernand was right, and Stanley or Estelle had murdered Bernard Katz. I wasn't so sure about Estelle; she had seemed genuinely distressed by her father-in-law's death, and her comment about bad timing made me think she didn't view his murder as a benefit.

I stepped over a clump of low-bush blueberries. Stanley had looked pretty shaken up when I told him Katz had been murdered. Maybe Stanley had killed his father, and had counted on it looking like an accident. I wondered why — and how — he had had his father's personal papers with him at breakfast. Had Stanley been the late-night intruder in his father's room? I'd always assumed that my arrival had interrupted the intruder before he or she found what they were looking for. Maybe I was wrong, and whoever had knocked me out had continued to search.

There was a lull in the rush of waves against the rocks, and I heard footsteps ahead of me on the path. A moment later, Estelle rounded the bend wearing pink lycra shorts and a matching crop top. She had done a better job of her hair and makeup today; like Charlene, her lipstick and nails matched her outfit perfectly. She pulled up short when she saw me, blinking her blue-lined eyes in surprise. "What are you doing here?"

"Heading home," I said. "I thought I'd come this way and see if the evaluators had finished." My eyebrows crept up a few millimeters as I took in Estelle's skimpy outfit. The weather was warm, but not that warm. Her arms were covered in goose pimples, and despite her fancy workout clothes, she hadn't been straining that hard; her powdered skin was unmarred by perspiration. "How about you?" I asked.

"I'm exercising."

"I thought you and Stanley had a personal gym." I remembered the weight machines coming over on the mail boat. The crew of the *Island Queen* had complained about lugging them over to the island for days.

"Of course we do," she huffed. "Since when is it a crime to get a little fresh air?" She glanced at her watch. "I don't have time for this." She pushed past me on her way back toward Cliffside.

"See you later, Estelle," I said to the cloud of perfume that hovered in her wake. *And you're welcome for the cookies.*

I started walking again, wondering why Estelle had suddenly decided to take up hiking. It seemed out of character. The path veered closer to the steep drop-off, and I moved over toward the edge of the cliff to look for the evaluators, but the rocks jutting out beneath the path eclipsed the view of the beach. As I turned back toward the main track, my sneaker caught a rock, and I sprawled onto the rock-studded path.

My battered body yammered in protest as I pushed myself up and brushed the dirt off my clothes and my knees. My fingers were disentangling a twig from my hair when a break in the ferns alongside the trail caught my eye. I peered through the trees; it was a trail, and it wound through the underbrush a good way before it disappeared. I bent down and fingered a few broken green fern fronds at the entrance; someone had been on this path recently. Estelle? I ducked under a low-hanging branch and followed the narrow track.

Although the path had been used in the last few days, it wasn't a regular thoroughfare. It had clearly been around for a while — the path had the kind of rut down the center that comes from years of use — but the narrow trail was so overgrown in places I was afraid I'd lose the track. Fortunately, whoever had been on this path recently had not taken pains to spare neighboring plants, so a hunt for broken or damaged leaves usually got me going in the right direction again quickly.

The trail wound through the trees and crested a hill, then headed back down again. I was beginning to think it might just be a shortcut back to the main road when I spotted a small building beneath the heavy spruce trees.

As I pushed branches aside and stepped closer, a sudden shaft of sunlight penetrated the thick tree cover, revealing a small log cabin. An old camp, probably. I pushed through the underbrush and made a cautious round of the perimeter. Cracks riddled the dirty glass windows, and some of the panes had been replaced with weathered boards. When I was satisfied the small building was unoccupied, I made my way to the front of the cabin and pushed at the big wooden door. It was wedged shut. I braced my shoulder against the rough door and threw my weight against it, and it lurched inward far enough for me to sidle in.

The camp might have been abandoned for many years, but someone had been here recently. Despite the musty smell of long disuse, the rough wooden floor had been swept clean — a broom stood next to the door — and a stack of blankets lay in the corner. Someone had made makeshift curtains out of dishtowels thumbtacked to the rough window frames, and a Coleman lantern stood on a wooden chest under one of the windows, but other than these basic amenities, the cabin was empty. No food, no clothes, no dishes or silverware: just the blankets, the lantern, and the broom.

I rifled through the blankets, hoping to uncover something hidden between them, but found nothing. I moved the lantern to the bumpy floor and opened the wooden chest. The smell of mildew threatened to overpower me as I eased open the rotting lid. The chest was empty, except for a few Captain Marvel comic books from 1970. I flipped through the moldy pages, but found nothing. Disappointed, I closed the chest and sat down on the floor, wondering if this was where Estelle and Bernard had had their assignations. A glance at the dishtowel curtains and the rotting wooden floor made me decide that it probably wasn't. I couldn't imagine Estelle agreeing to meet in a one-roomed shack with dishtowels for curtains.

Then again, if the price was right, maybe she would lower her standards a bit. It wasn't the Ritz, but at least it was somewhat clean, and very private. Still, why not meet somewhere else? And what had she been doing out on the cliff path a few minutes ago? My mind flitted back to her skimpy workout clothes. Had she been here? Maybe not; after all, I'd barely been able to get the door open myself, and I weighed a good bit more than Estelle. Perhaps she had been telling the truth, and was just out for some fresh air.

I took a last look at the cabin before heading through the door and pulling it shut behind me. It wouldn't close all the way — a good inch lay between the door and the frame — but I gave up after a few minutes and headed for home, deep in thought.

"Hey, Natalie!" John's voice jolted me out of my reverie, and I realized I was almost at my own front door. I looked around, trying to figure out where the voice was coming from. "Over here!" I squinted; John was calling to me from the front door of his workshop. His sandy hair gleamed in the watery light. "Still on for tonight?"

Tonight? I searched my brain for a moment before I remembered he had invited me over for dinner. With everything that had gone on during the last twenty-four hours, it had slipped my mind. "As long as you don't mind if I'm not the most sparkling conversationalist," I said.

"I heard about what happened last night. I'm glad everyone made it in safely."

"Are the phones back on, then?"

"No, not yet — I headed down to the store this morning, and Charlene filled me in. Oh — that reminds me — she sent some mail for you." He ducked into his workshop, and reappeared with a stack of mail, including a red and blue cardboard express mail envelope.

My heart thudded as I took the stack and shoved it under my arm. "Thanks," I said, stretching my lips into a smile. Had he looked at the mail? I assumed what I hoped was a nonchalant air. "So, what time tonight?"

His smile dazzled me. "Is six-thirty okay?"

"That would be great. Can I bring anything?"

"Nope. Just try to get a nap in beforehand. You look like you could use one."

"I haven't decided whether I'm going to make Gwen clean rooms today," I said. "If I do, I promise I'll sleep." I tightened my grip on the stack of mail. John was appealing, but I was dying to see what was in that express envelope. "See you at six-thirty, then?"

"Looking forward to it." John gave me a little wave and disappeared back into his workshop, and I walked back to the inn, forcing myself not to run. As soon as the kitchen door swung shut behind me, I pulled the envelope out and ripped it open, yanking out a thick sheaf of paper. I started reading the front page, then hesitated —

Grimes could reappear at any time — and decided to take it up to my room. I was in enough trouble with Grimes already; I didn't need to be caught reading someone else's mail. Particularly when the mail had been sent — at my request — under false pretenses. I took the narrow stairs two at a time.

I shut the bedroom door, threw myself onto the down comforter, and scanned the cover letter — just formalities — before flipping to the first report. It was on Tom Lockhart. I pored over the pages, but the investigators had found nothing unusual in Tom's dossier.

I was not surprised to find myself featured in the next report. I quickly skimmed my biographical sketch and the names of my family and friends dating back to high school — whoever had compiled the report had been very thorough. A shiver ran through me when I realized how much somebody could find out about you without your knowing. My entire life was laid out here in black and white, by someone who had never even met me. Although I was fascinated by the level of detail the investigator had discovered, like Tom's, my report was devoid of what I'm sure Bernard Katz would have considered interesting material, and I flipped to the next one.

I wasn't surprised by the name typed at the top of the last report. I was willing to bet I would find some interesting information in this portion of the neatly typed pages.

I found what I was looking for on page three. I sucked in my breath, read it twice, then flipped through the rest of the pages to see if there was anything else. There wasn't. Then I tucked the sheaf of paper back into the red and blue envelope and slid it under the mattress. It was time to pay someone a visit.

Seventeen

I knocked on John's door an hour later, smoothing my hair and feeling like a schoolgirl on a first date. As I waited, I wondered whether the makeup I'd troweled on to hide the circles under my eyes and the fading lump on my temple made me look overdone.

John opened the door and smiled a smile that made my already shaky legs turn to jelly. "You look like a new woman," he said as he ushered me through the door. He wore faded jeans and a deep blue shirt that intensified his golden brown skin and sunwashed hair. I tugged at my red blouse, wishing I'd worn something a little nicer than frayed jeans and scuffed brown loafers. On the other hand, pickings in my wardrobe were slim; I had been lucky to find a reasonably good-looking blouse. "Did you get your nap in?" he asked.

"No — Gwen was too wiped out from last

night. I let her sleep. Thank God the power is back on, though."

"Hard to cook breakfast without it, isn't it?" I followed him into the small living area to the left of the door. "Can I get you something to drink?" he asked. "Wine? Beer?"

I asked for a glass of wine and settled myself into John's big, wheat-colored couch as he bustled about in the small kitchen. I glanced at the dining table in the corner across from the kitchen; it was laid with a white tablecloth and candles. The downstairs of the carriage house had been converted into a living area, with the kitchen separated from the rest of the space by a narrow staircase. The walls between the tall windows were covered in bookshelves. The deep, comfortable couch sat across from two slightly down-at-the-heel armchairs, a blue braided rug lay across the scarred hardwood floor, and white sailcloth curtains framed the views of the water.

One of John's sculptures, a piece of driftwood that he had transformed into a basking seal, stood in the center of the small wood coffee table. I wondered if it was modeled after one of the harbor seals Eleazer had told me about. I had reached out to touch the seal's smooth gray back when

John emerged from the kitchen carrying two glasses of red wine. He handed one of them to me before settling in on the other end of the couch.

"This is beautiful," I said.

"Thanks. That was one of my first sculptures. I've improved with time, but I still like this one a lot." He reached out and stroked it.

"What got you interested in working with driftwood?"

He ran his hand down the seal's back for a moment before answering. His brown hand looked strong and warm against the soft gray wood. "I guess I noticed that most pieces of driftwood already look like something," he said. "On this one, before I even touched it, I could see the snout, and the long smooth neck. I just had to shape it a bit, bring it out of the wood."

I shook my head. "I could never do that. I just don't have that kind of vision."

"You might surprise yourself." I took a sip of wine. John's presence on the couch next to me was solid, and at the same time magnetic. I could smell his woodsy smell, with a hint of something spicy, over the aroma of garlic that was starting to drift from the kitchen.

"What smells so good?" I asked.

"Clams casino." He smiled. "We'll start with that, and then move on to lobster."

"Lobster? I *love* lobster, and I never get to eat it."

"Let me know whenever you need a fix. I've got a few pots out in the water."

"You're a lobsterman too? Is there anything you don't do?"

He laughed. "No, I'm just an amateur. I have a sport license, which means I can put out a few traps."

"Which buoys are yours?"

"The hot pink and blue ones," he said. "I put them out pretty close to home."

"And the locals don't give you a hard time?"

"I don't fish enough traps to be a threat. Four hundred traps are a problem; my measly five don't make a dent. Besides," he said, "at least I live on the island." He sipped his wine. "I'll have to take you out one day."

"I've got a boat of my own now," I said.

"I wondered whose skiff that was down on the dock. Eleazer just told me about it earlier today. She's a pretty little boat. You'd better take me with you the first couple of times you head out, though. Just till you get the hang of it."

"Eleazer already took me out once. It's

pretty easy to handle."

"I know," he said. "But be careful. That thing's not a toy, and weather can change quickly. I don't want you caught out at sea in a twelve-foot skiff."

I laughed. "You sound like me talking to Gwen." I thought of her wild night out at sea, and the amount of time she was spending with Adam. "You know," I said, "I'm worried about Gwen. I don't know what to think about her relationship with Adam."

John leaned forward, and a line appeared between his sandy eyebrows. "What do you mean?"

"I'm just afraid she's getting in over her head. She hasn't finished school, and getting serious about a lobsterman isn't exactly what her mother had in mind for her when she let her come up for the summer."

John raised his eyebrows. "What's wrong with getting serious about a lobsterman?"

"Gwen's mom, my sister, is worried about people's careers, and a lobsterman . . ." I trailed off. "It's just . . ." This was coming out wrong. My sister was the one with the problem, not me. "Oh, never mind."

John slid his wine glass onto the table and got up. "I'll be right back." As he disappeared into the little kitchen, I cursed my poor choice of words. John wasn't exactly what my sister considered a "career person," either, and it was fine with me. I hoped I hadn't given him the impression that I shared my sister's bias.

When John returned a minute later, he was carrying a plate heaped with clams on the half shell, loaded with garlicky golden breadcrumbs and bacon, and two plates. I was transported heavenward with the first bite. "I have *got* to get this recipe," I said. John smiled back through a mouthful of crumbs, and we ate in silence for a few minutes. I tried to think of a way to explain the issue with Gwen without alienating John further, and finally decided to abandon the topic in favor of something different.

"I noticed Stanley had a letter from Bernard Katz's lawyer at breakfast the other day."

John put down his clamshell and looked at me.

"Do you know who was in line to inherit his money?" I asked.

"Why are you so interested?"

I shrugged. "I don't know. Just curious, I guess."

He ran his finger around the rim of his wine glass for a moment before answering. "I guess it'll be public knowledge soon enough. Everything goes to Stanley. There was a change pending, but Bernard Katz hadn't signed the new will yet."

"Who was supposed to inherit according to the new will?" I asked.

He gazed at me levelly. "Estelle."

My eyebrows shot up. "So there *was* something between Bernard and Estelle." No wonder she had thought his timing was crummy. "She might have thought the new will was already signed, with everything coming to her, when Bernard Katz died. Heck, she could have murdered him herself." Berta Simmons had said that Katz had bought the necklace for an unhappily married woman he was hoping to wed himself. I thought about Estelle's off-handed response when I mentioned the sea-glass jewelry; either she didn't know about the necklace, or she didn't want me to know she knew about it. I shook my head in wonder. "And Grimes is still interrogating me?"

John shrugged. "I don't know what Grimes' take is on the murder." His lips twitched into a wry smile. "Sometimes I think he just keeps me around to pump me for inside information on islanders."

Was that why John had invited me over? To quiz me for the police? Then again, I was the one who brought up the murder, not him. "What kind of information?" I asked.

"Nothing much, I'm afraid. I don't get out too much." He laughed. "What he really needs to do is get plugged into Charlene's database."

"I hope you're not going to tell me you invited me over just to interrogate me."

"As long as you're not going to tell me you accepted my invitation just to find out what I know about the case."

"Nah." I grinned. "I just came for the free food."

We finished the clams in a lighter mood, and I was stuffed by the time John picked up the clamshell-littered plate and headed to the kitchen. He declined my offer of assistance, and I spent a few minutes studying the titles of the books in his bookshelves. The vast majority were dedicated to sailing. Propped up against a row of well-worn paperbacks was a small photo of a young boy and an older man, beaming as they displayed a giant codfish that dangled from the older man's hand. The tow-headed boy was almost certainly John, but I didn't recognize the man. I was replacing the photo among the books when John called me to the table.

Although my stomach was already distended from the clams (I resisted the urge to unbutton my jeans), my mouth began to water as John brought dinner to the table. My plate was dwarfed by what must have been a two-pound lobster, with a small bowl of melted yellow butter on the side. A blue crockery bowl held golden ears of corn, and another was filled to the brim with sliced cherry tomatoes and slender circles of leek, drenched in a glistening vinaigrette. John made a last trip from the kitchen with a basket of steaming rolls and refilled our glasses with a flourish.

"I think I died and went to heaven," I breathed, unfolding my soft blue cloth napkin. "If you're ever looking for another sideline, you might consider going into the restaurant business." I reached for a home-baked roll. "We could make the Gray Whale a full-service inn; my kitchen is yours."

"I'll keep it in mind." He grinned, and we both picked up our crackers.

"Why is one claw always bigger than the other?" I asked as I fished a morsel of creamy pink meat from the larger of the two immense claws on my plate.

"One's the cutter, and one's the crusher," he said. He held up the narrower of his lobster's claws. "This is the cutter," he said. "The big fat one's the crusher. They grow back if they lose them, but it takes a while."

"It's easier to enjoy them knowing they're not docile, peaceful animals," I said as I began excavating a leg.

"You know, the servants in Maine used to have it in their contracts that they couldn't be served lobster more than three days a week?"

"You're kidding me."

"Nope. It used to be considered a trash fish."

I pried out a chunk of meat and drenched it in melted butter. "They were nuts," I said, as I lifted the dripping meat to my mouth. "I could eat this every day, breakfast, lunch, and dinner."

"I'll have to have you over for lobster stew sometime."

"I'd love that." It may have been the wine, but I thought I saw his cheeks redden. I held his green gaze for a long moment before reaching for my wine glass. "You know, this is like a dream come true. Here we are, eating lobster together, in a beautiful island cottage with this stunning view." I turned toward the window, where the sun was receding over the mountains and painting the sea a luminous gold. "And the best thing of all is that this isn't a dream, or even a vacation. This is our life."

At the sight of the rocky hill rising up next to the inn, an image of Bernard Katz sprawled across the rocks flashed into my mind. "I guess it's nearing midnight, though," I sighed. John gave me a puzzled look. "Cinderella's carriage is about to turn into a pumpkin again," I said. More than ever, I wanted to stay here forever, and make the inn work. My eyes sought John's. "I'm afraid the inn might not survive."

John leaned forward. "What do you mean?"

"Well, even if the resort doesn't go through, Grimes thinks I killed Bernard Katz. I don't think I could make a go of it from jail." I grabbed my wineglass. "It's hard to be an innkeeper if you can't live on the premises."

"You're assuming he won't find the murderer," John said.

I sipped my wine and slid the glass back onto the table. "How likely does it seem to you that he will?"

He held my gaze and reached his hand across the table to squeeze mine. "I'll do whatever I can to make sure he does," he said.

My skin tingled as he rubbed the back of my hand with a calloused thumb. We were leaning toward each other when the phone rang.

A woman, calling from Portland, whom he would be calling back later tonight. Things didn't look good for the home team. I drained my wine and stared out the window at the evening sky. Neither of us reached across the table again.

We made polite conversation as we finished our meal. Just when it seemed I couldn't eat another bite without exploding, John stood up to clear the table. I joined him, and as we shuttled back and forth across the short distance to the kitchen, I made another brilliant conversational sally. "So," I blurted, "who do *you* think killed Bernard Katz?"

"Could be any number of people," he said.

"Do you think Stanley or Estelle might have done it? Stanley was strapped for cash, after all."

He raised his eyebrows as he collected our wineglasses. "How do you know that?" My mouth opened, then closed. I had been about to tell him about the past-due bills in Stanley's office, but decided that might not be the best idea. My brain grasped for a plausible answer, and finally I remembered what Charlene had told me. "He hasn't paid Polly Sarkes, his housekeeper, in months."

"That doesn't necessarily mean he's in financial trouble. He might have forgotten."

"Still, it's worth looking at. And then there were the people Bernard Katz was trying to blackmail . . ." I clamped my mouth shut too late.

John froze in the kitchen doorway with a blueberry cobbler in his hands. "Blackmail?"

"I heard a rumor that he was trying to blackmail people," I sputtered. "Trying to get them into going along with the resort. I have no idea if it's true or not."

"Who told you that?"

"I don't remember . . . it was just someone who suggested it, I guess, and it stuck in my mind." I stared at the cobbler in his hands. "Can I get some dessert plates?"

"They're to the left of the stove. But I still want to know more about this blackmail 'rumor'." He gave me a funny look. "You haven't been doing things you shouldn't be, have you? Like burgling people's rooms or houses?"

"It was just a rumor," I repeated, rummaging through a drawer in search of dessert forks.

"Well, I never heard anything about it." He brushed my arm as he passed me, and my body tingled in response. "Would you like some coffee?" he asked.

"Do you have decaf?"

"Yup." As he fiddled with the coffeemaker, I found a big spoon for the cobbler and retreated to the table, cursing my big mouth and wishing I had refused the third glass of wine.

The cobbler was delicious, and despite the gigantic dinner I had just consumed, I managed to put quite a dent in the huge piece John dished out for me. After finishing my coffee, I headed for the door. Part of me wanted to stay later, but John's promise to call the woman in Portland back echoed in my mind. The chemistry had altered after the phone call. Of course, it could have been my stupid comment about the blackmail, but things had definitely cooled off after the phone rang.

We stood at the door for a long moment, the cool breeze swirling around us.

"Thanks again for dinner," I said. "It was wonderful."

"My pleasure."

"It's my turn next."

"Name the time, and I'll be there."

I hesitated for a moment, wondering if he would reach for my hand again, but it seemed that whatever had passed between us earlier was gone. "Well, I'd better get back. Good night."

"Good night." The door closed behind me as I traipsed up the short path to the inn, wondering if he was already on the phone to Portland.

When I headed to the front desk to check for messages, the answering machine light was blinking furiously. I grabbed a pen and jabbed at the button, steeling myself for more bad news.

The first message was a booking! I jotted down the number and glanced at my watch; it was too late to call back, but I'd phone first thing in the morning. The second message was from Grimes. "Hello, Miss Barnes. I just wanted to make sure you'll be there tomorrow morning. Looks like your prints turned up in a lot of places they probably shouldn't have been." He continued, but I hit erase before he could say anything else, and Charlene's voice burbled out of the machine. "Bad news, Nat. The evaluators have weighed in — seems the nests are so disturbed they can't give it endangered habitat status. Looks like the resort's going to be a go."

Eighteen

The alarm rang at 6:45 the next morning, waking me with a jolt. I sat up fast and regretted it immediately; my head was throbbing from last night's wine. When I remembered how the evening had gone — from letting the bit about Katz blackmailing islanders slip to the call from Portland to the messages from Charlene and Grimes — I was tempted to lie back down and cover my head with a pillow.

It was the Bittles' last day, though, and on the slim chance the inn survived — I had, after all, gotten another booking last night — it was important that their last memories of the Gray Whale Inn be sweet ones. As I staggered out of bed, Biscuit glared at me and moved over to claim the warm spot I had vacated.

I pulled on some clothes and headed downstairs, and as the restorative aroma of brewing coffee filled the kitchen, began assembling the ingredients for Belgian waffles. I was folding fluffy egg whites into the batter when Gwen appeared at the doorway.

"You're up early." I finished folding the lemon-colored batter and set the bowl down next to the waffle iron, pouring the first waffle as Gwen fixed herself a cup of coffee and sat down at the kitchen table. Soon the warm scent of vanilla mingling with the aroma of fresh-brewed coffee permeated the kitchen, and my mouth started watering for breakfast.

"I think I've finally recovered," she said, crossing her long legs. Her outfit was subdued today: jeans and a purple-flowered blouse. "Since you covered for me yesterday, do you want me to take care of breakfast?"

Take care of breakfast? I blinked. She'd never offered to go above and beyond the call of duty before. "I think I've got it in hand," I said, "but if you wouldn't mind taking care of the breakfast dishes and running a vacuum through the dining room, I'd appreciate it."

"Sure," she said. "Those waffles smell great."

"You can have the first one." I pulled a container of strawberries from the refrigerator and turned toward Gwen. She still looked tired and pale, but her cheeks had a little bit of color in them. "Why don't you invite Adam over to dinner sometime this week?"

"Thanks, Aunt Nat. We'll see how it goes." Her wan face looked pinched. "I don't know when they're towing the boat back in. He's pretty down; he may end up missing half the season."

"Maybe a good dinner will help take his mind off things." I watched as Gwen took a long sip of coffee. "By the way, have you talked with your mother yet?"

She put her mug down with a jolt. "No. Why?" Her brown eyes were wary. "Have you talked to her?"

The waffle iron began to hiss. I lifted the lid; the puffy waffle was golden brown and tender. I eased the plump waffle onto a plate, sprinkled it with powdered sugar, and deposited it in front of Gwen with a fork. "She called the other day."

Gwen dabbed at the powdered sugar with her finger, then licked it. "What did you tell her?"

"Well," I said, pouring another thick stream of batter into the iron, "she knows you're seeing someone, but I didn't tell her much . . . just that he's got a degree from an Ivy and a career in boats."

Gwen picked up her fork. "So she took it okay?"

I poured a little more batter and cleared my throat. "I think she may need a little clarification on how he's involved with boats."

"What do you mean?"

My face felt hot with embarrassment as I closed the waffle iron. "I'm not sure, but I think she thinks he's a shipping magnate, or something," I mumbled.

Gwen paused with her fork suspended over the plate. "A shipping magnate? Aunt Nat, what did you tell her?"

"I only said he worked with boats. She jumped to conclusions."

Gwen groaned. "If the phone rings this afternoon, I'm not answering it."

"On the plus side," I said, "I saw your paintings, and I think they're incredible."

Gwen's brown eyes lit up. "Really?"

"Yes. I'd like to use the one you did of the inn in the next brochure, and in all our ads."

"You're kidding me!" Gwen sat up straighter, flushing, and her eyes shone. "I can do more, you know. Different angles, different times of day . . ."

I smiled to see the color return to her cheeks. "I can't wait to see them."

■ ■ ■ ■

My headache had begun to subside by the time I served breakfast, and I surveyed the golden waffles, crispy bacon, and mounds of strawberries and Chantilly cream with satisfaction. The woman who had called to make a reservation the night before had told me that she and her husband were planning to stay for two weeks in July, and I had recorded the dates with a growing sense of optimism. The resort might be inevitable, but maybe I could find a way for my fledgling business to survive despite it. The Gray Whale Inn wasn't going to go down without a fight.

The Bittles were delighted with the waffles, and with the bouquet of roses and sweet peas I had picked and placed on their table. When I asked them whether they would be interested in the retreat program I was planning with Fernand, Mrs. Bittles gushed in response. "Oh, of course! That sounds wonderful! We would love that; communing with other artists, practicing our craft . . ." She looked at me sidelong. "By the way," she added casually, "while you were at the studio, did you happen to see any of my paintings?"

The paintings? I'd almost forgotten about them. "Oh, yes. They're lovely," I answered, grasping for a positive way to describe them. "I can tell you were influenced by Monet."

Her little face scrunched up. "Monet? I had thought more the Dutch masters — you know, I strive for realism — but I guess I can see a touch of Monet."

"Definitely. I mean, the play of color and light . . ." I trailed off, remembering the grayish birdlike blobs, and decided to shift topics. "So, you'll come for the retreat?"

"We'll be up if we can. When you get it put together, please send us the information. I think we've both made great strides in our art, but there's so much more to learn, isn't there, dear?" Her husband looked up from his strawberry-covered waffle and grunted. I stayed to thank them again for coming and to make sure their arrangements with the mail boat were taken care of before returning to the kitchen.

Barbara and Ogden ate their breakfast simultaneously, but in silence, on opposite ends of the breakfast room. When I probed Barbara to find out what she'd been up to in Somesville, she just smiled and said, "You'll find out soon enough." I finally gave up.

It was just past 10:30 when I left Gwen to

clean up the dishes and clambered onto my borrowed bicycle. Fifteen minutes later, the red touring bike rolled up outside of a large, cream-colored house with black shutters and a gleaming brick-red door. The pots of pansies and alyssum lining the porch had miraculously escaped the rampaging goats, and the breeze was tinged with the honey scent of the small white flowers as I rapped at the front door.

I was about to knock again when the door creaked open an inch, and Ingrid Sorenson's blue eye peered out. "What do you want?"

"We need to talk, Ingrid."

"About what?"

"About Bernard Katz." She hesitated for a moment, then opened the door just enough for me to shuffle in sideways. I followed her into her tastefully decorated living room. The sofas were reupholstered Chippendale, and the room was crowded with expensive porcelain pieces crammed into nooks. Doilies decorated all of the dainty tables, and the smell of potpourri was overpowering.

Ingrid sat on the red velvet sofa. I selected a matching armchair across from her. My throat was dry — the bike I had borrowed didn't have a spot for a water bottle — but

Ingrid didn't offer me anything, and I didn't ask.

She crossed her legs, which were clad in crisp tan slacks, and rearranged her starched white blouse. Her short blond hair was neatly styled today, and she wore just enough makeup on her light skin to look polished. She looked as if she had just stepped out of *Town and Country* magazine; I half-expected her to pull on a tweed jacket. "What is it you wanted to ask me about?" she asked. Although her posture was one of studied casualness, her blue eyes darted around the room.

"How's your son doing at Cornell, Ingrid?"

Her pale skin blanched beneath her dusting of rouge. "Fine," she said quickly. "But I thought you wanted to talk to me about Bernard Katz."

"Ingrid, why did you vote in favor of the resort?"

She swallowed, and uncrossed, then recrossed, her legs. "I felt it was in the best interest of the island."

"You mean it didn't have anything to do with your son's recent arrest for drug dealing?"

She recoiled against the back of the sofa. When she spoke, her voice was as thin as wire. "Who told you that?"

I leaned forward. "I know Evan's not at Cornell. You've been making trips three times a week to visit him at a treatment facility in Vermont." Ingrid's mouth quivered, and her eyes filled with fear. "I know that Bernard Katz was threatening to expose your son's cocaine problem — and his arrest — if you didn't vote for the resort."

"It would have ruined his career. I couldn't risk that. No mother could."

"I wish I could believe that," I said, "but it doesn't make sense. I doubt your son would be applying for a job on Cranberry Island. Besides, any future employer could find out about his drug problem in a heartbeat, just with a simple background check." I glanced around at the expensive knickknacks and the polished floor, and my eyes came to rest on Ingrid's carefully made-up face. "I think you were more concerned about your own reputation on Cranberry Island than your son's career opportunities."

"You don't know what you're talking about!" she spat. Her icy eyes were slits. "You've never had a child. You have no idea what it's like when your child is in trouble." I remembered the cold feeling in my stomach when I thought my niece might be lost at sea. How would I have felt if Gwen were my child? Ingrid was right. I didn't know. I had an idea, but I didn't know.

"Lots of kids get into trouble with drugs," I said. "It's a terrible tragedy. It can wreck lives. I just don't think preserving your family's reputation is worth destroying the island."

"You're just interested in keeping your inn afloat." Ingrid's voice was cold. "You have *no* interest in this island, or the people on it. You've been here what — three months now? — and you think you know what's best for people who've been here for generations." She looked at me with disdain. "You know *nothing,*" she hissed. "In fact, I wouldn't be half surprised if *you* were the one who killed him. The only thing that surprises me is that you didn't do it earlier."

"Where were *you* the night Bernard Katz died?"

"Who are you, the police? You certainly aren't very smart. Don't you think if I wanted to kill Katz I'd have done it before the vote came up?"

I pounced on her words. "So *you* don't think the resort is good for the island, either."

Her eyes flickered. "I didn't say that."

"Maybe he was asking you for more than

your vote. Did he hit you up for money, too?"

She wrapped her arms around her thin torso. "What — are you going to try and blackmail me, too?"

"So he *did* ask for money."

"I don't know why I even let you in the door."

"How much did he want?"

"I'm not going to say another word to you. Now, if you'll excuse me, I have work to do."

She stood up and strode to the front hall. I followed, and the red door was halfway shut behind me when I turned to face her. "I think what you did was wrong, Ingrid. But nobody will hear about your son from me."

Relief flashed across her pale face, but her eyes were still hard as the door clicked shut behind me.

I had turned the bike's front wheel toward the inn when on impulse I swung it around to face the bottom of Seal Point Road. As I studied the arrangement of the houses, a new thought occurred to me. Instead of heading up the hill toward home, I continued down the lane.

The sound of hammering echoed in Eleazer's barn as my bike rolled up to the front porch at Eleazer and Claudette's house. That was good — I wanted to talk to Claudette alone.

I had barely knocked when Claudette opened the door, a ball of wool tucked under her arm and a half-knitted scarf in her hands. Her lips twitched into a half smile when she saw me on the doorstep. "Hello, Natalie. What brings you out this direction?"

"Claudette, I have something to ask you."

Her gray eyes grew guarded. "I guess you'd better come in, then." Instead of heading toward the kitchen, I followed her bulky form into her small, formal living room. The slipcovered furniture was covered in knitted throws, and the smell of mothballs dominated the earthy smell of wool and previous meals from the nearby kitchen.

I sat down on a big floral armchair and leaned forward as Claudette settled herself on the couch across from me. The furniture creaked beneath her as she adjusted her bulk and her knitting needles began clacking away, adding another row to the mauve scarf she was working on.

I nodded out the window toward the barn in the back. "Is Eleazer working on a new boat out there?"

"Ayuh. Young Adam Thrackton's boat'll

be in in a couple of days; he figures he'll get this one finished up so he can take care of Adam's in a hurry. So he won't miss the season."

"I know he'll be glad to hear that. I'm surprised they were able to salvage the boat; I thought once they foundered, they were gone."

"Oh, no," she said. "The *Diem* ran aground, but she didn't sink. Besides, sometimes they even tow them up from the bottom." She fixed me with a canny look. "But I don't imagine that's what you came to ask me about, is it?"

"You're right," I said. I took a deep breath and plunged in. "I know you were out the night Bernard Katz died."

She stared hard at the wad of mauve wool that was growing beneath her clacking needles. "What do you mean? I was at home the whole night."

"Someone saw a flashlight coming down the lane. I know it came from your house or from Fernand's studio; your houses are the only two down here. I also know you were out chasing your goats that night." Her wide face was impassive. "Look. I'm not saying you killed Bernard Katz. I just want to know if you saw him, or saw anything unusual."

She thrust her jaw out at me, knitting furiously. "What makes you think I was out chasing my goats the night he died?"

"Because," I answered, "not long after the night Bernard Katz was killed, Eleazer mentioned that you'd been out chasing them down and had come home soaking wet."

"So?"

"Until the night of the storm, it hadn't rained on Cranberry Island for at least two weeks."

Claudette's jaw wobbled for a moment. Then she slumped back into the sofa, her clacking needles suddenly stilled. "You won't say anything, will you?"

"What did you see, Claudette?"

"I didn't kill him, you know. I hated him, but I didn't kill him."

"What happened?" I pressed.

She thought for a moment before speaking. "Really, nothing. I didn't see Bernard Katz at all, I don't think. There was someone out on the cliff path, though. I never caught up with them — I was looking for Muffin — but I thought it was a strange place to be on a wet night." She wrenched her mouth to the side. "And then when I found out what happened that night . . . well, I couldn't very well say what I'd seen, could I? Not after what I said at the meeting."

"Which way was this person headed?" I asked.

"Well, I only saw the flashlight," she said. "But whoever it was was headed toward Cliffside."

"Were they anywhere near where Bernard Katz died?"

She shrugged. "I don't know. I'm not sure where he was killed. But the light was definitely closer to Cliffside than your inn."

Had the person holding the flashlight stopped off at the cabin in the woods? "Did it go all the way to Cliffside? Or did it disappear somewhere along the way?"

"I'm afraid I wasn't paying that much attention. I saw it a couple of times, but then it went away, and I didn't think much of it, until I found out Bernard Katz had been killed." I studied her broad face. Lines of worry creased the corners of her mouth and eyes, but her eyes were clear, and she met my gaze easily. I didn't think she was hiding anything else.

"Do you think you know who did it?" she asked.

I sighed. "I have some ideas, but I still don't know."

"You won't tell the police I was out that

night, will you?"

"I won't if I can avoid it. If it comes to it, though, I'll leave it to you to tell them." I looked at her solemn, careworn face for a moment. "By the way, have you given any more thought to contacting your son?"

She grimaced. "I have. I think about it all the time, actually." Her voice was strained. "I just don't know if it would be the right thing to do."

I reached across the small coffee table that separated us and squeezed her doughy hand. "If there's anything I can do to help, let me know," I said. "Thank you for being honest with me today."

"Do you think it will help? Knowing someone was on the path that night?"

"I don't know." A lone flashlight in the dark wasn't what I had been hoping for. What I needed was a face. "You never know, though. It might."

I pedaled home slowly, my eyes roaming over the green landscape, thinking about my conversation with Claudette. Despite her reputation as a battle-axe, I was beginning to like her; she had a tender side to her that was genuinely appealing. I hoped she got up the nerve to contact her son. Any kids would be lucky to have a grandma like Claudette.

I felt comfortable crossing Claudette off my list of suspects, but Ingrid was a different story. If Bernard Katz had blackmailed her for her vote and then followed up with a request for money, she might have decided he was better off dead than alive. I sighed. Would I ever narrow down the field enough to find the murderer? Stanley and Estelle were high on the list of potential suspects, but I couldn't cross Barbara Eggleby off, either.

As the hill grew steeper, I wondered who had been on the cliff path the night Bernard Katz died. Had Bernard Katz gone to Cliffside and been killed on his way back to the inn? Or had he been going to Cliffside and been killed before he reached it? My legs pumped harder and my breath shortened as the bike hit the steepest part of the hill, but my mind still wrangled with the puzzle of Katz's death. Why had he been out of the inn on a rocky path during a storm in the first place? The note that I had found in his room — *same time, same place* — floated into my mind. The only reason I could think of was a pre-planned secret meeting. Did someone know he was going to meet Estelle? Or had Estelle set up the meeting, and then killed him?

A whiff of roses floated up to me on the

breeze as I crested the big hill and started descending toward the Gray Whale Inn, and my eyes were drawn to the beach roses that flanked the path to the cliffs. Maybe the light Claudette had seen on the path had been the killer returning home. Then again, just because the light had been headed toward Cliffside didn't mean that Cliffside was its destination. I shook my head in frustration; I had been hoping Claudette could provide me with a little more detail than a flashlight glimpsed in the distance. Still, it was time to pay another visit to Estelle and Stanley.

I stowed the bike in the shed and walked around the side of the inn, bending down to pluck a few stray weeds from the flower beds along the way. Just before I turned the corner, a familiar voice floated to my ears. I froze mid-step.

"Based on those prints," the voice drawled, "she spent a little more time in Mr. Katz's room than she let on." The odor of stale tobacco mingled with the scent of roses on the breeze. It was Grimes, talking to somebody on my back porch. I sidestepped a trellis dripping with sweet peas and pressed myself against the rough shingles on the wall of the inn, cursing my luck. My plan had been to grab a quick bite to eat and head over to Cliffside. It appeared Grimes had other ideas.

As I flattened myself against the wall and contemplated an exit strategy, Grimes' gravelly voice continued. "You know, I'm not sure there was any intruder at all. I told her I needed her to be here today. If I can track her down, I'm tempted to take her down to the station this afternoon."

Nineteen

"Why would you take Natalie in?" The mild voice was John's.

"I told you, her prints were all over that room. She had the motive, she had the means, she had the opportunity — heck, she found the stiff herself. Got stuck on that cliff trying to conceal evidence, if you ask me."

"If she were going to kill him, don't you think she would have done it before the Board of Selectmen voted?" John asked. *Thank you, thank you, thank you,* I breathed silently.

"I'm guessing it was a crime of passion," Grimes responded. "Miss Barnes strikes me as a pretty passionate woman."

"I'd agree with passionate. She's not stupid, though. And what about Estelle, and that business with the will? She could very well have thought Bernard Katz had already signed the new version, and that everything was coming to her. Or Stanley — he was being cuckolded by his own father, for God's sake. Besides, he's the one in line to inherit."

"Estelle? That young lady? She couldn't hurt a fly. And her husband's a pansy. No, my gut says it's the lady innkeeper. And I've got the evidence to back it up."

"Weren't there other prints in Katz's room? Prints that haven't been identified?"

"Yeah, but you know how inns work — there are always people in and out of those rooms. Could be from a previous tenant."

"Or from the innkeeper who takes care of the rooms," John said drily. I cheered him on silently from my post at the side of the inn. "Don't you think it would be a good idea to get a few more islanders' prints? Surely lots of folks weren't too happy about the big resort coming in. And the issue of the intruder was never really cleared up, was it?"

Grimes sighed. "Mr. Quinton, I know you're the island deputy, but don't interfere with the workings of the real police. This is a homicide investigation. We've seen it all. We know what we're doing."

"I still think there are more angles that need to be examined."

"Are you sweet on your landlord, or something?"

"It's just that the investigation doesn't seem as . . . as thorough as I would have liked to see. As I would have *expected* to see."

"You got a problem with it? Call my boss. He'll set you straight. Anyway, I'm going to stick around here for a while, see if Miss Barnes shows up. If you see her, let her know I'm looking for her."

"Aye aye, captain." Sarcasm tinged John's voice.

"And if you like being deputy, I'd recommend you shut your trap."

I heard the sounds of footsteps receding. Apparently the interview was over. My throat tightened. Grimes really had pegged me as the murderer. At least John had stood up for me.

Panic began to well in my chest, and I struggled to regulate my breathing. How was I going to run the inn if Grimes detained me on the mainland? Gwen was helpful, but she couldn't take over the whole operation. And if I was tried and found guilty . . . I shivered, wondering how Maine dealt with capital murder cases, then dismissed the thought from my mind. It was time to find out who the murderer was. Fear would accomplish nothing; the most important thing was to use every minute of my remaining time as a free woman.

I crept around the side of the inn and hurried past the front, crouching down to avoid being spotted from the windows. It was now or never. I picked my way over toward the cliff path and headed up the rocky slope toward Cliffside.

Despite my dark state of mind, it was a beautiful day — the sun was high in the now-cloudless blue sky, and the cobalt water was frisky in the strong breeze. The aroma of the beach roses intensified as I navigated the path, ducking past the thorny branches.

As I threaded through rocks and clumps of blueberries, my thoughts turned to Estelle and Stanley Katz. Estelle might not want to see me, but I had a few questions to ask her about Bernard Katz's will — and about the little cabin I was increasingly convinced she had visited the day we met on the path.

Estelle had a strong motive — Katz's money, direct, not filtered through Stanley. According to John, a woman would have had the strength to commit the murder, and although Estelle was small, she kept herself in good shape. I thought of the letter in Katz's room — *from Ess,* it had said. Could the promise of a tryst with a beautiful woman have lured Bernard Katz out into the storm?

I remembered Stanley's shocked reaction when he learned his father had been murdered. Had he been shocked because he realized his wife had committed murder? Then again, Fernand had suggested there was no love lost between Stanley and Estelle. Still, regardless of how you felt about your spouse, it would be a shock to discover that the person you lived with was a murderer. Of your own father, to boot.

At the break in the undergrowth that marked the path to the old camp, I decided to check out the cabin one more time. I pushed through the low-hanging branches and climbed over a fallen tree. Maybe I had missed something the first time through. Something that would link the cabin to Estelle, or at least to Bernard Katz.

At first glance, the cabin looked exactly the same as it had yesterday. On closer inspection, however, the door seemed farther ajar. Yesterday, only an inch or two remained between the door and the frame; now the distance approached half a foot.

The undergrowth shielded me as I squatted down where I stood, listening. If whoever had come to the cabin was still here, it would be good to know about it while escape was still possible. A long moment passed, and nothing stirred but the calls of seagulls and terns and the wind through the tops of the tall spruce trees.

I crept closer, trying to move as quietly as possible. My heart hammered at my ribcage as I tiptoed into the clearing and approached the nearest window, scuttling over crablike and crouching beneath it. I braced myself and peered over the rough windowsill.

The cabin was empty.

The blankets, the lantern, even the dishtowel curtains — everything was gone. I moved around the cabin to the front door. The rough wood scraped my stomach as I sidled through the narrow gap into the cabin. Somebody had cleared the place during the last twenty-four hours, even down to the broom that had stood in the corner. I walked around the cabin with a mounting sense of frustration. All that remained was the old chest the lantern had stood on. The comic books still moldered beneath the rotting lid, but everything else had disappeared.

I circled the cabin's interior several times, searching for a clue that would tell me who had cleared the place out. Outside the cabin, my search for footprints was in vain; any mark was lost in the heavy carpet of pine needles.

I walked around the cabin again and again, pushing aside the fallen branches and needles with my feet, hoping to find something someone had dropped. My search yielded nothing. After one last pass, I admitted defeat and turned back toward the narrow path.

Why had someone cleared out the cabin? Had Estelle been startled by my presence on the path, and decided to remove all evidence that the cabin had been in use, just in case? My arm shielded my face from prickly branches as I trudged back up toward the cliffs. I had a long list of questions for Estelle.

When the narrow trail rejoined the cliff path, I turned left and headed toward Cliffside, pausing briefly at the sight of the few terns that had survived the disruption of their homes. As they wheeled in the sunlight, unaware of the doom that had been pronounced on the home they had inhabited for centuries, I was sickened to realize what one man could do to the lives of so many others. The fabric of Cranberry Island, which had been woven for centuries, would be rent irreparably by Bernard Katz's desire to make the island his next conquest. My own life would suffer as well; in fact, it already had.

I gazed at the terns for a long time before continuing up the path toward Cliffside, wondering how many more times I would take this high, narrow road before the bulldozers flattened it. My eyes turned from the sky to the rocky path in front of me as I walked. One of the lumps of granite was smeared with red. I bent down instinctively to touch it, raising my fingers to my nose, and the brief whiff of copper sent a current of fear through my body. It was blood.

I jerked my hand away from my face. My heart thundered in my chest as I wheeled around. *Think, Nat, think.* A few branches had snapped off the low-growing bushes nearby, and the ground was scuffed, as if a struggle had taken place. My eyes avoided the red smear on the rock as I debated what to do next, fear prickling my skin. The options were to head back to the inn and get John, or to stay and look for the person who had been injured.

If Grimes weren't sitting at the inn, like a fat spider waiting to catch a fly, I would have run back to fetch John. Instead, I stood frozen with my arms wrapped around my body, weighing my options. Searching for the person whose blood I had found could lead me not just to the injured person, but to whoever had inflicted the wound. *The murderer,* my mind whispered, and a tremor of fear coursed through me. On the other hand, returning to the inn meant delivering myself to Grimes.

I decided to risk going it alone. I walked farther up the path, scanning the underbrush and calling out in a loud voice, hoping that if whoever had been hurt was capable of speech, they'd respond. My eyes strained to catch movement, peering into the bushes lining the path and darting between the tall pines and spruce. I combed the woods with my eyes, expecting a murderer to leap out at me at any moment, but saw nothing, and heard only the low moan of the wind over the craggy rocks and the calls of the wheeling birds. After twenty minutes of calling and poking into the undergrowth, I abandoned the search.

As I traipsed back to the spot where I had found the blood, a sick feeling welled in my stomach, and my eyes crept to the edge of the cliff. If someone was hurt down there, it was important to get help. I steeled myself, took a deep breath and sidled over to the lip of the cliff.

When I saw what lay below, my stomach

lurched. I stepped back and closed my eyes, swallowing back the bile in my throat. I couldn't bring myself to look a second time, but I didn't need to; the image was seared on the backs of my eyelids. On the rocks, about ten feet down, Estelle Katz lay sprawled like a broken Barbie doll, a trickle of blood leaking from a red matted gash on her pouf of blonde hair.

I turned and hurtled back down the trail toward the inn, struggling to catch my breath. The murderer had claimed a second victim. As my arms flailed through the thorny rose bushes, I tried to think of what Estelle could have known that had made the murderer strike a second time. I cursed my bad timing; if I had made it to Cliffside just an hour or two sooner, maybe the grisly scene on the rocks behind me could have been forestalled.

John was in the back of the inn, sitting among the sweet peas, a large piece of glass propped up beside him. He must have been working on replacing the window when Grimes had come looking for me.

"John!" I called, gasping for breath.

He looked up, surprise in his green eyes. "Where have you been?" He hauled himself to his feet, wiping his hands on his jeans. "Grimes was here looking for you a little while ago. I told him to check Charlene's store."

"I need you to come," I panted. "There's been another murder."

John's brown face paled. He dropped his tools to the ground and grasped my shoulders with work-roughened hands. "Who? Where?" His dark green eyes bored into mine. "Are you okay?"

"It's Estelle. She's up on the cliff — near where Katz was."

John's voice was urgent. "Are you sure she's dead?"

"I think she is . . . she's just lying there, she looks broken, and there's blood in her hair . . ." I shuddered, lifting my hands to cover my face. I jerked them away when I realized my fingers were still stained red with Estelle's blood.

John ran toward his house, his plaid overshirt flapping in the breeze behind him. "I'm calling the paramedics," he called back over his shoulder. "I need you to head back up there — I'll find you, and you can show me where she is."

"Got it." I jogged back up toward the trail, not wanting to go back to where Estelle was, but knowing that somebody needed to. I was still reeling from the scene on the cliffs as I pushed through the thick rosebushes, trying to shield myself from the thorns. Why Estelle? My foot caught on a rock, and I regained my balance just in time to avoid crashing into yet another thicket of thorns.

As I climbed closer to the rocky place where the murderer had struck not once, but twice, I turned the problem over in my head and tried to shut the image of Estelle's matted hair out of my mind. The same person had most likely murdered both Bernard Katz and Estelle: the location and the MO were the same. What had she known that she shouldn't have? A frisson of fear crept up my back, and I pushed away the thought that my destination was the scene of two recent murders — one *very* recent. Despite the fact that my hairline was damp with sweat, a cold tingle ran down my spine as I remembered the cut brake lines on my bike. I had been poking around a good bit myself. What if the murderer decided I would be better off out of the way, too?

Whoever had killed Estelle was long gone, I told myself. If there had been any risk, wouldn't the killer have dealt with me when I found Estelle? Besides, John had called the police, and might be on his way to join me already.

Even with these rational thoughts streaming through my brain, I felt very vulnerable and alone when I reached the windy spot above Estelle.

I stood a little way from the edge of the cliff, not daring to look down, my eyes instead scanning the underbrush for movement. Suddenly the bushes rustled behind me, and I whirled around to an explosion of white wings. My heart was about to burst out of my chest when I realized with a flood of relief that it was only a seagull.

By the time I heard footsteps on the path, it felt as if several hours had passed, even though it couldn't have been more than twenty minutes. "John?"

"It's me." John's sandy hair appeared among the bushes, gleaming in the sun. His lean face was dark. "Where is she?"

"Down there." I pointed toward the rough edge of the cliff, averting my eyes as he leaned over and looked down at Estelle's sprawled body. "I can't believe there's been another murder," I said.

John leaned over and stared down for a long moment. "She's still alive."

"What?"

"I can see her breathing." He scanned the blue sky over the craggy humps of Mount Sheffield and Mount Pearl. "She still looks pretty banged up. I wish I could climb down to take a look, but I think I'd better wait for the helicopter. I hope it gets here soon."

We kept our vigil together in silence, straining our ears for the thump-thump of a helicopter, but hearing only the moan of the wind, the crash of the water against the rocks far below, and the occasional lonely call of a gull or a tern. As we sat together near the edge of the cliff, ready to stand up and signal at the first sign of help, I caught a whiff of his woodsy smell on the wind. The desire to lean over and bury my head in his solid chest flooded over me. Instead, I sat motionless, resisting the magnetic pull of the quiet man beside me.

"Who do you think did this?" I asked.

John paused for a moment before answering, his green eyes fixed on the horizon. The sunlight reflected the gold flecks in his irises and highlighted a small scar on his chin. "I don't know. I just wish you hadn't been the one to find her." He turned the full wattage of his forest-green eyes my direction.

Despite the heat emanating from John, my stomach turned to ice. "Grimes really *does* think I killed Bernard Katz, doesn't he?"

John twisted his lips into a grimace. "I'm afraid so."

"But if Estelle's still alive, won't she be able to say who tried to kill her?" I could hear the desperation in my voice.

"*If* she lives, and *if* she saw her attacker. There are no guarantees." We lapsed into silence, scanning the empty sky, as I tried to quell the panic that pressed against my throat and prayed that Estelle would live.

Finally, the whir of a helicopter's blades reached our ears, and a small speck appeared in the crystalline sky. John stood up, ready to wave them over to where Estelle lay. I hoped they hadn't come too late.

The speck quickly grew larger, and soon the wind from the blades was whipping my hair across my face. Before long, two paramedics and a stretcher descended from the belly of the helicopter like spiders on a thread. After several minutes, they lifted the stretcher. The sun glanced off Estelle's platinum hair as she disappeared into the hovering aircraft.

"Is she still alive?" John yelled into the thunder of the whirling blades.

"Yes," a paramedic yelled back. The small flame of hope burning in my chest burned stronger. But before John could ask any more questions, the doors closed, and the helicopter sped away into the distance.

Twenty

"They'll send another police launch over soon," John said as we watched the helicopter recede into the sky. "You might want to head back to the inn. Grimes is looking for you." His smile was grim. "I'll bet he has even more questions for you now."

"Aren't you coming?" I asked.

"I'm going to wait here for the police to show up. If you see Grimes, let him know what's happened. It might get him off your back for a while, anyway."

"Can I bring you anything?"

"No, thanks," he said. "I'll be fine."

The phone jangled as I swung the kitchen door closed behind me. It was Charlene, her voice bright with excitement. "I hear another helicopter was out over the cliffs. What's going on over there?"

"I found Estelle," I said, swallowing hard. "It looks like someone tried to do the same thing to her that they did to her father-in-law."

Charlene drew in her breath. "Tried? You mean she survived?"

"Barely, I think. But yes."

Charlene let out a long, low whistle. "Man, I never thought I'd say this about Estelle, but I hope she's okay." A slurping sound passed down the phone line, and then she continued. "Jeez, Nat. You're always in the wrong place at the wrong time, aren't you?"

"You're telling me."

"At least you can knock another suspect off your list."

"I hadn't thought of it that way, but I guess you're right."

"Well, keep me posted. But before you ring off, I have news for you, too. And I think you're going to like it, for a change."

Good news? I couldn't believe it. "What is it?"

She paused for another sip of whatever it was she was drinking. "Well, first, we've had lots of requests for more chocolate chip cookies down here. You've been slacking off, missy. If you could bring yourself to whip up a batch, my clientele and I would be much obliged," she said in a fake Texas accent.

I rolled my eyes. "And?"

"And . . ." Charlene paused dramatically. "I finally know what Barbara's been up to."

"Well? What is it?"

"She was putting together an expose on Premier Resorts International." She slurped again. "It looks like there's not going to be a resort after all."

The resort wasn't going to be built? "But how is that possible? The board already voted, and the evaluators said the endangered habitat status was a no-go."

Charlene cackled. "Well, it looks like Katz has been robbing Peter to pay Paul. PRI is broke, and so is Bernard Katz."

I paused to let this information filter through my brain. Bernard Katz, broke? I knew Stanley was having problems, but his father seemed to be doing just fine. "You mean PRI is a Ponzi scheme?"

"It didn't start out that way, but it looks like that's what it turned into. Two of their resorts never got finished, contractors haven't been paid in over a year, and the money for the few bills Bernard Katz has been paying has come out of the funds he's been drumming up from new investors. His own coffers are empty."

My thoughts turned to the bank statements I'd seen in Bernard Katz's room.

They hadn't been wrong; he and his company really had been in dire straits. At the board meeting, he had hesitated before outbidding Barbara Eggleby. Now it made sense. I would have hesitated too, if I was bidding on a big piece of land I didn't have the money to pay for. If he'd been killed for his money, somebody had made a pretty bad investment.

"How come he was willing to fork over two million dollars for the land here, then? Where was the money supposed to come from?"

"I don't know," Charlene said. "Either he was planning on getting some big investors to cover it, or he didn't know how bad things had gotten."

I leaned up against the wall. "Didn't know how bad things had gotten? How could you *not* know your company was going belly up?"

"Maybe someone else took care of the finances."

"So Barbara's spent all this time putting together an exposé?" I laughed. "So *that* was what she meant by alternate tactics." Despite the horror I'd seen just an hour ago, I felt giddy. The resort wouldn't be built! "Do you think the Shoreline Conservation Association will end up getting the land after all?"

"I don't see why not." Charlene giggled.

"What?"

"I just can't wait to see the look on Murray Selfridge's face when he finds out he's been hoodwinked by Bernard Katz," she said.

A smile spread across my face as I hung up the phone. I might be going to jail, but at least the island had a reprieve. My stomach gurgled, reminding me that the issue of lunch still needed to be dealt with. I grabbed a few cold waffles and sat down at the kitchen table, thinking about what this new information meant to the murder investigation. If Katz had no money, I thought as my teeth sank into the first buttery waffle, then maybe the will wasn't the motive for his murder. Then again, maybe Stanley didn't know how dire his father's financial situation was.

A fishing boat steamed across the water outside the kitchen window as I chewed. Even if the Gray Whale Inn didn't survive, at least the slow pace of life on this island would continue unchanged. As the events of the last week replayed in my mind, I sat up with a jolt. I was convinced I knew who had murdered Bernard Katz. The only problem was, I needed to get to the mainland to prove it.

I grabbed my windbreaker and hurried down to the dock, a half-eaten waffle still in my hand. This might be my only shot at getting to the mainland. Grimes could be back at any moment, and now that I had found the murderer's second victim, chances were excellent that my freedom was about to be curtailed.

As I trotted down the path to the dock, I eyed the *Little Marian* with trepidation. Handling the little boat had seemed easy when Eleazer was with me, but could I do it alone? I didn't even know how to tie a proper knot, much less find somewhere to tie the boat up in the event I actually managed to get her over to the mainland. The small, white boat bobbed jauntily in the blue-black waves as I clambered in and untied the ropes, pushing wildly against the dock to avoid bashing the boat's sides. I slid onto the bench in front of the engine and pulled the cord as Eleazer had shown me. The engine whined, but sputtered and fell silent. I took a ragged breath and tried again, with the same result. Great. The boat was drifting away from the dock — I'd untied the ropes and pushed off — and now the engine wouldn't start.

I yanked again. This time, the engine sputtered twice and caught, and the *Little Marian* surged forward. I sighed with relief, then yelped as I realized the boat was headed straight for a barnacle-encrusted rock. I grabbed at the rudder and pulled hard to the right, holding my breath at the low rasp on the left — port, I corrected myself — as the skiff grazed the barnacles. I hoped the scrape hadn't done too much damage to the *Little Marian*'s paint job. As long as she had no gaping holes, though, that was good enough for me.

I guided the small craft out toward the open water, reflecting that whatever seamanship ran in my family's blood had clearly not been passed on to me. John was right; I should have gone out with him a few times before embarking on this fool's errand.

As I pulled farther away from the Gray Whale Inn dock, my eyes slid over to the cliffs. If John was up there, he might recognize me. I decided to veer south until I was too far away for John to see me before heading for the mainland.

As the nose of the little boat turned toward Sutton Island, the dark cleft in the rocks that Eleazer had pointed out to me caught my attention: Smuggler's Cove. In all the excitement of the last few days, I'd forgotten about it. Yet someone had been there the night of the murder. As the cove slipped away behind me, I promised myself that if the *Little Marian* survived the trip to the mainland, I would visit it on the way back.

The cliffs receded from view, and the *Little Marian* was almost all the way to Sutton Island before I decided to risk crossing the open water. I steered the boat toward the mainland and pulled my hood over my head, hunching down as low as possible in the back of the boat as my eyes probed the rocky harbor. Where could I put the *Little Marian*? Was it okay to tie her up where the mail boat docked? My eyes were still trained on the harbor when the thrum of an engine caught my attention, and I looked up to see George McLeod waving at me from the *Island Queen.* I groaned. Now the whole island would know I'd slipped my leash. I ducked my head and gunned the engine.

The engine whined as I crossed the rest of the water at high speed, feeling like a criminal on the lam. A shiver ran through me. As far as Grimes was concerned, I *was* a criminal on the lam. I hoped the *Little Marian* wouldn't encounter the police launch next. I also hoped my hunch about Bernard

Katz's killer was correct. If it wasn't, I didn't know what else I could do.

Finally, the Northeast Harbor dock came into view. I threaded the small boat through the moored yachts and sailboats and came up alongside the main dock, ramming the bumper hard. I winced at the sound of splintering wood as my fingers scrabbled at a cleat, wrapping the rope around it several times before cutting the engine and jumping out onto the dock. I fastened the other rope as best I could and jogged up toward the harbormaster's little booth.

"I'm from Cranberry Island," I said breathlessly to the young man behind the cloudy, pitted window. His brown eyes were expressionless, and he scratched at one of the pimples that were scattered across his cheek like a constellation. "Can I leave my boat down here for a few minutes? I have an emergency errand to run."

He leaned back in his chair. "Sure. No problem."

"Thanks. I'll be back as soon as I can." I ran up through the cracked asphalt parking lot toward my little Celica. I had to get to Somesville fast, before the police came looking for me. The little green car was right where it was supposed to be, and my hand dug in my pocket for the keys. My heart sank when I realized they were still at the inn.

"Damn." How was I supposed to get to Somesville? I hurried back to the harbormaster's booth. "Is there a place I can put in at Somesville?"

"Yeah," he said, scratching another pimple, this time on his bristly chin. "You just head down a ways south, go round the bend into Somes Sound, and it's the first harbor you come to."

"Thanks," I said, and ran back down to the *Little Marian.*

I hopped aboard and untied the ropes from the cleats, but this time I held onto them until the engine was up and running; I was learning. Fortunately, the *Little Marian* roared to life immediately, and I pulled in the ropes and shoved myself away from the dock, chugging past the expensive boats in the harbor and the equally expensive houses perched among the towering spruce trees on the mainland before veering southward down the coast.

Before long, I was pulling up to the weathered gray wharf in Somesville, and docked only slightly more gracefully. Then I checked in with the harbormaster to make sure I hadn't put the skiff where it would be run over by a yacht, and headed for the library.

Somesville was a picturesque town, and images of its main street, which was decorated with brilliant flowerbeds and boxes, often appeared in the pages of Maine guidebooks. As I trotted toward the main square, two otters played together in a little cove beside the road, and the rows of bright red geraniums lining the quaint bridge glowed in the afternoon sunshine. I made a mental note to come back and spend a little more time in this attractive town, in the event Grimes didn't arrest me. Now that I had a boat, it would be a lot easier to do.

It was only a short walk to the library, which was housed in a white clapboard building that appeared to be a former church. I stepped in through the heavy wooden door and inhaled the familiar scent of old books that always catapulted me back to childhood. I passed through the small space that had once done duty as a nave and found myself in a long, high-ceilinged room with heavy brown beams reminiscent of the hull of a ship. After nodding a greeting to the librarian, a white-haired woman whose ringed fingers jangled as they flew across a computer keyboard, I grabbed the most recent *Wall Street Journal.* The article

Barbara had put together was on page two, but it told me no more than Charlene had. I tossed the paper aside and hurried over to the computer area.

I sat down at the first empty station and pulled up the Premier Resorts International Web site, whose home page featured a picture of a gigantic resort on a white sand beach. Was this the North Carolina resort that Barbara had fought so hard to prevent? I said a silent prayer of thanks that Cranberry Island wouldn't have a similar monolithic structure plunked down on its rocky shores, and clicked through the pages to a list of the companies associated with or owned by Premier Resorts. As I suspected, what I was looking for wasn't there.

I pulled up another Web site and typed in a name. The entry appeared immediately; it was located in New York City, and the address was a post office box. My pulse picked up. I was on the right track. When I clicked to find out who the registered owners were, though, the site informed me that a paid membership was required for access to that information. When I saw the price of membership, I sat back in frustration.

What I wanted had to be public record; how could I find it? I walked back to the librarian. She pushed her bright red reading glasses up on the bridge of her nose and joined me at the computer, her ringed fingers whizzing over the keyboard as I stood back and watched in awe. She might not be a child of the information age, but she sure knew her way around the Internet. Within two minutes, she had guided me to exactly where I needed to go.

I typed in a name, and my breath quickened as the entry came up immediately. I clicked on a link, and a list of names unfolded on the glowing screen in front of me. The first name on the list came as no surprise, and the calmness of certainty settled over me as I stared at the small black letters. The second name puzzled me for a moment, but as I sat back and sifted through all the things I had seen and heard, it made perfect sense.

I printed the list, gave the librarian my appreciation for the help and ten cents for the printed page, and headed back out into the bright Somesville afternoon. The floating ramp to the pier was steeper than it had been when I climbed it; the tide was on its way out. It was time to pay a visit to Smuggler's Cove.

Twenty-One

I cast off with a bit more ease this time — I was beginning to get a feel for the *Little Marian* — and puttered past the boats moored in the harbor, debating the best way to approach the cove. Four eider ducklings bobbed by me, following their mother in a noisy line, and I smiled despite the tightness in my stomach. Eleazer had said the landing would be tricky. I hoped I'd be up to it.

Instead of bearing directly for the cliffs — I knew John was still up there, and it was likely that by now both Grimes and the police from the mainland had joined him — I veered back north toward East Bunker Ledge. At least I thought it was East Bunker Ledge — I was still a little hazy on my Cranberry Isles geography. My plan was to turn toward Cranberry Island at its northern tip and then work my way along the shoreline toward the cove. There was still a chance that John would see me, but it was better than making straight for my destination across the open water.

East Bunker Ledge wasn't much more than a rock sticking out of the water with a couple of pine trees growing at the top of it. I scanned the water around me as the *Little Marian* chugged toward it; I didn't want to encounter a police launch along the way. As my eyes swept the horizon, a seal's snout protruded from the water in front of the boat. I thought of John and his beautiful sculpture and smiled. While the conversation I'd overheard earlier today with Grimes had chilled me to the marrow, hearing John come to my defense had brought a flush of warmth to my heart.

I finally reached the small island, which was swarming with seagulls, and turned the skiff toward Cranberry Island. The short stretch of blue water passed quickly, and before long I was puttering along the rocky shore south of the Gray Whale Inn. The shattered granite looked as if someone had bashed it with a hammer, sending large chunks spiraling to the ocean floor below. I scanned the water in front of me, searching for the telltale break in the waves that would reveal a submerged rock. Despite my life jacket and my proximity to the shore, I didn't relish a dip in the icy water.

I hunched down into my jacket as the Gray Whale Inn slid by over my left shoulder, steering the skiff so that it hugged the shore. The entrance to the cove wasn't visible from John's rocky perch. If the little boat veered off too far from the shoreline, though, he — or Grimes — would be able to spot me. My knuckles whitened as I gripped the rudder and steered past a trio of rocks jutting up from the silky blue water.

As the boat thrummed closer to the rocky entrance to Smuggler's Cove, a huge boulder reared up out of the water in front of me like a craggy gray elephant, the waves breaking hard against its weathered hide. I had no choice; I was forced to veer out away from the base of the cliff. I turned the rudder and glanced up toward John's high perch, catching a flash of his red T-shirt and a glint of sunlight on his hair before I gunned the engine and turned back toward the cliffs, steering the boat as close to the rocks as I dared. I hoped he hadn't seen me. I needed time to find evidence to clear myself before Grimes descended upon me with dangling handcuffs.

Finally, the entrance of the cove appeared, like a black mouth lined with vicious gray teeth. I examined the narrow opening with a sinking heart. Even though the tide was at its lowest ebb, exposing enough room under the ragged arch in the rock for the boat to pass through, I remembered what Eleazer had said; when the tide came up, the entrance was completely submerged. I'd have to get in and out fast.

The opening was barely six feet wide, just enough to squeeze into, if I could avoid the cove's jagged edges. The tops of rocks jutted out of the water like the fins of sharks, all along the narrow corridor leading to the cove.

The waves slapped up against the boat as I idled the motor and examined the approach to the cove with growing unease, wishing that I had taken a few test drives with Eleazer or John before attempting a maneuver like this. Suddenly, the boat lurched, almost knocking me off my seat. A rogue wave had nudged the *Little Marian* sideways, and its fellows were rapidly pushing the small boat into the rocks. I suddenly realized the skiff was inches away from slamming into the rocks.

I threw the engine into reverse and gunned the motor. The *Little Marian* lurched backwards, then jerked to a stop with a sickening thud. I threw the engine into forward gear, but the boat didn't move. I gunned it again. The engine whined in protest, but the skiff was drifting, rudderless. When I pulled the outboard motor up out of the icy water, the problem was obvious; the propeller was gone. I must have hit a rock and sheared it off.

As I sat, helpless, the waves sucked at the *Little Marian,* pulling her closer and closer to the jagged rocks. Panic welled in my throat. *Think, Nat. Think.* I scrambled to the floor of the boat and grabbed one of the oars Eleazer had pointed out to me on our first boat trip. I leaned over the side and positioned the oar against the nearest rock and pushed with all of my strength. A wave pushed back, so I heaved a second time, and this time managed to get the *Little Marian* moving away from the rocks. I breathed a sigh of relief and sat back on the bench before realizing that the boat was now drifting out to the open water. A flurry of terns was already visible overhead; if the skiff drifted much farther, I would be exposed to the eyes on the cliffs above. I considered giving up and rowing back to the Gray Whale Inn, but dismissed it. This might be my only opportunity to explore the cove.

I eyed the narrow entrance. It was only about six feet wide at its narrowest point — nowhere near enough room for oars. To row into the cove, I'd have to pick up enough speed to carry me through before the boat got to the entrance. The rocks on the sides looked vicious, but I figured I could use the oars to keep the boat from scraping along the sides, and maybe even add a little momentum by pushing the boat along off of the walls.

I fumbled the oars into the oarlocks and sat down on the hard wooden bench. It was now or never. I gave the oars a few experimental swings and then dipped them into the blue-green water, pulling with all of my strength and stealing a glance over my shoulder at the narrow gap. I pulled again, praying that the waves wouldn't push me too far to one side, and the little boat began picking up speed. By the fourth pull, the boat was almost to the mouth of the cave. I had dipped my oars into the water for a final thrust when the left oar cracked against something, spinning the *Little Marian* around toward one of the walls.

I dug the left oar into the water again frantically, trying to get the boat on track, and the right oar dragged hard against the other wall. I pulled it out of its oarlock and stabbed at the walls with it, trying to keep the skiff from scraping against the rocks. As I swung the oar from side to side and pushed against the walls to avoid the rocks that protruded from the water like spears, I prayed that the entrance was short and involved no turns.

The slice of sky above the boat narrowed as I fought my way into the cove, the oar slipping against the slick rocks. Despite my efforts to push deeper in — I was sweating hard under my windbreaker — the boat was slowing down, and the slapping of the waves had taken on an eerie, sucking sound. I stabbed at the rocky walls with the oar, trying hard to steer the sluggish boat through the narrow waterway, and hoped that the little skiff wouldn't hit any underwater surprises.

I was beginning to wonder if I'd be floating in the cove forever when a shallow shelf loomed on the right side of the *Little Marian.* I dropped the oar into the boat and fumbled for a hold among the rocks, my hands skittering over the lumpy surface and closing around a rough metal loop. I reached back for a rope and threaded it through, then grabbed the other rope and clambered out of the boat, searching the shelf for another place to tie up. When my fingers closed on a second rusted loop driven into the granite floor, I relaxed for what felt like the first time in days. Then I remembered that I'd have to find my way back out of the cove, and tensed up all over again.

I looked at the iron loops driven into the rocks. As difficult as it was to get into the narrow waterway, apparently someone had visited it regularly at some point. My mind flitted back to Eleazer's comments about rumrunners. I knelt down to examine the stone around the base of the loops; it was stained orange with rust, and the iron was pitted and corroded. Whoever had driven these loops into the rock had done it a long time ago.

I checked to make sure the boat was secure, then stood up and looked around. The sunlight had been reduced to a narrow slit in the rocks above me, and the small space around me felt more like a cave than a cove. I took a few steps forward and cast my eyes around the dim walls. Nothing was visible but jagged walls, and disappointment welled in my throat. Still, if somebody had once tied a boat up here regularly — and someone else had visited the cove the night of the murder — there had to be something here. I ran my hands along the wall, looking for a concealed shelf, and edged along toward the back of the cove. The small walkway ascended sharply, and I was almost at the end of it before I found what I was looking for: a small opening, about three feet high, hidden behind a bulge in the rock.

Excitement tinged with fear welled in my chest as I bent down and stepped into the hole. I stood up slowly to avoid bashing my head against the granite ceiling, but I needn't have worried; although the entrance was low, there was enough room to stand up easily in the small chamber. The darkness was inky — this part of the cove was truly a cave — and the sound of the water slapping against the walls behind me was muted.

I stood still until my eyes adjusted to the faint light, wishing I had brought a flashlight. After a few minutes, I could make out the shape of the rough walls, but not much else. I'd have to fumble around with my hands and take anything I found out into the main part of the cove to examine it. As I glanced back toward the mouth of the cave, a dull gleam caught my eye. When I reached out to touch it, my hand closed around a flashlight. I perked up; my luck was turning. When I flicked the switch, the cave was suffused with light. My initial excitement was tempered with a frisson of fear as I realized that the working flashlight meant somebody had been here recently, and evidently planned to return.

As I swung the flashlight around, the beam illuminated two shovels leaning up near the cave's entrance. I focused the light on the nearer of the two and knelt to examine it. The gray metal shone in the flashlight's beam, and at first glance, looked as if it had never been used. On closer inspection, however, I noticed fine scratches on the blade and few grains of sand wedged between the metal blade and the handle. Was this the shovel that had been used to destroy the terns' nests?

I scooted over and trained the beam on the second shovel. This one was much older; the blade was rusted through in spots, and it wobbled on the handle as I picked it up. A few rusty red streaks marked the wood at the base of the handle, and a shiver passed through me. *Blood,* a little voice in my mind whispered. Then again, it could just be a rust stain. I released the shovel hastily and ran the beam of the flashlight around the rest of the cave.

On the second sweep, I spotted what looked like a small fireproof safe tucked into a crevice at the far end of the cave. My heart leaped in excitement, but began sinking stomachward as I walked over to take a closer look. It *was* a safe. And like most safes, it was locked with a key. I flashed the light around the cave, hoping that whoever had left the safe here might also have left the key, but my luck wasn't that good.

I stared at the tan plastic box with mounting frustration. I was stuck in a cave with no easy exit, the police were after me, and it looked like the evidence I needed to clear myself might be locked in a box, two feet in front of me. I reached out and gave the lid a tug, just to be sure. It didn't budge. Now what?

I slumped against the wall of the cave and forced myself to think. It wasn't an expensive safe; if I knew anything about picking locks, I probably could have had it open in a few minutes. Unfortunately, however, burglary — the breaking part, anyway — wasn't among the skills listed on my resume. How could I open it without the key?

I examined the safe again. It was a garden-variety safe; sturdy, but not bulletproof. I could try bashing it against the rock walls, but it looked as if it had been made to withstand that kind of abuse. I swept the beam of the flashlight around the cave, hoping to find something that would help me out of my predicament. The beam was swinging around a second time when my eye fell upon the shovels next to the entrance, and an idea flashed into my mind.

I pulled the box out toward the middle of the floor and laid it on its side, with the latch face-up. Then I walked over and picked up the newer of the two shovels. I slid the narrow blade into the space between the box and the lid, right under the keyhole, then gripped the spade with both hands and bore down with all of my weight.

Nothing happened.

I drove the shovel down again and again, frustration fueling my attack, until the arch of my foot throbbed from the impact and the palm of my hand began to blister. I was about to give up when the lid flopped open with a bang and a stack of files slid out onto the granite floor.

I tossed the shovel behind me and fell to my knees, grabbing the top file. I paused at the sound of an engine in the distance — had John discovered me? — but it didn't seem to be getting any closer, so I turned my attention back to the green folder lying open in my hands. It was filled with invoices. I flipped through the pages; every bill was labeled *For Construction Services.* The amounts due were huge: a hundred thousand, three hundred thousand, even one for five hundred and fifty thousand — and the invoices had been issued on a regular basis over the past eighteen months. The billing company was Holding Construction Company, and Premier Resorts International was listed as the recipient on every single invoice.

I opened the next folder and found a stack of bank statements, neatly filed by date. The bank's address was in the Bahamas, and the holder of the $4.2 million account was, once again, Holding Construction Company. As I grabbed the next file, two passports slid out. The sound of the boat bumping against the rocky shelf echoed in the cave as I opened the first little blue booklet. The name was unfamiliar — Dennis Wiley — but the face was well known to me. I opened the second one, and once again, though the name was wrong, the face was instantly identifiable. I slid the passports back into their folder and was about to examine the next folder when the familiar scent of a man's cologne wafted into the small rocky chamber.

I whirled around. There, next to the opening to the cave, stood Ogden Wilson, the light gleaming off the thick lenses of his glasses. My eyes leapt to his hands, and the file folder slipped from my grasp. His pale fingers were wrapped tight around the handle of the rusty shovel.

Twenty-Two

I scuttled toward the back of the cave like a crab, keeping the flashlight trained on Ogden's pale, waxy face. He looked more than ever like some kind of cave-dwelling amphibian as he advanced a few steps toward me. My eyes shot toward the shovel I had cast behind me earlier.

"I might have known I'd find you here," he said. He raised one hand to shield his eyes from the light, but kept a firm grip on the rusty shovel with the other. "You've been nosing into things that don't concern you from the very beginning."

"Nosing into things that don't concern me?" Despite the fear coursing through my veins like liquid ice, I snorted. "That's rich. First, your boss plans to build this huge eyesore right next door to my inn, and before long I find out he's planning to bulldoze the inn entirely. Then he gets himself killed, and the police start asking me all kinds of questions, as if I'm the one who did him in. And you think that doesn't concern me?"

"You should have just kept out of things," Ogden said in a low voice, and took another step toward me. My eyes skittered around the room, coming to rest on the shovel I had discarded earlier. It was about five feet behind me. I had begun edging toward it when Ogden's voice cut through the cave's damp air like a knife.

"Don't move." I froze; there was a tinge of iron in his voice I had never heard before. If I didn't come up with a strategy fast, it looked as if I would be joining Bernard and Estelle.

"When did you come up with the idea of making up a fake construction company?" I blurted, hoping to buy myself a few precious minutes.

Ogden relaxed his grip on the shovel. "Holding Construction? I'd been toying with the idea for a long time," he said.

"You've been pulling it off for a year and a half. When did Stanley get involved?"

"Stanley?" Ogden smiled. "Stanley was involved from the start. Once Estelle got her claws into Bernard, Stanley started to get nervous about the will. So we figured out a way to get around it."

"How did you manage to get those huge invoices past him for all those months?"

"Easy," he said. "Bernard is . . . pardon me, *was* . . . a schmoozer, a delegator." Ogden sneered. "He didn't want to handle piddling little things like paying bills, or auditing accounts. He just relied on good old Ogden to do his bidding, and look out for his interests, like a faithful servant." His teeth gleamed as he smiled. "So I just started issuing and paying the invoices, and I made up some fake balance sheets for him to look at from time to time, to give him a false sense of security — that's all he needed."

"Where did the will come into things?" I asked, trying to keep the flashlight beam immobile as I edged toward the glint of the shovel behind me.

Ogden sighed. His eyes were black coals against the stark white of his face, and I had to force myself to breathe. "Stanley was worried his father wanted to — shall we say — *formalize* his relationship with Estelle. The choice was to kill Bernard before things progressed any farther with Estelle, or find a creative way to move the money. Stanley chose deception. I was more than happy to help."

I was confused. "If you had already moved

the money, though, why kill Bernard? And why keep hanging around?" I glanced at files spilling out of the upended safe. "All you had to do was head to Rio."

Ogden grimaced in the glare of the flashlight. "Bernard found out that Stanley and I were together. He tailed us one night — the night of the storm — and stood outside while we met."

"At the cabin?" I asked.

His pale face registered surprise. "You know about the cabin?" I nodded. "Stanley found it a long time ago," he said, "when he was a kid. Anyway, I don't know how Bernard found out about it, but he was there."

"He had one of your notes in his room," I said. "It took me a while to figure out who Ess and Oh were, but Bernard Katz must have caught on quicker than I did."

"Ah, yes, Ess for Stanley and Oh for Ogden. Stanley's little pet names."

"I found it the night you hit me over the head."

Ogden's eyebrows lifted in surprise. "Hit you over the head?"

"In Bernard Katz's room. The night after he died."

"No," Ogden said, looking puzzled, "that wasn't me. Someone else must not like you much either."

I scooted a few more inches toward the shovel and shifted back to the subject of Bernard Katz. "What did Katz do when you left the cabin?"

"When we came out, Bernard was standing outside the door." Ogden's face twisted with anger. "He called us perverts, called his own son a *fag.* He said he would disown him." Ogden's smooth voice was suddenly ragged with rage. "Then he told us he'd found out about Holding Construction, and that he was reporting it to the police the next day. Everything we'd worked for, planned for . . . it was all going to go up in smoke."

"Did Stanley kill him, or did you?"

It was Ogden's turn to snort. "Stanley? Stanley's not good with confrontations. He just ran into the woods, sobbing. It took hours to console him, afterwards." I wondered if Stanley's flashlight had been the one Claudette had seen, retreating toward Cliffside.

"No," Ogden said, "it was just me and Bernard." His eyes darkened, and he looked as if he were reliving the scene a second time. I took the opportunity to inch a little closer to the shovel. "I couldn't stand to see everything we had worked for destroyed," he said. "So I grabbed the shovel . . ." His eyes strayed down to the shovel in his hand. "It was lying next to the door — had been there for years, I guess — and I whacked him over the head with it. After all that bluster, he just crumpled up there on the ground." Ogden was quiet for a moment before he continued. "Afterwards, I dragged him up the path to the cliff, and tipped him over the edge. I figured it would look like an accident that way . . . as if he slipped and fell."

"Why didn't you leave immediately?" I asked. "You had the money, so why not skip town?"

"If we did that, the police would be suspicious," he said. "Rio's nice, but I'd prefer to be able to come and go as I please. I was hoping the death would be ruled an accident."

"Did Stanley know you'd killed his father?"

"Not until you told him, that day when you were out at Cliffside. He suspected, but he didn't know." Ogden shook his head. "Bit of a nasty shock for him, I'm afraid. But he came around when I explained how it was." I remembered how shaken Stanley had looked; now I understood. Ogden continued. "And when the police figured out Katz *was* murdered, I was guessing that you would be the one to take the fall for it — after all, Grimes was hot on your tracks. I helped that along with a little leak to the local paper about PRI's plans for your inn. A little something to help establish your motive." His thin lips jerked into a smile. "Stanley didn't want to leave, either — he thought there was still a chance he might inherit something. He's hungry for money. I've kept him on a pretty tight leash, just to make sure his resolve doesn't waver." He grimaced. "If we'd played our cards right, we could have settled down and not had to leave the country — we might even have been able to stay at Cliffside, after we sent that tramp Estelle packing. Even if PRI went under, we'd still have a hefty cushion to fall back on."

"So what happened with Estelle?"

"Stanley was careless. He left some papers where he shouldn't have, and didn't notice when Estelle followed him out to the cabin. She confronted us, just like Bernard had." Ogden shrugged. "I really had no choice."

"Same shovel?"

"No, not this time," he said. "I walked her out to the cliff and bashed her head with a rock. Then I tossed her over. I was just coming down here to clean up. I'm afraid we're headed out to Rio, after all."

"She's still alive, you know."

Ogden's eyebrows rose. "Not conscious, I hope. She certainly wasn't when I left her."

"I don't think so; she may be in a coma."

He looked relieved. "Well, then, that's nothing a little visit to her hospital room won't fix." He advanced toward me, raising the shovel as he came.

"How long have you and Stanley been together?" I asked, desperate to buy more time. I inched a little farther toward the shovel, which was still just out of reach.

"Since just after we met, about two years ago." He smiled dreamily. "It was kismet, I guess you'd call it." He took another step forward.

"Were you the one who cleared out the cabin?" I tossed out as my arm stretched out behind me, trying to close the gap between my hand and the shovel on the ground before Ogden attacked.

"If Estelle could figure out where it was, anybody could. There wasn't much to incriminate us in there, but I figured better safe than sorry."

"How did you find out about Smuggler's Cove?"

"Once again, another find from Stanley's youthful summers. I explored it after taking care of the terns' nests for Bernard."

"So you destroyed the nests?"

"Boss's orders. Anyway, once Bernard found the cabin, I decided this would be a much safer place for sensitive documents."

"But it's hard enough getting here in calm weather . . . how did you do it during the storm?"

He laughed. "Fortunately, I know my way around a boat." He glanced back toward the cove where what was left of the *Little Marian* was moored. "Better than you do, evidently. And now," he said, "enough chatter. I've got a timetable to meet."

I glanced back wildly. Another foot to go. "How does Stanley feel about the fact that you murdered his father?" I scooted backward as I spoke.

"Stanley?" He shrugged. "Oh, he's still a bit shaken up, but it's nothing that a few months sunning ourselves on a beach won't fix. In fact —" he glanced at his watch, "as soon as I'm done dealing with you, we'll be headed to the airport. We were originally going to wait until the will was probated, but now . . ." He moved closer.

I glanced back at the shovel; I was still six inches shy of where I needed to be. "Did you throw the rock through the window?" I blurted in desperation. "And cut my brake lines?"

Ogden's eyebrows rose higher on his pasty forehead, and he paused. "My, you really are unpopular, aren't you?" he said. "No, I must say, I was unaware of any of that." He stepped forward again; he was only a few feet away from me now. "At least I'll have the pleasure of knowing you won't be much missed."

In a flash, he raised the shovel over his head and brought it down toward me. I dropped the flashlight and rolled backward toward the shovel on the ground, and as my hand closed on the handle a searing pain exploded in my left thigh. I grabbed the shovel and held it in front of me like a shield. The beam of the flashlight illuminated Ogden, standing over me like a demon from hell, pale face twisted into a horrific mask, shovel upraised.

"Let's not make this more difficult than it has to be, Natalie," he said. Then he brought the shovel thundering down at me again. I gripped the handle of my shovel as hard as I could, but it still threatened to leap out of my hands as I deflected the blow. As he raised the shovel again, I tightened my grip and lurched forward with all of my strength, slamming the blade of my shovel into his stomach. His bulging eyes widened in surprise, and he stumbled backward toward the mouth of the cave before raising the rusted shovel a third time. I could feel blood pouring down my leg as I staggered to my feet and lifted my own shovel. Before he had a chance to strike another blow, I squeezed my eyes shut and brought it down on his head.

When I opened my eyes, Ogden lay crumpled in a heap on the floor of the cave. I limped over toward the flashlight, the pain in my thigh throbbing as I moved, and trained the beam on Ogden. He was still breathing. I turned the beam on my leg. The shovel had opened a huge gash, and as I watched, what looked like pints of my blood poured out, blackening my jeans and growing into a dark, wet pool on the floor. As the blood leaked from my body, my vision began to close in around the edges. I swayed to the ground and struggled to pull off my windbreaker. I needed a tourniquet.

My head felt swaddled in cotton as I tied the arm of my jacket around the top of my thigh and pulled. Water thundered out in the main part of the cove — soon, I realized fuzzily, the cave would be filled with water, and I would be trapped here with Ogden until the next low tide. Despite my muddled state, a seed of panic took root. I grabbed the flashlight and pulled myself toward the small opening in the wall, dragging my wounded leg behind me. When I peered through the low hole, my throat closed up — the cove was already half full, and the water was rising quickly. Ogden's skiff was tied up behind mine. If I could make it into his boat, I had a chance.

As I clambered through the hole in the wall and stood up, blackness encroached on the edges of my vision. I wasn't sure I could make it to the boat — I'd lost too much blood — but I had to try. Water licked the soles of my shoes as I leaned against the rocky wall for support, and I had only made it halfway to the boat when my legs gave out. I sank down onto my knees in the icy water. The cold jolted me — I couldn't give up now — and I crawled the remaining few yards through a shallow puddle of seawater, my leg screaming as the salty waves kissed the open wound.

I pulled myself forward on my hands and knees for what felt like miles before I finally reached Ogden's boat and heaved myself over the side. My head cracked against the seat as I tumbled into the boat's wooden belly, and I lay there on the cold wet boards for a moment, listening to the water thundering into the little cove. *You're not out of the woods yet, Nat.* I dragged myself to my knees and lurched toward the front of the boat, fumbling at the rope with thick fingers. After several clumsy attempts, I managed to loosen the knot, but as the rope snaked into the water, the skiff immediately turned sideways, slamming the bow into the wall opposite the shelf. I staggered to the back of the boat, scrabbled at the second rope until it came loose, and with my last remaining strength, pulled the starter to the engine.

Nothing happened. As the water hurled the wooden boat against the rocky wall again, I pulled a second time, but the engine remained still; I didn't have the strength to start it. The boat was now careening around the cove like a ball in a pinball machine. I braced myself for a third pull and heard a splintering noise. As I squinted in the dim light, trying to find the source of the noise, icy water began pooling around my feet. I soon located the problem; one of the rocks had ripped a gaping hole in the left side of the boat, and the sea was gushing in. Soon, the cold crept past my feet to claim my calves, and I realized with frightening clarity what was going to happen next. I was going to drown.

Suddenly, the sound of a boat's motor filled the cove. "Natalie!" Despite the cold seeping through my limbs, I felt a sudden rush of warmth at the sound of John's voice. I waved feebly, then slumped to the bottom of the rapidly filling boat and let the blackness enfold me.

Twenty-Three

I opened my eyes to a pale fluorescent light embedded in a ceiling of acoustic tiles. As I sat up with a groan, I realized my hand was attached to something — an IV tube. A dull pain throbbed in my leg, and my finger was hovering above the orange "nurse" button on the side of my bed when the door opened and John walked in with a vase filled with beach roses.

"Hey," he said, his green eyes crinkling into a smile. Despite my weakened condition, I found myself admiring the fit of his faded blue jeans as he turned to set the vase on a shelf in front of the small room's only window, and my pulse picked up as he turned and pulled up a chair next to my bed. I hoped he wouldn't notice it on the monitor.

"Thanks for the roses," I croaked. Their heady perfume was already drowning out the antiseptic smell of hospital, reminding me of Cranberry Island and the inn.

"Prickly little buggers, aren't they? I think my hands are permanently perforated."

I laughed. "Next time, wear gloves." As I drank in his disheveled sandy hair and the sprinkling of gold and gray whiskers on his tanned face, it occurred to me that I had no idea where I was or what day it was. "Where am I, by the way? And how long have I been here?"

"You're at the Mount Desert Island hospital. You've been here coming up on twenty-four hours now. You lost a whole lot of blood out at Smuggler's Cove, and the salt water didn't help. Ogden nicked a big artery with that rusty shovel of his. Major tetanus shot material." His face grew serious. "If you hadn't had the presence of mind to tie that tourniquet, you might not be here."

I shivered. "And if you hadn't shown up when you did . . ." Goosebumps prickled my arms at the memory of the cold water rushing into Ogden's boat. "What happened to Ogden?"

"You gave him a good wallop, but there's no permanent damage, unfortunately." He grinned. "He's recovering under police guard, and they've arrested Stanley, too. As soon as Ogden's well enough to be moved, they'll be transporting him to other quarters."

"How did Grimes take the news that I'm not a murderer?"

John rolled his eyes. "He acted as if he'd known it was Ogden the whole time, of course."

"All the evidence was intact?"

"Yup. Right down to the plane tickets to Rio. I hope they were refundable." His woodsy scent wafted over me as he shifted on the orange plastic chair.

"And Estelle?"

"She came out of her coma just a few hours ago. The doctors were worried at first, but she's already complaining about the bed, the food, the service . . ." He chuckled. "I think the staff is ready to declare her recovered just to get her out of their hair."

I laughed. "I never thought I'd say it, but I'm glad she's okay."

John leaned forward in his chair. "It's a good thing you found her when you did. Otherwise, she wouldn't be bugging the hospital staff much." The scent of beach roses wafted over to the bed, and I sat up with a jerk.

"Oh my God — what about the inn?"

John patted my hand. "Relax. Everything's taken care of. Gwen and Charlene have it under control — and besides, now that Ogden's out of the picture, it's only Barbara, and she's heading back this afternoon."

I sat back, relieved. "It was Barbara's article that got me on the right track, you know. That, and a bank statement I saw in Ogden's room just before the board meeting. I have to thank her for writing that article. If she hadn't, that resort would probably have been a go . . . and it might be me in custody now." I stared at the brilliant pink roses for a moment. A few lavender sweet peas had been tucked in among the pink blooms.

John's eyes followed mine. "I got them from your garden. I hope you don't mind."

"Mind? No, I'm delighted. I was just wondering, though. Now that I've found the money Ogden and Stanley embezzled from PRI, do you think the resort will go through?" The thought of losing my inn was like a brick in my stomach.

"I think Katz was in more trouble than just Ogden's scam," John replied. "The funds you found may be enough to pay back investors, but I doubt they'll be able to scrape up enough money to make the land deal go through, much less develop it. Besides, if they did anything, I imagine they'd work on finishing the resorts they already have under construction."

"Or thought they did." I grinned. "I don't imagine Holding Construction Company has a lot to show for the last eighteen months." John rubbed the top of my hand, and the warmth of his touch tingled as it traveled up my arm.

"You know," I said, "one thing that puzzles me is, who threw that rock through my window and cut the brake lines on my bike? I thought it was Ogden, but he didn't know anything about it."

John tilted his head back. "I forgot to tell you — the prints came back from the rock."

"You mean Grimes actually did something with it?"

"Amazing, isn't it? At any rate, it turns out they belong to one Murray Selfridge. Looks like he was trying to protect his investment by scaring off the opposition."

I blinked. "Murray Selfridge? If he's the one who cut my brake lines, he almost killed me. I have half a mind to press charges."

"You probably should," John replied. "What I don't understand is why he didn't try to scare you off earlier, *before* the board meeting. And he really didn't start getting that coalition of his together until after the vote, either."

"I can answer that question."

John's lips twitched into a grin. "This wouldn't have anything to do with breaking or entering or anything else I don't want to know about, would it?"

"Not breaking or entering, no. But I think I'll keep my sources secret. I haven't decided what to do with the information yet. If I tell you, will you promise me you won't tell Grimes?"

He sighed. "No can do. That might be obstructing justice."

"Okay, then, let's just say I'm pretty sure Katz knew how the vote was going to go before it happened, and I imagine Murray knew too."

"How?"

"I think Katz did a little bit of information gathering on certain key individuals, and that he found a few of the things he uncovered — how shall I put it — *useful.*"

John's green eyes widened as he worked this out. "You mean he blackmailed Ingrid?"

"I said nothing of the sort."

"Who else did he go after?"

I grinned. "If you want to know, you'll have to find out for yourself. But if you have any unidentified prints from the night I was brained in Katz's room, I would recommend comparing them with the prints of certain prominent islanders."

John raised his eyebrows in disbelief. "You mean Ingrid knocked you out?"

I smiled at John, but didn't respond. I wasn't one-hundred-percent sure it was Ingrid, but I couldn't think of anyone else it could be. She had been at the store when I told Charlene the forensics crew was coming to examine Bernard Katz's room — she'd dropped something right after I mentioned it to Charlene — and I knew she was paranoid about exposing her son's drug arrest.

"How did you find all this out?"

I fluttered my lashes at him. "Feminine intuition?"

John groaned.

"Speaking of finding things out, how did you know to come find me at Smuggler's Cove?"

"I caught a glimpse of a familiar boat while I was waiting for the forensics team to show up. I didn't know what you were up to down there, but with your lack of experience on the water, I was afraid it wouldn't be good." He shook his head at me. "You know, I almost didn't check the cove. I didn't know you knew about it." I shivered, thinking of what would have happened if I hadn't swung out from the cliffs far enough for him to spot me. Suddenly the phone jangled, startling both of us.

"Hello?"

"Natalie? This is Gertrude Pickens." Before I had a chance to respond, she rushed on. "I just want to say how sorry I am about the article in the paper earlier this week. I don't have to say it too often, but it looks like I was way off this time. I want to make full restitution, write an article that really shows your point of view, and details how you caught the killer. I hope you'll be sure to talk to the local paper first."

"Thanks, Gertrude. I'd love to, but I'll have to call you back later. I have a visitor." She was still talking as I replaced the receiver on the hook.

John eyed the phone. "Persistent, isn't she?"

"At least she's not trying to get me put behind bars anymore." I leaned back against the pillow. "By the way, I hate to ask, but how's the *Little Marian*?"

"What, you mean aside from the splintered sides and the sheared prop?"

I looked at him sheepishly.

"We had her towed over to Eleazer's shop. Once he's finished working on Adam's boat, he'll get her back into shape." He fixed me with a stern look. "He's under strict orders not to return her to you until you've promised me you'll take me with you for at least the first ten times you go out." He shook his head. "I'm afraid to ask how you managed to get into that cove with no propeller."

I blushed. "I got lucky, I guess."

"You call that lucky?"

"Well, I'm not the primary suspect in a murder case anymore, am I?"

"True. I guess that is pretty lucky," he said, then leaned down and kissed my cheek, his bristly chin hot against my skin. The warm, woodsy scent of him overwhelmed me, and I was glad I was lying down, because my legs turned to jelly. "You'd better hurry up and recover quickly," he murmured into my ear. Goosebumps traveled up and down my body — the good kind, this time. "I'm expecting dinner after all of this."

The thought that had been squirming in the back of my mind wriggled to the surface. I pulled my eyes from John's deep green ones with difficulty. "What about your girlfriend in Portland?"

I glanced back at John. He looked stunned. "Girlfriend in Portland? What girlfriend?"

"You know, the woman who called when I

was over to dinner."

He looked puzzled for a moment. Then his face cleared. "Oh, you mean Olivia?" He laughed. "She's married to my brother. She just likes to call me all the time to complain about him."

"She's your sister-in-law?"

"Yup." He sat up straight in his chair. "Scout's honor."

I laughed. "Well, for once Charlene's grapevine is wrong."

"Charlene told you I had a girlfriend? I'd better go set her straight." He eyed me sideways. "Although if I play my cards right, maybe soon that won't be a lie."

He got up and stretched as I tried to form a response, and saved me from answering. "I've kept you up long enough. The nurses will be after me if I don't leave you alone. I've got to run into town for a little bit, but I'll be back this evening." He leaned down and gave me another quick, heart-quickening peck on the cheek. "They say you'll be out of here soon. Get as much rest as you can, so I can hurry up and get you back home." He smiled one last, dazzling smile and disappeared through the door.

Get me home, I thought, and drifted off to sleep smiling, the heat of John's kiss on my cheek and the smell of beach roses enveloping me like a familiar blanket.

A week later, I took my coffee outside and leaned out over the back deck, gazing out at the terns wheeling over the sapphire water. The Cranberry Point lighthouse was an ivory spire in the distance, and a few lobster boats dotted the water's surface, along with a smattering of buoys bobbing in the waves. It was a crisp, beautiful morning, and promised to be a cloudless day, which was a good thing, since Gwen and I were planning on heading out to pick wild strawberries later on.

Gwen had sent a few of her sketches to her mother, who had reluctantly agreed to let her stay and continue her apprenticeship with Fernand, and then started talking about putting together a show at one of the galleries on the west coast. Gwen had apparently cleared up the misunderstanding about Adam, but I didn't ask how — I was just glad I wouldn't have a fire-breathing dragon after me, even if she did live three thousand miles away.

I lowered myself into my favorite white chair — my leg, though mending, was still sore — and sipped my coffee with satisfaction. Fifteen minutes and I'd have to start putting together breakfast for ten guests.

Reservations had started pouring in after all of the news coverage — although I had given the initial scoop to the *Daily Mail,* the story had been picked up nationally, and I suddenly found myself with bookings all the way through to September.

And tonight, I thought with a tingle of anticipation, John and Adam were coming to dinner. I listened to a bell buoy tolling in the distance and took a deep breath of the salt-laced air. I sat, silent, enjoying the morning light, until the sun crested the roof of the inn behind me. Then I turned to go back into the kitchen. It was time to whip up another blueberry coffee cake.

THE END

RECIPES

Wicked Blueberry Coffee Cake

1/2 cup butter or margarine
1 cup sugar
3 eggs, slightly beaten
1/2 teaspoon vanilla
1 teaspoon baking powder
1 teaspoon baking soda
1/4 teaspoon salt
2 cups flour
1 cup sour cream or vanilla yogurt
2 cups blueberries (fresh or frozen)
1 cup brown sugar
1/4 cup butter
1/4 cup flour

Cream the butter and sugar. Add next six ingredients. Add the 2 cups of flour and sour cream (or yogurt) alternately to egg mixture, mixing with a spoon. Fold in blueberries. Pour mixture into greased

9″×13″ baking pan. In a separate bowl, cream brown sugar and remaining butter. Add flour to get a semi-dry mixture. Spread on top of batter. Bake in 350° oven for 30 minutes.

Natalie's Famous Oatmeal Chocolate Chippers

1 1/2 cups plus 4 tablespoons flour
1/2 cup oat flour (or oatmeal pulsed in food processor until finely ground)
1 teaspoon baking soda
1 teaspoon salt
1 cup sugar
1/2 cup brown sugar
2 eggs
1 1/2 teaspoons vanilla extract
1 cup butter, softened until almost melted
1 cup semisweet chocolate chips
1 cup milk chocolate chips
1 cup coarsely chopped walnuts (optional)

Mix flour, oat flour, baking soda, and salt together with a fork. Add sugars, eggs, vanilla, and butter and beat with a wooden spoon until smooth and well combined. Stir in chocolate chips and nuts. Drop by table-spoonfuls onto ungreased baking sheets (place dough about 3 inches apart) and bake at 375° for 8–10 minutes. (For chewier cookies, refrigerate dough first: cooking time might be slightly longer.)

Cranberry Island Blackout Brownies

6 squares unsweetened baking chocolate
1 1/2 cups butter, separated
3/4 teaspoon salt
3 cups sugar
4 eggs
1 1/2 teaspoons vanilla extract
1 1/2 cups flour
3/4 cup chopped walnuts (optional)

Melt chocolate with 3/4 cup butter and salt. Beat remaining 3/4 cup butter in an electric mixer until soft, gradually adding sugar until well blended. Add eggs and vanilla, and mix. Add melted chocolate. Add flour and mix at low speed until just blended. Mix in nuts (optional). Turn the batter into a greased and floured 9″×13″ pan and bake for 35–45 minutes. Let cool and frost with Fudgy Frosting.

Fudgy Frosting

1 1/2 ounces unsweetened baking chocolate
1 1/2 cups sugar
1 pinch salt
3/4 cup heavy cream
1 1/2 teaspoons vanilla extract

Melt chocolate in double boiler with sugar, salt, and cream. (Do not overstir, as it may cause fudge to sugar.) Cook to soft-ball stage and transfer to bowl of an electric mixer. Beat at medium speed until it has cooled. Add vanilla. Beat until it loses its sheen and becomes thick. Frost cooled brownies.

Killer Cranberry Scones

3 cups flour
2/3 cup sugar
2 1/2 teaspoons baking powder
1/2 teaspoon baking soda
1/2 teaspoon salt
3/4 cup firm butter, cut in small pieces
3/4 cup cranberries, chopped if desired
3/4 cup walnuts
1 teaspoon grated fresh orange peel
1 cup buttermilk

Topping

2 tablespoons coarse sugar
1 tablespoon milk (approximately)

In a large bowl, stir together flour, sugar, baking powder, baking soda, and salt with a fork. Cut in butter with a pastry blender until it resembles coarse cornmeal. Stir in cranberries, walnuts, and orange peel. Make a well in the center of the mixture and add the buttermilk. Stir the mixture with a fork until the dough pulls away from the sides of the bowl. With your hands, gather the dough into a ball and turn out onto a lightly floured board. Roll or pat into a 1/2-inch thick square. Cut into 2 1/2 inch circles (use a cookie cutter or an empty can) and place 1 1/2 inches apart on lightly greased baking sheets. Combine cinnamon and sugar. Brush scones lightly with milk, then sprinkle with coarse sugar. Bake at 425° for 12 minutes or until lightly browned. Makes about 18 scones.

Buttery Belgian Breakfast Waffles

4 eggs, separated
1 teaspoon vanilla extract
3 tablespoons butter, melted
1 cup flour
1/2 teaspoon salt
3/4 cup sugar
1 cup milk

Beat egg yolks until very light. Add vanilla and butter. Combine flour, salt, and sugar and add with milk to egg mixture, alternating. Beat well. Beat egg whites until stiff and fold into batter gently. Spray Belgian waffle iron with cooking spray and bake until golden. Serve with a sprinkle of powdered sugar, sliced berries, and Chantilly Cream.

Chantilly Cream

1 cup heavy whipping cream
2 tablespoons sugar
3/4 teaspoon vanilla extract

Whisk the cream, sugar, and vanilla together until satiny.

Gray Whale Inn Blueberry Compote

1 1/2 cups blueberries
1/4 cup maple syrup
Juice of half a lemon
1 teaspoon vanilla extract
2 teaspoons cornstarch (dissolved in a small amount of cold water)

Bring blueberries and syrup to a simmer and cook until blueberries are hot and bubbly. Add lemon juice and vanilla and simmer a moment longer. Stir in cornstarch. Serve warm over pancakes, French toast, waffles, or even ice cream.

ABOUT THE AUTHOR

Although *Murder on the Rocks* is **Karen MacInerney's** first novel, she has been writing ever since she could pick up a pen. She has whiled away many of her summers on small islands in Maine and Newfoundland. Currently her home is Austin, Texas, where she is a full-time writer as well as mother of two.

The employees of Thorndike Press hope you have enjoyed this Large Print book. All our Thorndike and Wheeler Large Print titles are designed for easy reading, and all our books are made to last. Other Thorndike Press Large Print books are available at your library, through selected bookstores, or directly from us.

For information about titles, please call:

(800) 223-1244

or visit our Web site at:

www.gale.com/thorndike
www.gale.com/wheeler

To share your comments, please write:

Publisher
Thorndike Press
295 Kennedy Memorial Drive
Waterville, ME 04901